THE EAGLE WILL FLY

The Time Has Come

Ernest Barber

AuthorHouse™ UK Ltd.
500 Avebury Boulevard
Central Milton Keynes, MK9 2BE
www.authorhouse.co.uk
Phone: 08001974150

This is a work of fiction; all characters, including names and descriptions, are the product of the author's imagination, and any resemblance to any actual person, living or dead, or to any real-life events, is entirely coincidental.

© *2010 Ernest Barber. All rights reserved.*

No part of this book may be reproduced, stored in a retrieval system, or transmitted by any means without the written permission of the author.

First published by AuthorHouse 9/3/2010
ISBN: 978-1-4520-6234-1 (sc)

Library of Congress Control Number: 2010913313
The author would also like to point out that while the 1990 Battle of Britain Fiftieth Anniversary Commemorative Flight takes off, in the novel, from Duxford, Cambridgeshire, the British Memorial Flight is, in actual fact, based at Coningsby. Lincolnshire.
The location was changed to suit the author's own purposes, and does not reflect historical fact.

This book is printed on acid-free paper.

Dedication:

*I dedicate this book
to my late wife, Muriel -
She would know the reason why.*

Acknowledgements:

I would particularly like to thank
Norfolk Legend, Keith Skipper, MBE, for his encouragement,
Keith's wife, Diane, who kindly typed the first script,
and my son Paul, who kept pushing me, with dictionary also in hand.

Also to
Guy N. Smith, who kept me riding the range,
and not least Ashley Ford, my editor,
who put up with my constant quibbling.

FOREWORD

Keith Skipper, MBE, DL.

I have known Ernest Barber - or Dick Barber, as he is known to me - for several Norfolk chapters, a down-to-earth character prone to an occasional flight of fancy. And now, in the form of *The Eagle Will Fly*, is his impressive lift-off as dispenser of thrills.

Born at Kissing Cross, the romantic quarter of Moulton St. Mary, near Acle, in Norfolk, Dick went to school in Upton, then worked on the land in that same village. Many other callings followed, including a spell running a fish-and-chip shop, and years on the roads in and around Norwich as a taxi driver.

I first met him in my role as host of BBC Radio Norfolk's Dinnertime Show in the 1980s, a popular refuge for homely personalities. Dick settled easily behind a microphone to play his melodeon and warble self-penned compositions in between sharing fond reflections of his Norfolk journey so far.

Dick hinted then that there was much more to come on the creative front, as soon as he'd polished his joined-up writing and tied up various strands of vibrant imagination.

The Eagle Will Fly has far more twists and turns than any of Dick's countless taxi trips. A sizzling climax reaches his most hectic of sessions with a deep-fat-fryer. The triumph of good over evil runs through this gripping saga as smoothly as one of Dick's melodeon medleys.

This is a Barber specialising in close shaves. Take a seat, and savour a journey bristling with action.

WHEN BRAVE MEN FLY.

When brave we fly, with fear,

Will God be there?

Voices whisper, in silent prayer -

Silver wings, carry me home.

To where white cliffs,

Green fields, are ours to roam.

Thou be blest; they are here.

When brave men fly in fear,

God is there.

PROLOGUE

The summer of 1990 had occasioned various headlines; the *Today* newspaper reported, on August 3rd, that a temperature of 99F had been officially recorded at Cheltenham, an advertisement announced that, to cool yourself down, you could have bought a Gainsborough-style electric shower from B&Q, for a mere £99.95. The Queen Mother reached her 90th birthday, and the Iraqi dictator, Saddam Hussein, invaded Kuwait.

Sport was also not far from the headlines; England cricket captain Graham Gooch scored three hundred and thirty three runs in the first leg against India, Boris Becker lost his Wimbledon crown to arch-rival Stefan Edberg, while in Rome the England football team, captained by Bobby Robson, were out of the semi-finals of the World Cup, beaten on penalties by West Germany. If you happened to be a fan of the comedian Frankie Howard, you would have been pleased to note that, rather than tour Australia, he had opted instead to perform at Great Yarmouth, a British seaside resort in Norfolk, popular with people from across the country as well as the locals.

Now, September had arrived almost unnoticed. The "breaking news" was sporadic, but, as newspapers relentlessly rolled off printing presses up and down the land, editors were forced to sit and wait for the next front-page sensation.

They would not have to wait long. On September 15th, 1990, a lone vintage aircraft, wearing the colours of a former enemy of Great Britain, prowled the skies above central London.

Why was it there, almost half a century after that war ended?

CHAPTER ONE

Tim "Watto" Watts lounged in an old deckchair, just outside the dispersal hut. The nickname Watto had stuck with him since his schooldays. He had just returned from London, where he had been on a 48-hour rest period. He had enjoyed the two-day getaway, the chance to relax away from his station at Biggin Hill. It had been good to see Joan again, too. They had danced at the Cafe Royal, then had dinner at Chez Moi, a small club/restaurant frequented by many of the fighter pilots. London had been busy; not much sign of war, apart from the huge silver barrage balloons. He had stayed on, at the Regent Palace, when Joan had gone to catch the train back to Hornchurch, where she was stationed. As always, Tim had driven his trusted Riley to London, and back to Biggin Hill. As always, he had had to scrounge the petrol from Transport.

Mid-afternoon had been and nearly gone, and there had been no action yet. The sun was hot, and a few bees buzzed around a clump of clover. Tim watched them lazily, his eyes half-closed, feeling sleepy. In the grass, Jim Cross lay on his stomach, reading a paper. One of the tabloids, Tim noted, with its lurid print. He shook his head. He had never understood how people could read those rags, which seemed to be published more for entertainment than the imparting of news. Someone, somewhere, was humming the tune of a popular song, slightly off-key. It was the waiting that got to him, always the waiting. He dreaded that bloody telephone. It would ring, and you'd tense up, ready for action, only to learn it was the Naffi on the way with the tea. But when that ring finally came, and it was a scramble, the tension would suddenly lift.

The ringing of the telephone interrupted Tim Watts' thoughts, as though his thoughts themselves had caused it to ring. The word came – *Scramble!* - and everyone was off and running.

Tim Watts was a flight lieutenant, today taking the position of Blue Leader Number One, with Jim Cross his Number Two. Grabbing his helmet, and Mae West, he made a dash for his Spitfire, already prepped by his two riggers, Teddy Bates and Henry Clark, and waiting in the dispersal pen. He clambered into the cockpit as Teddy called out "You give 'em hell, sir!" Giving the man a thumbs-up, he pressed a button, and the huge Merlin engines burst into life, a tremendous roar shooting from the exhausts.

Brakes off...ease the throttle open...rudder straight...more throttle... the big bird is moving, picking up speed, the nose comes up and they're flying. The Controller's voice comes over the R/T; "100 bandits approaching Dungeness, including snappers." Snappers – the code name for Messerschmitt ME109s. Tim glanced in his mirrors, checking on his Number Two. Jim Cross was there, tight on his tail. The R/T crackles again, and the Controller's voice comes over, calm and clear.; "Two-hundred plus over Dungeness. Look out for the snappers." Tim glances at the altimeter on his instrument panel. They are holding steady at 10,450ft. Time to turn on the oxygen. He felt the flow inside the mask, cold against his face. The R/T crackles, and Control comes through again; "You are getting close now, Blue Leader. Good luck to you." Tim Watts gazed ahead into the distance; the vast sky seemed to be filled with fat black insects, well over a hundred – he could never remember seeing so many. This was going to be some show.

He flicked his mike; "This is Leader. It's time for the show, boys. Just get stuck in, and watch your backs."

The 109s were coming in around six o'clock, 2000ft above. Things were going to be rough. Bowing his head, Tim "Watto" Watts whispered a brief prayer. Below him, he could see the Dorniers. He assessed the situation, then descended at speed, picking out one of the Dorniers that had foolishly got a little out of formation. Lining up the orange circle and central dot of his sights, he pressed the gun button. As he pulled away, soaring upwards to avoid a head-on collision, he thought he saw bits and pieces of debris flying off the big bomber.

Stick back...ease up...full throttle...regain height....back into the battle... every man for himself now.

A 109 screamed across his front, far too quick, a waste of ammunition to fire after it now. Suddenly, the bright flash of tracers tears past him, inches away. Looking over his shoulder, he sees, almost too late, the 109 behind him.

"Where the hell did you come from, Jerry?" Tim thinks, cursing himself for being caught napping. He yanks the Spitfire round, pulling off one of the tightest turns he has ever done, a turn the German plane, with its inferior handling, could never make. There are puffs of smoke, more tracers flash past. Tim keeps turning, but the 109 sticks to his tail, doing well, considering its disadvantage at this sort of height, in terms of speed and maneuverability Swearing under his breath, cursing the 109's pilot, he realised he was up against it this time – it was going to take everything he had to get out of this one. He was up against a pro, a man who knew how to fly.

"Must be some sort of bloody ace," he muttered, summoning all his knowledge and skill, readying himself for the fight of his life.

In fact, "Watto" Watts wasn't wrong in his assessment of the German pilot. Hans Lux was a well-decorated hero, bearing the Iron Cross and Oak Leaves Plus, a Luftwaffe ace with 26 kills to his name already. He was looking forward to taking down this English pilot, to proving that flying skill could always more than make up for lacklustre engineering. The English were so proud of the crafting of their Spitfires, thought Hans, so quick to trumpet the fact that they were faster than the German Messcherschmitts, could make tighter, more abrupt turns, did not lose momentum at height...but all that, thought Hans, was so much gibberish when your plane was falling earthwards in a cloud of smoke, and you yourself were dead. He readied his guns once more.

During the next few minutes, a furious battle took place; for a time, it was a close call on who would emerge victorious,

Slowly but surely, however, Tim Watts got the better of his opponent, reversing their positions as hunter and hunted, and pulling himself out of a jam. From behind and slightly above the 109, he gave a short burst on the guns, the sound of the heavy browning cannons sweeter to his ears than any music.

Smoke billowed from the Messerschmitt's engine, glycol appeared on the fuselage. Another sharp burst, and there were holes in the port wing – but the plane didn't go down. Instead, the pilot turned his struggling craft, and headed for home, hell for leather. Tim Watts gave chase, a furious desire to finish this burning in him.

Suddenly, he became aware that they were crossing the French coast. Glancing quickly at his fuel gage, he saw that it was low; just enough, he thought, to finish this, and make it back, back to the White Cliffs, and Biggin Hill.

The Messerschmitt fell lower and lower in the sky, the fact that it stayed up at all a testament to the pilot's skill, and nothing else. It was time for the kill. Lining up the Brownings for one last burst, Tim swore to himself that he was going to blast the German out of the sky. He pressed the gun button, but the Brownings were silent. He was out of ammunition, nearly out of fuel, and could only watch the Messerschmitt's final descent, as it seemed to almost float from the sky before coming to an abrupt halt in a field at the rear of a sprawl of farm buildings. There was no sign of it bursting in to flames, it just sat there, silent and still, as though thinking of its narrow escape. *I'm home, Englishman,* it seemed to say, albeit mistakenly, *home, and safe. Aufweidersehn, Englander!*

Berlin, 1940.

Berlin was enjoying itself; the Boulevards were packed with people, and a feeling of buoyancy was in the air. Cafes were full, night-life was swinging, the shops were spilling over with goods, and sales were soaring. Life for Berliners couldn't be better. It was almost as though there was no war going on at all, or at least not one Berlin was involved in.

In one upper-class suburb, however, the good times were about to end. It was a warm day in August, and Eva Lux was startled by a knock on her door. She opened it, and felt her body stiffen, a cold sensation gripping her. A high-ranking Luftwaffe officer stood there. That could only mean bad news. The man bowed slightly, and clicked his heels together.

"Frau Lux?"

She nodded, not trusting herself to speak, then, said, slowly, "Please, Herr Kommodore, come in." Closing the door behind him, she led him into a pleasant, spacious room, furnished with evident good taste in the style of 1920's Berlin, a style which, as styles do, was becoming fashionable once again.

Eva Lux turned and faced the man, her face calm. "You bring bad news, Herr Kommodore." It was a statement, not a question.

"I am afraid so, Frau Lux. The news came this morning. Your husband, Hans Lux, was involved in a brave and glorious battle, for which he will never be forgotten. He managed to land his plane safely, although, we believe, badly damaged, but unfortunately, he did not survive."

After assuring her of the Luftwaffe continued support, and saying that the funeral arrangements would be taken care of, he took his leave, allowing Eva Lux to privately mourn the loss of her husband. For a long time she simply sat in silence, her hands clasped tightly together. However ridiculous, it was always so easy to believe this would never happen to you, that it would never be your husband the Luftwaffe had to report as killed. Easy to think it couldn't happen – but it had. Reluctantly, she got to her feet. Her son was in his room, at the back of their rambling house. Erik would not have heard the arrival of their visitor. Eva Lux would have to go and tell her ten year old child that his father was dead.

She knocked softly, just once, before entering her son's room, which she did, as always, with a sense of foreboding. The room had a dark, sombre feel to it, and seemed to belong to someone much, much older than the ten year old Erik Lux. Eva Lux shivered, as she did every time she entered her son's room. A large portrait of Hitler hung over the mantelshelf, while other, smaller, photographs, depicting Third Reich marches and rallies, hung on the walls. The swastika flag was everywhere. Her son rose from his bed, where he had been sitting, reading.

"Sit down, Erik. I have some...bad news for you."

Erik cried out in German; "No! Don't tell me Papa is dead! He can't be dead!"

Eva Lux held her son tightly. "The Kommodore who came said he was a very brave man, Erik. We should always be proud of him."

"I shall be", Erik said, and his mother was shocked to see that his tears had all but ceased.

At ten, Erik Lux was already grown up, particularly in his politics. A committed member of the Hitler Youth, he admired the Fuhrer almost as much as his father. He loved to watch the Stormtroopers parade down Unter Den Linden. With his small fists clenched at his side, Erik whispered, fiercely;

"I will kill the Englander! I hate England! The brave Reich will conquer them, and, if he lives, I will kill the Englander who killed Papa myself!"

Turning away from his mother, he faced the portrait of Hitler. Clicking his heels together, he saluted, shouting "Heil, Hitler!" - in the manner of one who truly believes what he is saying, rather than the casual, half-muttered way of most Berliners, who speak not from love but from duty. Watching him, Eva Lux could not believe the hatred that suddenly seemed to consume his ten-year-old body; his face was the face of youth gone mad.

In time, Erik Lux grew to be a powerful figure in the Hitler Youth, and was promoted several times, but his dreams of becoming a soldier, of advancing the cause of the glorious Third Reich, of conquering England

and her allies under the swastika-banner, were not to be. Germany was defeated.

The defeat nearly killed Erik Lux, and the suicide of his beloved Fuhrer turned his soul bitter – not with disillusion, which would have been natural, but with a raging fire of wholly unnatural hatred towards the English, a fire which was to burn for the rest of his life, and, through its flames, forge a vengeful madman.

Berlin was a shambles, a city in despair. Her citizens were cold and starving, short of the very basics of life – of food, of fuel, of good clothing, even. The black market flourished, and Erik Lux, now almost sixteen, took full advantage of this. If one was careful not to get caught, it was a lucrative trade. Erik Lux was careful, and he didn't get caught. In the house she still shared with her son, Eva Lux was doing what so many Germans were doing; shrugging their shoulders at the passing of Hitler and the Third Reich, accepting Germany's defeat, and getting on, as best they could, with their daily lives. Eva Lux did not venture far from her house in those first few months after the war's end. There were chores to be taken care of, and the garden to attend to. Life went on.

Seeing the things Erik brought home – real coffee, ham, American cigarettes – and knowing he could never buy them on the wages he earned at the American canteen where he worked, Eva knew what her son was doing, knew also there was nothing to be gained by remonstrating with him. There was an aggression in him that terrified her at times. As time went by, and Germany began to find some sort of normality, Eva Lux found her own friends, and would go out with them, to the theatre, a cafe, a quiet bar. It was in a cafe, after an evening theatre performance, that Eva Lux was introduced to Major Walter Chiltern, of the US Army, who soon became her regular consort on social occasions. In time, their friendship turned to something more intimate. It was on New Year's Eve of 1947 that Walter Chiltern asked Eva Lux to marry him, and it was on New Year's Eve of 1947 that Eva Lux said yes, knowing that Berlin held nothing for her now, knowing that she wanted a new life, for herself and for her son. Perhaps, she thought, Erik's demons were bound to Berlin, and would leave him when he left the city. Walter's parents, she had learned, had been very wealthy, living on a ranch in Montana, and owning several thousand acres of land. They had died a few years before, both peacefully, and of old age. Walter had told Eva that their nearest city would be Great Falls, population 50,000 – hardly a city at all, really, if one was to judge by numbers alone.

On a chilly day in March 1947, Eva Lux left Berlin for good with her husband, Walter Chiltern. Her son Erik did not come with them, feeling that there were more lucrative pickings to be had in Germany's black market, where he was deeply involved, and doing very well for himself. A few months later, however, Germany seemed to shake herself, to resolve to begin a brand new life after the horror of war. The laws were tightened, and the Politzai turned vigorous attention on the black market and its traders. Several of Erik's friends were arrested, and he had intelligence enough to know that no friendship would hold in the face of harsh questioning. That fall, one step ahead of the law, Erik arrived in Montana.

CHAPTER TWO

At first, Erik Lux hated his new environment. That first winter was much colder than any he could recall from Berlin, with the huge, forbidding mountains topped by snow, and the many small streams and rock-forged rivers frozen to solid ice, and he soon found the work of a ranch-hand – rising at dawn to feed and water the horses, then turning them out for the day, taking their muck to the top of the largest field, where it was placed on a huge, steaming pile that, Walter told him, would eventually make capital fertiliser that they could sell to the local farmers, all before breakfast, with the prospect of rounding up recalcitrant cattle for milking and branding once that first meal was finished, along with many other tasks, such as fixing and painting fences, repairing saddlery and killing vermin, far harder than that of a slick young trader peddling black market goods around a devastated city. Erik also struggled to come to terms with his lack of status; being the purveyor of desirable goods had made him someone special, someone to be respected and revered. Now, he was just another labourer. No one cared that his mother was married to the ranch's owner. In Montana, it wouldn't have mattered a damn if he had been Walter Chiltern's natural son – he couldn't carry as heavy a load as the other hands, couldn't ride as long or as well, couldn't handle a bucking steer the way they could, and these things meant that, in their eyes, he was nothing. They were not cruel, they would allow him time to adapt, to learn, to prove himself, but, for now, he was a child to them, and a grunt, someone to mock, to fob off the hardest and dirtiest work on. They had all served their time in this place, and, once Erik Lux had truly become a man, there would be others who would take his place as the weakest of the ranch team. That was the way of life, in Montana.

Walter Chiltern, however, was an amiable man, and one who knew the strains of being a young man in the middle of nowhere – his ranch was the only home for twenty miles, aside from the line cabins dotted around and about, which provided somewhere to take a much-needed rest from a long ride along the cattle trails. He took Erik under his wing, tolerated his moods, and slowly taught his stepson a new way of life – Montanan first, then American, the way it had always been in these parts. The way Walter's father, God rest his soul, had been raised, and the way he had raised Walter. Walter reckoned the boy would turn out to be a top rancher with the right guidance, more than able to fill his boots when the time came, just as he had taken over from his father ten years ago, five years before the old man's last, long ride into that eternal sunset. There would be no children for him and Eva – a necessary operation a few weeks before Erik's arrival had seen to that. Erik was all they had. Walter thought he could probably tame the boy – horses, dogs, boys, they were all the same; just needed the right handling.

Over the next few months, and with Walter's patient guidance, Erik settled into the routine of his new life, making friends with the other rugged cowboys, from whom he learnt the many tricks of roping, branding and handling unbroken colts. His muscles grew with his skill, and soon he was no longer the weakest hand, no longer the worst rider. He could handle a steer as well as any of them, and, after barely a year in Montana, was deemed ready for the toughest challenge of a cowboy's life; the summer drove, where spring cattle were herded along ancient trails, through the rugged, inhospitable terrain of Montana, to the large cities, to be sold for breeding or slaughter. In the winter, the drove only went as far as the freight station; the snow could easily fall to three feet or more in a day, and the going became quickly too treacherous for long droves. In the summer, though, the men took the cattle all the way themselves, without benefit of cattle trucks, which were deemed a city farmer's indulgence. The way went through mountains and forests, along deep, dry river valleys, passing through places where hardly a soul lived. Almost every year, the drove was attacked by bandits – sometimes rogue Indians, sometimes rustlers – and, almost every year, at least one of the men didn't make it home.

Erik's first drive, as it transpired, was attacked only once, the Montanan police patrols having decided to tighten up their duties around the borders of the Indian reservations. There was a short, brief skirmish, some minor injuries, but no lives were lost, no cattle harmed, and the herd continued on, travelling through the night to make up the time they had lost.

As the years passed, Erik found an interest for the little spare time ranch life allowed – the huge United States Air Force base at Malmstrom, near Great Falls. He would watch the planes taking off and landing, almost obsessively, and, keen to encourage this interest, Walter was easily persuaded to buy his stepson a small biplane, and to pay for flying lessons. It would do the boy good, he thought, to get away from the ranch for a few hours a week, to meet other people, city dwellers his own age. Once he had his pilot's licence, and was accepted in the community of men who loved and flew small planes, Erik considered himself more a Montanan than a Berliner. He had an accent, of course, but the farming country around Great Falls, and the city itself, was home to many different accents, traces of lives left behind in other lands – Russia, China, Sweden and Mexico, among others – in order to find fortune in America.

In keeping with this new identity, Erik enjoyed hunting, fishing and skiing, and exploring this new land that he now called home. It was on a trip to Missoula that he met a young student from New York, Patricia Harvey, and was swept off his feet. There was a whirlwind romance, and, three months later, Patricia Harvey was Patricia Lux, and she and Erik were living together on the ranch with Eva and Walter, who were quietly making plans to retire from the day-to-day running of the ranch, and move to a small annexe on the ranch land. Erik was of an age where he could easily handle the running of the ranch, and both Walter and

Eva felt it was time he was made to feel like a man, rather than kept in the dependence of childhood.

Life seemed good for Erik, and he almost believed the past was behind him. But, one day, as was only natural, Patricia asked about his father, about Berlin. Erik fell silent, and told her, stiffly, that he didn't talk about that time, that it was over, and long since in the past. Afterwards, he was withdrawn, sullen and moody, and Patricia found herself unable to get through to him – he would shut himself in his childhood bedroom, with the door locked, for hours on end. Behind the locked door, he would look at old photographs of his father, would read old newspaper cuttings dealing with Hitler's rise to power, covering the glorious rallies, reporting German victories during the years of the Second World War. Erik Lux had kept none of the coverage of Germany's defeat, nothing dealing with speculation around Hitler's death, none of the reports of the sanctions imposed on the ruined nation after the war. For him, in the world he had created, such things did not exist, had never happened. He remembered hearing, all those years ago, his mother's voice as she broke the news of his father's death, remembered too the oath he had taken, that he would find and kill the Englishman responsible for his hero father's fate.

Some nights he would saddle his horse and ride for miles out into the dark prairie, to sit on the banks of a creek, and allow his mind to wander, allow the flame that Patricia's innocent questioning had rekindled to burn furiously within him.

These night time trips kept the nightmares he had started to experience at bay; terrible, dark dreams, in which he saw his father, his beloved Papa, as dark, swirling clouds, and flashes of lightning, a storm of energy. Suddenly, the clouds would shift, would take on the shape of a ghoul, a ghoul that had his father's face, and wore a German pilot's uniform. Grabbing at his father's throat was a faceless English pilot – just a uniform, a helmet, and bony, skeletal fingers. Suddenly, Erik would see himself in these dreams, as he had been when he had heard of his father's death, a young boy, dressed in his pyjamas. He has a parachute, a parachute of swastikas, and his plan is to rescue his father, but, instead, he finds himself falling, falling...he would reach out for his father, but the faceless Englishman would pull him away...he would always wake up with the image of his father's ghostly face fading away as he fell further and further, would always wake with the sound of the Englishman's cruel, mocking laughter ringing in his ears...

He wondered if the English pilot had survived the war, if he was still flying. It was time to find out.

CHAPTER THREE

Tim "Watto" Watts had survived the war, and was, indeed, still flying, albeit only privately now. He kept a Cherokee Piper, and the restored Spitfire he'd flown in the Battle of Britain, both of which he regularly displayed. He was preparing to go out in the Piper now, regarding himself in the full-length mirror in the hallway.

Time had turned his sandy hair grey, but it was still thick and full. Daily exercise, much fresh air and a good diet had kept him trim, and, as he looked at his reflection, he acknowledged, without vanity, that the man in the jumpsuit could easily be his younger self, ready and waiting for the call to come through.

After the Battle of Britain, Tim Watts had moved from 555 squadron, seeking action abroad. He had done a stint in Malta, and then in North Africa. He had left the RAF at the end of the war at the rank of Wing Commander, with eighteen kills to his name – ten in the Battle of Britain, three in Malta, and the remaining five over the shimmering sands of the North African desert. He had been awarded the DFC and Bar, and it was generally acknowledged throughout the RAF that Watto Watts could, if necessary, land a plane on a postage stamp. The end of the war had seen him dutifully return to the family accountancy business, but debtor and creditor ledgers weren't Spitfires and dogfights, and a London office wasn't the open sky of Britain. Flying was in his veins now, and, staring out of his office window over the dreary rooftops of London, he longed to fly again. One day, flicking through the *Times,* looking for the crossword, an advert caught his eye; "Test Pilots required, apply Handley Page." A PO Box number followed. Almost without thinking about it, Tim wrote out a letter of application, including details of his RAF career, and posted it when he went out to buy his lunchtime sandwich and cup of tea. He received a reply the very next day; he had been accepted, and could start as soon as he liked. He arranged to start the following Monday, seeing out the week, and leaving the accountancy firm in the capable hands of his father and older brother, neither of whom were at all surprised that Tim was heading for the skies again. Least surprised of all was his wife, Joan, whom he had married the day his discharge came through, their romance having survived the long years of war since they had met in 1939, when she had been a WAAF, and they were both stationed at Croydon.

"I always remember you coming over to Cromer to visit my parents – you never stopped talking about your planes, about flying. I never did get used to seeing you in that suit and tie, you know. It wasn't you, somehow."

And it hadn't been. Tim Watts remembered those days in Joan's hometown, which he loved for its quiet solitude, its self-containedness. Joan's father, Herbert Randal, had made friends among the local farming elite and the wealthy landowners, and was regularly invited on shoots with them. When Tim was visiting, he too was taken into the field, something which he enjoyed. Joan was right; he had never really been a town man, and had certainly not been cut out for life behind a desk. Life at Handley Page was exciting; this was the age of the jet engine, and faster, more powerful planes were being built all the time. Tim was in his element. Flying, for him, was far more than just a job.

In time, of course, Tim Watts would find himself climbing from a Handley Page cockpit for the last time, shaking hands with his colleagues, receiving a gold watch, drinking champagne and staring at retirement.

He and Joan had lived in Surrey since their marriage, but both had always enjoyed their visits to Norfolk to see Joan's parents, and so it seemed only natural to both of them that they should start this new chapter of their lives in the county they both loved. Handley Page had no objection to Tim Watts keeping his Spitfire, and the Cherokee Piper, in one of their hangars, or of using their airfield at weekends. He had been an excellent test pilot, and a popular member of their team, after all. It was the smooth tarmac of the Handley Page airfield onto which Tim now guided the Piper, following a fantastic flight over the surrounding countryside, during which he had proved to himself that he was more than capable of pulling off all the stunts and manoeuvrings that had made him famous in the RAF, and, later, the most popular test pilot at Handley Page. Climbing out of the cockpit, he smiled at the woman waving to him from the grassed viewing area. His wife, Joan, the same woman he had spent his rest-days with during those hectic years of war, and whom he had married shortly after the end of hostilities. Although their marriage had produced no children, it was a happy one, and their love for one another was as strong as the day they'd first met.

As the airfield crew attached the Cherokee Piper to the tractor, and towed it towards the row of hangers at the far side of the field, Tim loped over to his wife.

"Did you have a good flight?" she asked, as he draped an arm around her shoulders.

"Splendid, my dear. I do feel bad for abandoning you so often, though!"

Joan laughed. "Don't – it gives me a chance to clean the place without you under my feet all the while!"

'The place', as Joan called it, was the Georgian manor house she had bought with Tim when they had decided to move from Surrey to Norfolk. At the centre of the village of Middle Upton, the Manor

House, as it was called, was less than fifty miles from Cromer, where Joan's now-aging parents lived, nine miles from the town of Thetford, which was handy for shopping, and a short gallop to Newmarket. Tim liked a flutter now and again, and was good friends with Mark Havers, a successful racehorse trainer who lived and worked out that way. As they walked home, Joan thought, as she often did, how very lucky she was. Tim Watts was still as slim and handsome as he had been when they'd first met, and she loved the fact that they had truly grown old together, sharing their interests throughout these years. Although Joan didn't fly herself, she loved watching her husband in the air, the way mothers enjoy watching their children play, and she enjoyed listening to him talk about aircraft, about the shows and displays he took part in. She wondered, briefly, if he would change once he finally stopped flying, then, with a shake of her head, dismissed the idea. Of course he wouldn't. He would always be the same old Tim, and she would always be in love with him. This wasn't empty reassurance; Joan Watts knew it to be the truth.

"I spoke to Dad earlier; he and Mum are going to go out to Duxford for your show."

Tim smiled. Joan's parents never missed a flying display if he was in it, just as he never passed up the opportunity to play a round of golf at the course in Cromer with old Herbert, smiling as the man pranced around in his plus-fours, braces, cloth cap and shiny shoes, the very image of a country gentleman taking his leisure, Tim thought.

"That'll be good. How did they react when you told them I'm retiring from flying altogether in a couple of years, after the fiftieth anniversary fly-past?"

Joan shook her head, playfully. "You can tell them that yourself. But I think they'll understand, and they'll certainly agree doing the fiftieth anniversary flight is the right thing. How do *you* feel about it, though?"

Tim shrugged. "It will be the right time, I think. It had to come eventually, and I'd rather go out while I'm still at the top of my game. I don't want to be remembered as some old has-been!"

Ernest Barber

"Oh, you'll never be a has-been, Timothy Watts! Is the fiftieth anniversary going to be quite a big thing, then?"

"Oh, yes. They've already started planning it. There'll be a lot going on; I think it'll be the most dramatic fly-past yet, a perfect performance to bow out with."

Wing Commander Timothy "Watto" Watts couldn't have known how true his words were.

CHAPTER FOUR

Over the years, as and when his funds allowed, Erik Lux had gathered quite a fine collection of vintage aircraft, with his dream being to one day own a working Messerschmitt ME109, the plane his father had flown. Hearing one day of an auction of vintage transport in London, Erik Lux announced to his wife that they were to take their first trip to England, something which delighted Patricia, whose sister Catherine had, a year or so before, got a job, at a very junior level, in the American Embassy in London. Thus husband and wife would not spend too much time together, which suited Erik, for whom the vintage transport auction was merely an excuse – he knew that planes almost never came up in such events, and those that did were mere wrecks that would never fly again. His real purpose was a mission to search and find, and he would set about his task with dedication and precision. He spent many hours in libraries, museums, public archives and private collections, but it was at the Imperial War Museum, in their treasure trove of records, that Erik Lux was finally rewarded.

Timothy Watts, Royal Air Force 555 Squadron, on August 8th 1940, claimed a damaged, believed destroyed, Messerschmitt ME109 over France. The plane was recovered, and the pilot confirmed dead in the cockpit, identified as Hans Lux, Luftwaffe squadron JG26, under the command, that day of Adolf Gollands. The flame of hatred that burned steadily in Erik Lux's mind erupted in a fireball, burning away all sense and reason. This fire it was that would drive him to obsession, to the madness of revenge, and, finally, to the fight of his life. Smiling as a little of his control returned, Erik Lux was already sketching out a plan; he would find this pilot, this Timothy Watts, and lure him to his death with the guise of friendship. The old man – for he would be old by now, as old as Erik's father would have been, had he lived – wouldn't have a clue until it was too late.

"Are you alright there, sir?"

It was one of the Imperial War Museum's archives staff, a smiling, friendly blonde. Erik looked up.

"Ah, yes, thank you. I have found what I was looking for – I am doing research, for a book about former Second World War pilots. Tell me, please, where would I go to find out more about this man, this Timothy Watts?"

"Wing Commander Timothy Watts? He should be flying in one of the Duxford displays later this year. He usually does – takes out the Spitfire he flew in the War."

"Really?" The plan was becoming more defined in Erik Lux's mind. "And I would be able to meet him there?"

"Oh, yes – the pilots love talking to the crowd after the flight. They love what they do, you see, and, well, they want to share that enthusiasm with everyone. I suppose it's the same with you and books, as you're a writer?"

Erik hesitated, having almost forgotten his cover story. "Oh, of course. Yes, to talk about something one enjoys – there is nothing better, as you say."

"Would you like me to get you details of the display, sir?"

"If you would – I think I shall enjoy it."

"Did you find what you were looking for at the auction?" Patricia asked, as they sipped their drinks in the bar of their hotel that night.

"Ah, no. There were a few planes, but not a Messerschmitt. I am thinking of going to see my cousin, Kurt Hahn, in Hanover, Germany...he knows about such things, the planes, what happened to them, through his job. We will also be coming back, in a couple of months – there is a display at Duxford which I would like to see. They will be having some German planes there – perhaps one of the pilots might have information regarding the Messerschmitt."

Patricia looked at her husband. She couldn't really explain the sense of unease she felt when he spoke about finding this Messerschmitt; after all, she knew he collected World War Two aircraft, and guessed, from his age, that the father he never mentioned had probably flown with the Luftwaffe during the war; it was natural that Erik should want a Messerschmitt, and yet...and yet, his interest in obtaining one seemed almost *un*natural.

"You haven't been back to Germany since you left for Montana, have you?" she asked. Erik shook his head.

"No. And that is why, I think, I shall go alone – there are...memories... that I couldn't face were there someone with me."

Patricia felt a hot flash of something she couldn't name, the same something that overwhelmed her when her husband locked himself in his childhood room back at Big Sag ranch. A hot flash of unreasonable fear – the fear that her husband wasn't himself.

"I shall call Kurt tomorrow" Erik said, standing up abruptly. "It will be easier, if it is convenient for him, for me to fly to Germany from here. You go back to the ranch – if I can arrange to go to Germany, I shall call Zeke, to let him know of the change of plans. He is more than capable of running the ranch in my absence."

Helplessly following her husband up to their room, Patricia reflected on all the things she didn't know about her husband. It began to dawn on her that the list of things she didn't know about Erik Lux outnumbered the list of things that she did know. And that it was the things on the former list that were most important.

The following morning, Patricia was woken by the harsh sounds of the German language. *Erik*, she thought, *talking to this cousin, Kurt, that I'd never heard of until yesterday.* There came the sound of the receiver being replaced, then picked up again. The sound of a number being tapped in.

Then her husband's voice, speaking in English this time, telling their ranch manager of the change of plans. Idly, Patricia wondered if Zeke missed Walter Chiltern, who had passed away the summer before, six months after Eva had died following a short, sudden illness. Walter, who had been a true rancher, from a line of ranchers. Zeke, who had worked for Walter Chiltern, was always polite to her, always respectful to Erik, but Patricia couldn't help thinking that old Zeke must know her husband only kept the ranch and the horses because of the respect they gave him in the rugged community of Montana, a community built of men who owned land and horses, which was deeply suspicious of anyone who made their living any other way. Patricia knew the ranch wasn't, and had never been, Erik's main interest, and she thought that Zeke must know it, too. But the old Montanan never gave so much as a hint of what he thought of "the master" as he called Erik, and had called Walter before him.

Erik came back into the bedroom, his eyes blazing with a strange light.

"It is arranged. I shall be going to Germany the day after tomorrow. Kurt will book the tickets, and meet me at the airport. You will fly back to Montana, as we had planned. Zeke will meet you at Great Falls International."

Patricia nodded. "Are you sure you don't want me to come to Germany with you?"

"No – I must be there alone. Kurt and I, we have a lot of catching up to do...he does not have a wife; it would make things uncomfortable if you were there as well."

As Erik went into the bathroom, it occurred to Patricia that he really hadn't meant to be rude to her; it was characteristic of Erik not to think how other people might be affected by the things he said, the way he said them.

Sighing, she got up, and began to dress. She had enjoyed seeing Catherine again. Her sister had arranged to take a few days off work, and had spent the previous day showing her little sister all the important sights of the capital. Today, the two women were going to go shopping, a thought that thrilled Patricia, who had been shocked, when she had first moved there, at how few shops there were in Great Falls compared with her native New York. Indeed, Montana didn't seem to notice that people shopped for pleasure, and enjoyed buying fine, impractical things. The stores in Great Falls sold tools, guns, work clothes and boots, animal feed, harnesses, bridles, whips, parts and fuel for farm vehicles, staple foodstuffs and liquor. Of course, she had got used to this, but all the same, it would be nice to shop for the joy of shopping, to buy things she might wear at most twice a year, things her husband would barely deign to notice, and that Zeke and his wife, Montanans to the core, would laugh about in the privacy of their accommodation by the stable-block.

Hanging up the telephone in his apartment in Hanover, Kurt Hahn stared thoughtfully at his reflection. He was tall and slim, with thick blond hair that was only now beginning to be touched with grey, and piercing blue eyes. He rubbed the faint stubble on his jaw, and wondered what Erik Lux wanted.

Kurt Hahn was much older than Erik Lux, and had also seen service in the Luftwaffe during the second World War. Like Hans Lux, the husband of his father's youngest sister, Kurt Hahn had not loved Hitler, but had loved, and did love, Germany. It was his love of his country, rather than love of the Fuhrer, that had seen him volunteer for service, and it was his love of his country, combined with his life-long passion for history, that found him working as an administrator for the Luftwaffe Museum archives.

He sighed, and began to dress for work. Whatever it was his rather strange youngest cousin wanted, he would find out soon enough. As he stepped out of the door, he had a vague sense of unease, a feeling that he should not have encouraged this visit of Erik's, a sense that he should certainly not help the man, if he asked for it.

He shook his head. Erik Lux was his cousin, and he hadn't seen him since that day, in 1947, that he had left Berlin, and Germany, for the open spaces and big skies of Montana. It would be good to catch up, Kurt thought.

A couple of days later, Erik Lux sat in a window seat of a Lufthansa flight, bound for Hanover. He was nervous, although he didn't show it. He could not have said why he was nervous; he did not think it had anything to do with his return to Germany after so long, although he admitted to himself that it might have. He had been away a long time, after all; perhaps, he thought, he was afraid his home country would have changed beyond all recognition, would no longer seem like home to him.

Kurt Hahn, in his days as Oberleutenant, had been a rising star in the Luftwaffe, almost as good as Erik's father. Erik remembered him talking with passion about Germany, about how powerful the country would be when the war was won. He hoped the end of the war had not seen the end of Kurt's passion, hoped that his love of Germany was not restricted now to cataloguing records of her glorious past. Erik regretted that he had not kept in touch with his cousin as much as he ought to have done, but, once life in Montana had succeeded in casting its spell on him, he had all but forgotten about Germany. Until Patricia reminded him of the country of his birth, and of the oath of honour he had sworn in the dark light of his father's death, the promise that he would kill the Englishman who had taken his father's life, if that man still lived. Once more, he felt the fire of hatred raging inside him, and was warmed by its flames.

On the flight back to Montana, Patricia found herself growing increasingly worried about Erik. He had refused to speak to her about why he suddenly had to go to Germany, except to repeat that she wasn't welcome, that it would make things difficult. Patricia was no fool – she knew that Erik's reason for going to Germany was no innocent visit to his older cousin, no man-to-man catch up. Erik had had years in which he could have returned to Germany to see this Kurt Hahn, but he hadn't. It was only after that day when he'd gone to the vintage transport auction in London, and failed to find a Messerschmitt there, that he had even spoken of his cousin. Once more, Patricia got the feeling that there was something terribly wrong with her husband's desire to obtain a Messerschmitt ME109, that it was about something far more sinister than a man's hobby of collecting World War Two aircraft. She shivered, closing her eyes as if to shut off her thoughts.

"Erik." Kurt's voice was expressionless, and his heart was heavy. His cousin looked exactly as he had in his Hitler Youth days, minus the uniform – the same close-cropped hair, as blond as Kurt's own, the same shine to the leather of his belt and boots, the same gleam of metal buttons and buckles, the same stiff, upright posture, as though he might, at any moment, be expected to snap to attention. Kurt looked into his cousin's eyes, and his heart sank; he saw there the same light he had seen in the eyes of another man, when that man had been stirring troops and citizens to a bloody, exhausting war, spinning a pretty tale of the glorious nation that would rise from the ashes of armed struggle, of the life of luxury that country's people would lead, of the wealth they would enjoy. Like all the others, Kurt Hahn had believed these impassioned speeches at the time, although he had his misgivings regarding the speaker. He had dreamt of a golden Germany, a land of power and wealth, envied across the world.

But that dream had died in the defeat of Germany, and Kurt had seen the man who had conjured the dream for what he had been; an insane monster, using the hopes and fears of a troubled nation for his own ends.

Looking at his cousin Erik Lux, Kurt Hahn was reminded of the man made infamous by the horrors he had brought about, the man whose name still inspired deep reactions in almost everyone who heard it. Looking at his cousin, Kurt Hahn was reminded of Hitler.

"Kurt. How are you?"

"*Ja.*" Kurt shrugged, the affirmative seeming to encompass everything, as it often did with Germans. Erik nodded, understanding.

"Come," Kurt said, gesturing ahead, "the car is waiting."

On the drive to Kurt's apartment, Erik was silent, looking out of the window. Hanover seemed to have never seen a war, and he wondered if the same were true of Berlin, if Germany had managed to rebuild herself so completely everywhere? The city seemed to be thriving; men and even a few women walked the streets in smart suits and well-polished shoes, striding along with purpose. Other woman strolled at a more leisurely pace, dressed in good clothes, looking into elaborate shop-window displays. Young people sat around on low walls, or lounged against the sides of buildings, their hands in their pockets, talking, laughing, calling out to one another. There were expensive-looking cars on the roads.

"What do they say about the war, Kurt?" he asked suddenly, his voice sounding very old, older than Kurt's, who was nearing retirement.

Kurt shrugged. "What war, my friend? The war has come and gone. It did not go our way. What is there to speak of?"

"But the young ones..." Erik gestured to a group of teenagers sitting around the edge of a fountain, laughing, swigging from cans of Coke, and smoking cigarettes.

Kurt shrugged again. "They know the facts. Sometimes their schools bring them to my museum, they seem to listen, or at least have the manners to make a good pretence...it is history to them, Erik, and should perhaps be so to us."

"Never!" Erik's voice was louder than he had intended, and Kurt was startled. Calming himself, Erik realised it wasn't just Germany that had changed, and that he would have to be careful in his cousin's company. Laughing a little, as though mocking his passion, he continued, his voice softer; "I mean, we should not forget what happened. We should not allow it to be forgotten. It was important, terrible. We should not only remember the good things, is it not so, Kurt?"

As much as he was able to whilst driving, Kurt Hahn studied his cousin. He sensed there was something deep, and darkly disturbing, going on in his cousin's mind. He was thankful when they arrived at his apartment.

"I will let you freshen up, change your clothes, perhaps. Then we shall have dinner, a beer. Talk about old times. The business you mentioned on the telephone, it can wait until the morning, ja?"

Erik was disappointed, but hid it well. "Of course, Kurt – we must catch up first before I make demands on you!" He laughed, a disconcerting sound, and the sense of unease that had troubled Kurt when he had first spoken to Erik Lux returned. Something was terribly wrong with his young cousin, and he had a feeling he was about to get caught up in whatever madness Erik carried inside him.

The next day, Kurt announced that he was going to take his cousin back to Berlin.

"You will not recognise her, Erik. The city. She is so changed, so successful. It is as if the War, the destruction, never happened." Kurt caught Erik's look, a look of anger, and disgust. He softened his voice, calming his excitement.

"It does not mean the War is forgotten, Erik. There are memorials, museums – but it is recognised that these things speak of the past. There are other things, other buildings, that speak of the future."

"The future." His cousin spoke the words, in German, as if they belonged to a culture, a language, entirely alien. And, with a shiver, Kurt Hahn sensed that something in Erik Lux was preventing the man from having a future. What, after all, did he do with himself, except live off the inheritance from his wealthy step-father, and occasionally give flying instruction to visitors to Montana? Sometimes, he would sell one of his vintage craft – they had discussed the subject of Erik Lux's employment on their drive back from the airport, when Kurt had explained that he had taken a week's leave from his own job, in order that he could be a good host to his cousin.

"Ah, that is where I am fortunate," Erik had replied. "I do nothing unless I choose to do something, my time is my own."

"But you need to make your living, cousin" Kurt had replied, puzzled. Erik had laughed. "My stepfather and mother died whilst they were on vacation in Canada. I inherited the ranch from them, and promptly employed a manager. True, there are still some things I must take care of myself, but, ever since my mother and Walter died, and the ranch became mine, it has made money for me without much effort on my part."

Erik had sounded proud. Kurt had kept his feelings carefully hidden. He had been raised, as most Germans were, to value hard work, to view having an occupation as a thing of duty. Yes, there was leisure, but the Germans reserved it for the times they set aside as holiday, or for the weekends. The weekdays were for working, for providing for your family and contributing to the economy of your country. There was neither patience nor understanding of those who did not work.

Berlin had indeed changed. Where Erik remembered crumbled buildings, the stumps of trees, scruffy patches of grass ripped apart by bombs, the city now gleamed with clean, sleek, modern lines, huge glass buildings, neatly-kept parks with shiny railings and tidy dogs on leads, trotting beside expensively-groomed owners. Where Erik had once walked through dust and dirt, along narrow roads cluttered with the garbage of ruined lives, the streets were broad and even, swept clean, Kurt explained, by a machine which came through twice a day, in the morning and the evening. On the equally-clean pavements were tidy, almost artificial-looking stands selling *knockwurst, bratwurst, schnitzel* and other snacks. There were even American ones, selling pretzels and popcorn, and Italian vans, less tidy, selling cheap ice-cream. Erik shook his head sadly.

"I know you call this progress, my cousin, but to me, it does not seem real. To me, this is not Berlin. It is a fantasy, a pretend city." He laughed, a forced, false sound. "I feel as though I am dreaming, and am about to wake up!"

Suddenly, his ears were assaulted by the sounds of...English. And not the heavily-accented English of students who were practising, the English of *haff* and *vish* and *vill*. This was English that had never had to be learned. He turned, trying to find the source of the sound, and spotted it in the pack of suited men and women emerging from a glass building.

"*Was ist das, Kurt?* Who are those English, and why are they here, in Berlin?"

"It is an English bank, Erik. Ours were struggling, had been since the War. Five, six years ago, one of the largest was in danger of closing. An English bank went into partnership with them, brought staff over here. They kept as many of our people in jobs as they could. It was a good thing. There are many Englishmen working here, now – they say there is very little work in their country, because everyone wishes to come there, for a better life."

"So they come here. And steal from us once more." Erik was angry, and could not keep the anger from his voice.

Kurt shook his head. "*Acht, neine, Erik* – it is not like that. They help us, they are our friends now."

Erik had stood, resolutely silent, the look in his eyes conveying more than even the strongest shake of his head.

"I would like to see Unter den Linden", he had said, speaking quietly, but his eyes burning with a fire too bright to be merely that of a son of Germany newly returned home. He longed for something familiar, and believed he would find it in the street where he had marched in those long-ago days of the Hitler Youth. They had gone, Kurt and Erik, to the street down which the younger man remembered marching in his Hitler Youth uniform, a street which the older man would always associate with boys pretending to be men. Erik had been disappointed; Unter den Linden was not as he remembered it; there was no sense of pride or glory their. Instead, it was crowded with teenagers in dark clothing, with too much makeup and overly-elaborate hairstyles – and that was just the males. These strange creatures spoke of politics, true, but their politics were not the politics of the Third Reich. They hardly seemed German, to Erik, except for the language they spoke. They even identified themselves as "European", with no sense of the insult that one word contained. They did not seem to realise, Erik thought, that they were serving those over whom they ought to be masters.

Erik turned to his cousin. "Let us return to your apartment, Kurt – before I find myself incensed beyond endurance." Kurt sighed, but knew better than to argue with his cousin when he got like this. The fire that seemed to burn in Erik's eyes frightened Kurt. He had seen such fire before, in the eyes of men whose unswerving devotion to the Reich and to Hitler had driven them mad. He hoped this would not happen to Erik, but feared that it would.

"I want to find out whether my father's Messerschmitt is still flying."

It was breakfast time in Hanover, the day after they had been to Berlin, and Kurt Hahn, who found, as he aged, that he didn't get going as quickly as he used to, wasn't ready for a veneration of Berlin's war-dead. He stared into space, swallowed some coffee, and speared a chunk of sausage before answering.

"Your father's Messerschmitt – why do you want to know what has happened to it, Erik? The war was a long time ago."

Kurt Hahn spoke with the wisdom of one who is growing old, one who sees historical events as just that – events that happened in history, and thus should be left to those whose sole field of interest is history to deal with.

Erik Lux spoke with the fire of the fanatic, a fire normally reserved for youth, and quenched by a man's late-twenties.

"I must have that plane, Kurt – my collection will not be complete without it. I can do mechanical work – an American taught me how – so, even if it cannot fly, I will take it, will work on it. But I must have it..." realising how strangely Kurt was looking at him, Erik calmed himself, and said, "it is the last, most powerful memory of my father, Kurt. It is important to me to have this plane in my collection, you see?"

Kurt nodded, briefly.

"There are many ME109s, Erik, although most do not fly, and are beyond repair – the best mechanics in Germany have been called to look at them, and there is nothing they can do, they are too badly damaged, have suffered too much neglect. But, yes, I suppose it is possible that Hans's plane still exists, and can still fly – the records, alas, are poorly kept, and remain, despite my best efforts, woefully incomplete. You say you have a record of the markings?"

Erik Lux nodded. "In my suitcase. I will fetch you the photograph after breakfast."

Kurt Hahn shivered. He wondered if this was why his cousin Erik had not returned to Germany before; many Nazi sympathisers kept away, finding it easier to spread their ideology in countries that had not known how badly the unwanted war had hit Germany. Kurt Hahn knew what he was talking about; his best friend, now living under an assumed name in Switzerland, had been a Werwulf, part of an elite, unacknowledged specialist unit of the Third Reich, equivalent in expertise and ability to the English SAS. The Werwulfs were superior in all aspects to the Waffen SS, although the latter received the acknowledgments, the plaudits. Even Germans weren't meant to know about the Werwulfs. Heinrich Weiss, the name adopted by Reinhardt Schwartz, had left Germany six months after the war's end, as had most of his former comrades, the platoon he had commanded scattering to the four winds. Kurt Hahn did not know whether he was alive or dead, but, if he lived, he was a wanted man. Somehow, Kurt Hahn sensed that Erik Lux did not know about the Werwulfs, and knew it was very, very important that his cousin never found out about them – all those who had been Werwulfs loved Germany, loved the Third Reich, and loved Hitler – and not necessarily in that order. If Erik was some sort of neo-Nazi, a former Werwulf was the last person Kurt wanted him to be in touch with.

"I would be happy to see such a picture, and happier if I could help you find the plane." Hahn was good at lies, at dissembling, and he could see that Lux was taken in.

Erik Lux smiled. "Good. You understand, Kurt, why this plane is important to me?"

Kurt Hahn regarded his cousin, thinking before he answered. "You were young when Hans was killed. It is natural that you should...that you should want something that was so much a part of him. And I am glad you came to me – it has been too long since we spoke, my cousin."

"Indeed." Erik nodded, then got up from the table. "I will fetch you the photograph now, and the details of the squadron my father flew with. I have a record of the mission in which he was killed."

"You have been working hard!" said Kurt, smiling in spite of his concerns. He couldn't help but admire such thorough research.

"Yes – the English Imperial War Museum, at Duxford, keep very good records of the scenes of their murders." Erik tried to keep his tone light, but failed. Seeing wariness cloud his cousin's eyes, he turned away. "I will get you the photograph, the records."

Over the next few days, Kurt Hahn followed the same procedure that Erik Lux had followed in England, of sorting through many hundreds of files, archived newspaper reports, and records. In addition, he spoke with colleagues at the Luftwaffe museum, and with private collectors of World War Two planes that he knew.

"I am sorry, Erik" he said, on the last day of his cousin's visit "our records are not complete, alas, many files are lost, not all who collect aircraft tell us about their collections...I could find nothing this time, not about your father's Messerschmitt, at least, but I will keep looking, and I have contacts who will also keep an ear to the ground for you."

Although disappointed, Erik Lux managed a smile, and shook his cousin's hand.

"Thank you, Kurt. I appreciate the effort you have gone to for me already."

Kurt smiled, too, and shook his head. "Really, Erik, it was nothing. I enjoyed it. Have a good flight back to Montana, and keep in touch, *ja?*"

"Of course. I may even have something to tell you, soon."

And, without explaining his last words, Erik strode off across the concourse, to board the plane that would take him back to Montana.

CHAPTER FIVE

A few weeks later, Patricia Lux stood beside her husband on a grassy field in England, shading her eyes as she gazed upwards at the flying display going on above their heads. Erik Lux, whilst appearing to scan the skies, kept his binoculars trained on one particular plane, an original Spitfire, evidently either well-kept or else very carefully restored. It had been a pleasant day at Duxford, Erik reflected, talking to other vintage aircraft enthusiasts, people who did not look askance at him when he said he was trying to track down a particular Messerschmitt. His obsession was shared, here, was treated as entirely natural. The day was drawing to a close, finishing with this fly-past of vintage planes. Erik marvelled at how many planes from the Second World War were still flying – surely, he reasoned, his father's plane must be one of them? It had been with intense interest that he had watched the cocky pilot of the Spitfire pull off several complex, low-level manoeuvrings, manoeuvrings that a less skilfull pilot would have got into serious trouble even attempting. As he watched, his mind was busy with the plan to avenge, once and for all, what he saw as his father's murder. He watched as the planes came in to land, the Spitfire leading them down. Lowering his binoculars, he watched the pilot clamber from the cockpit, watched him shake hands with his fellow pilots. As the man walked towards the main building, chatting to people as he went, Erik Lux took a deep breath.

"Wing Commander Watts?"

Tim Watts stopped, turned, and looked at the man who had called out to him. Five feet ten, with close cropped blond hair and piercing grey eyes that unsettled Tim; they seemed to stare straight through him.

But the man seemed friendly enough, smiling and holding out his hand. "My name is Erik Lux, and I believe we have a...mutual interest."

"Oh, yes?" Tim smiled, picking up another accent under the harsh American twang. German, he thought. "What would that be?"

"I am...a researcher, of sorts, Wing Commander, and a pilot myself, as well as something of a collector. My interest, like yours, is in vintage aircraft, particularly those that flew in the Battle of Britain."

"Really? I must say, you don't look old enough to remember that scrap, Mr Lux!"

Erik felt the rage rise inside him. That scrap, indeed! But he smiled, and shook his head.

"Ah, no. I was still a boy when the war ended. But the planes interest me, all the same. I have a fine collection of them at home – vintage planes, I mean."

"And where is home, Mr Lux?"

"Montana, in America. I live on a ranch there, Big Sag, with my wife." He indicated Patricia, who stepped forward, unable to take her eyes off the pilot. Fortunately, Erik didn't seem to notice.

"Hello, Mrs Lux. Your husband was just telling me about his vintage plane collection – very interesting, I must say. I can't really chat now, but, look, there's a dinner taking place tonight, at the Limes Hotel, in town -" Tim gestured to an elegant lady with a clipboard "- go and see the lady over there, tell her Timothy Watts has said you're both to come as his guests. My own wife, Joan, will be there – I'm sure you and she will have something in common to natter about while your husband and I discuss our toys, Mrs Lux."

"Patricia, please. And I'm sure I will enjoy your wife's company." She smiled, hiding her sudden dismay that the man was married. Although why should it matter? She was also married. She looked at Erik, and wondered what he was up to, certain this friendliness was a sham, but not sure what it could be covering.

The dinner was a great success, with the two couples getting on very well. Erik Lux felt it was rather going his way, as he and Tim discussed planes and flying.

"You must come to Montana, and visit our ranch there, Wing Commander. We could fly together – it is the best way to see the area."

Tim Watts laughed. "Well, that's kind of you, but I'm not sure I'd be much use as a cowboy!"

They all laughed, Patricia loudest of all, still unable to shake the attraction she felt for this charming, soft=-spoken, well-mannered man, who was so utterly unlike her husband, and who seemed devoted to his wife, who, in turn, seemed devoted to him.

Joan Watts spoke now. "We've never been to the States – we tend to holiday in Europe. The Alps, mainly, and Austria. Tim loves his skiing. Montana's an awfully long way, isn't it? But I'm sure it would be fascinating to visit – I do so love new places. Are there any Indians still there?"

"Yes," Patricia replied "they have their own reservations, now." Turning to Tim, she continued, "There's also a large airbase, Malmstrom, over near Great Falls, which I'm sure you'd enjoy, Wing Commander. They do conducted tours there."

Erik Lux broke in. "And we also have mountains there, Wing Commander. I regularly fly over them – and miss them every time! Not everyone can do that, there have been many accidents."

Tim found himself liking the chap, but he wouldn't commit to Montana. Joan had been a little under the weather, and at times seemed very unwell indeed. He was worried about her. However, both parties exchanged telephone numbers, and agreed to keep in touch.

Later that evening, Joan said; "I'd like to go, Tim, when I'm feeling more up to it." Tim had smiled, kissed his wife, and said; "Perhaps in the spring, when the weather's better, old girl. We'll see how you go."

Sadly, that winter, Joan Watts became very ill, and, on Christmas Eve, with Tim holding her hand, she passed away.

Tim was desolate, all thoughts of Montana forgotten. Devastated, feeling the world a bleak place without his wife, he mourned her deeply, and wondered if he would ever have any reason to smile again.

In Montana, Erik Lux was in a buoyant mood. He had found the man responsible for his father's death, had made his acquaintance, had left him with the impression that he was most definitely a friend, not an enemy from the past. He felt sure that Tim Watts and his wife would come to Montana, and then he could carry out his plan to avenge his father's death.

In March of the following year, growing impatient, he decided to call the Englishman, as he had heard nothing.

In Middle Upton, the butler answered the phone, and informed a Mr Lux that the master was away on business for the day. In response to the stranger's question of was Mrs Watts available, the butler felt it was not his place to tell the man that the lady was no longer with them, and simply replied that no, the mistress was not available. If Mr Lux would be so good as to leave his telephone number, Mr Watts would be sure to return his call.

Two weeks later, at the beginning of April, feeling as though he could, in fact, face the world without Joan, Tim Watts did so. But, because of the time difference, he made a huge blunder.

"Hello? Who is this?" A sleepy female voice answered the phone. "Do you realise the time – it's three-thirty in the morning!" Tim Watts felt rather foolish. It was, of course, only mid-evening where he was, in Middle Upton.

"Mrs Lux – I do apologise! It's Tim Watts, from England. I'm afraid I forgot about the time difference."

"Don't worry, Wing Commander – I'll be the talk of Montana, getting a phone call at three thirty in the morning from an English gentleman! I assume you want to speak to Erik, but he's away in Arizona, looking at one of his vintage planes."

"Well, really I'm just returning your husband's call, enquiring as to whether Joan and I had decided about Montana…you see, I don't think… well, it's not practical. You see, Joan…Joan passed away, at the end of last year."

"Oh, I'm so sorry. But, Wing Commander, don't you feel a change of scenery would do you good?"

Finding himself oddly comforted by Patricia's voice, Tim Watts agreed, and said he would call them again once things had been arranged. "At a more sensible hour, this time!"

In May, Erik Lux received two pieces of excellent news. The first was that Kurt had, finally, located his father's Messerschmitt, and could arrange, if Erik wanted, to have it flown over from the scrap yard where it had been found, with other vintage war planes, in the Hague area of Holland. The second was that Wing Commander Timothy Watts would be coming to Montana – alone. Erik decided that the collection of his father's Messerschmitt could wait – he told Kurt he would collect it himself, soon, after ascertaining from his cousin that the scrapyard's owner had no intention of selling the plane to anyone else at that time.

"How was your flight, Wing Commander?" Patricia asked, as she led Tim to her car, having gone to meet him at Great Falls airport.

Tim smiled. "Wonderful, thank you. Rather long, but it gave me time to catch up on my reading, in between snoozing!" he laughed, and tapped the guidebook he carried under his arm.

"I'm glad you enjoyed it. I've a feeling you're going to love Montana. Erik's just got back from some business upstate – he absolutely can't wait to get talking to you about those planes of his! You'll have time to freshen up, and chat a little, before we eat."

"That sounds perfect," Tim smiled, climbing in to the car and settling back against the seat.

As they drove, Tim took in Montana, the dusty plains, whose sand was almost red in colour, the mountains that seemed purple, the brilliant blue of the sky, the colours overlaid with the scent of hay and horses, diesel and cattle. Wild things called to one another in the gathering twilight; horses and steers answered them, an occasional dog joining in the argument. Porch lanterns burned low, white post-and-rail fencing gleaming, paintwork obviously well-tended. Everyone they passed was wearing a Stetson, and, to a man, they took them off and waved as the car drove past.

"Supper's ready, you two!" Patricia called. Erik turned to Tim. "It won't be steak tonight, more likely some concoction of chicken or turkey curry – my wife's only real culinary talent is curry, I'm afraid."

Patricia came through from the kitchen, carrying a large dish, the steam coming from it scented with spices. "Yes, Tim. Erik is right – I never have managed to get his steak to come out the way he likes it, so I let him cook it himself. But, of course, tonight he wanted to be free to chat with you, so I offered to cook. I hope chicken curry is alright for you?"

"Perfectly, thank you," Tim replied. After the meal, he would think that there was nothing wrong with only having one talent, if it were as well honed as Patricia Lux's for making curries was.

During the meal, Patricia suggested they take a ride across the valley. "It will be light for quite a while yet", she said. Tim nodded, saying he would be very interested in seeing the local area.

"Ah, you and Tim go out, my dear" said Erik, suddenly unable to contemplate continuing to play at being this man's new best friend. "I have some paperwork to catch up on. I'll arrange for Zeke to have the horses ready for you."

Zeke was a short, stocky man, Montana born and bred, who had been a rancher since he was fourteen years old, more than forty years ago now. He prided himself on the fact that he could still ride rings round all of the young bucks in town, could show most any man in the county a thing or two on a horse.

His skin was the skin of a man who spent his life outside in all weathers, the colour and texture of old leather, and his hair and mustache were snow-white, the latter stained yellow with pipe tobacco. His life in the saddle had bowed his legs, and he swayed as he walked, his cowboy boots and stetson hat making him appear taller than his five feet five inches. As Tim and Patricia stepped out onto the front porch, Zeke led two saddled horses round from the corral at the rear of the ranch.

"Mister?" Zeke called out. Tim turned around, smiling. "I brung yah the chestnut geldin'. He'll give yah a good ride – fine, steady hoss he is. I'll be a-listenin' for yah and Miss Patricia here when y'all come back. No need ta worry 'bout wakin' me – these old bones don't need much rest ennamore."

Tim thanked him, and assured him that they didn't plan to be out too late in any case. He and Patricia saddled up, and rode out together, Tim fidgeting a little, as the Western saddle was rather different to what he was used to back home.

As he watched them leave, Zeke scratched his head. Strange, he thought, that Mister Erik never rode out with his lady – didn't even come with her when she went out with this British fella. Strange too how much more relaxed Miss Patricia looked with the British man than with her own husband. Still, Zeke reasoned, shrugging his shoulders and walking back to the stables, it wasn't his place to question how people conducted their lives. He was paid to take care of the horses and the land, and that was all. Nothing else was any of his business.

Patricia looked well on horseback, thought Tim, as he followed her through the hay meadows that surrounded the ranch, heading towards the distant hills along roads lush with buck brush, chokeberry and elderberry, riding against an evening sunlight Tim had never known in England, not even in Norfolk, where the skies were more dramatic than in most other counties.

After a while, Patricia reined her mount in, wheeling about to face back the way they'd come. Copying her, and drawing level, Tim saw the glow on her cheeks brought about by the cool evening air. As his knee accidentally touched hers, Tim felt a jolt of pleasurable pain; this was how he and Joan had been, he recalled, riding out together in the long summer evenings.

"Well, Tim. This is Montana – what do you think of it?"

For a moment, Tim couldn't speak, drinking in the sight spread out below him, rivers and creeks sparkling like silver snakes, the Rockies in shadow in the very far distance, the soft, dimming light seeming to belong more to a painting than reality, pinpricks of lamplight from scattered homesteads.

Tim knew instinctively that this was a sight that would stay with him until the very end of his life, one he would look back on again and again.

"It's wonderful" he said, words seeming inadequate.

Patricia kicked her mount on, suddenly, calling back over her shoulder; "Come on, Wing Commander! Last one back to the ranch makes the coffee!" Spurring his own mount on, Tim rode hard towards the sound of her laughter, which sounded like water whispering over crystal.

CHAPTER SIX

When he woke the next morning, Tim couldn't remember where he was for a moment. Then, blinking in the sunlight streaming through the uncurtained window, he remembered he was in Montana, and smiled as he remembered the previous evening's ride with Patricia, although he thought it odd that Erik hadn't accompanied them – he would never have let Joan ride out alone with another man!

As he got up, Tim remembered the sight of Patricia, waiting to meet him at Great Falls International airport the day before, dressed in blue jeans, check shirt and cowboy boots. It had been cool when he'd arrived, the long flight having allowed him not only to catch up on his sleep, but also to read a few key points in his guidebook.

Big Sag ranch, he discovered, was named for the local area, as it was the largest of the ranches around Great Falls, comprising of some 23,000 acres. The city of Great Falls had a population of 50,000 at last count, which, though it seemed small to Tim Watts, was not unusual for a frontier city. Great Falls was famous for its rich Lewis & Clark history, and had been home to several famous persons, including the artist Charles M Russell. Patricia had driven him back to the ranch, a journey during which he had convinced her to stop calling him Wing Commander, and she had got him to stop calling her Mrs Lux. They were Tim and Patricia by the time she was pointing out the sites of deactivated MinuteMan Intercontinental ballistic missiles, which had been primed for use during the Cold War. As he washed and shaved, Tim remembered Patricia asking, nervously;

"Do you think there'll ever be another?"

"Another what?" he'd asked, puzzled. "Another war? There will always be wars, I'm afraid."

"I meant another Cold War, really."

Tim had smiled and shaken his head. "I think the Reds are too busy shaking skeletons out of their own cupboards to worry about some humble westerners. And I don't just mean cowboys."

As he buttoned his shirt, Tim sighed, remembering Patricia's slightly awkward condolences on his loss of Joan, from which she had seemed to rush on to explaining that Erik would be back shortly, he had had to go over to the vet in Great Falls to collect some medication for an ailing horse. Erik had returned an hour or so later, and had taken Tim out to see his collection of vintage planes.

"The bi-plane there is Patricia's – she flies, too. A present...my wife has expensive tastes, you might say."

Although Erik Lux had smiled, the smile hadn't reached his eyes. Tim Watts had thought he saw the shadow of something dark and disturbing on those proud Aryan features...but, of course, he told himself as he went downstairs, it had been a long journey, he had been tired. He'd probably just imagined it. After all, Erik Lux had never been anything other than friendly towards him.

Arriving downstairs, he greeted his hosts, who were sitting at the table. Patricia got up to make him some coffee.

"Erik wondered if you might want to do some flying with us, after breakfast? There's a local feature, Square Butte. It's quite an eminent landmark around here; legends say an outlaw Sheriff, Sheriff Plummer, is meant to have buried loot he stole in a bullion robbery or some such there, back during the Civil War. When he was hanged, he said if he was pardoned, he'd take the townsmen to the exact location – but they didn't believe him. Even today, people still go out there, looking for Plummer's gold."

"Square Butte is over 2000ft high" Erik Lux chipped in. "All the local youths who can fly go over there, daring each other to see who will fly the lowest."

As Tim frowned in obvious disapproval at such recklessness, Patricia laughed.

"I'm afraid there's not much else for them to do round here. And they're all very skilled pilots; most of them have fathers who own small planes, you see – the distances around here are so vast, a plane really is the only viable form of transport sometimes, especially for those who own more than one ranch – the children are taught to fly practically before they can walk!"

"But there have been accidents" her husband said, looking at Tim. Once again, Tim saw that dark shadow – only this time, he knew it wasn't simply his imagination.

"I would be more than happy to take a flight with you, Erik – it certainly looks like the perfect morning for it."

And indeed it was, a clear, mist-free morning, with the temperature neither too high nor too low, the sun at the perfect level of brightness, bright enough to bathe everything in an impossibly beautiful, soft light, but not so bright that you would be blinded when you gained height.

"Good". Erik said, smiling. "You and I, Tim, shall take my two Mustangs – I regret to say I will not share the second one, my latest acquisition! The other Mustang is in perfect order, though, I assure you – I have my planes serviced regularly. And Patricia shall join us in her bi-plane, the one I showed you yesterday. I have a feeling she may give us both a run for our money! We shall fly the tourist trail first, then finish the day with some youthful folly over Square Butte – because how will these young ones learn, Tim, if old dogs like us don't show them a few tricks?"

Tim laughed, but couldn't help feeling that he was being set up, somehow, that Erik Lux had something in store for him. He tried to tell himself he was being ridiculous – surely, if the man were up to anything, he would have insisted they head straight for Square Butte? You didn't show the sights to someone you planned to harm in some way, after all. But Tim Watts couldn't shake the memory of the shadow he'd seen on Erik Lux's face, and, making some excuse about needing to feel real sunlight on his skin, he left them to their breakfast, and went outside, to check Lux's Mustang 51-P over for himself.

Everything was in order, including the fuel level, and Tim Watts chastised himself. Paranoia was a symptom of depression, wasn't it? And who could blame him if he'd been feeling a bit low after Joan's death? But Joan was gone, she wasn't coming back, and he was still here. It was time, he thought, to pull himself together, to stop imagining things; time to stop seeing enemies where none existed. When he looked inside the plane, however, he noticed that there was no parachute.

"Erik – do you have a parachute at all?"

"Ah, no. I am afraid my only spare was damaged. My own fault – I neglected to fix a small hole in the roof of the supply shed. Two days later – the worst rainstorm Montana had seen for years! You may take mine, of course, if you feel you may need it."

At the implied insult to his skill, Tim smiled and shook his head, as Erik had hoped he would. "No, I don't think so – no need for a parachute when you know what you're doing, I always say. Thank you for the offer, though." Tim had not noticed the slight panic in Erik's voice, the panic of a man who is not convinced that his gamble will pay off.

The day passed well enough, Erik and Patricia taking Tim, as promised, over the tourist trail. They landed on a private runway at Great Falls International, and explored the city together, Tim finding the place wholesome, family-orientated, and not too lively. When he commented on this fact, Patricia nodded.

"That's how Western towns are – nothing like your London!" Tim laughed. "I wouldn't want it to be," he said, and meant it. He would have been disappointed to have come all this way just to find an American version of London.

After they had spent an hour or so wandering around Great Falls, taking in the sights, and visiting the city's museum of old Western equipment and memorabilia, with a meal at Bar-S Supper Club, where Tim ate what he heartily declared the best steak of his life, the trio took to the skies again, cruising low over the Broadwater Overlook, where the Missouri and Sun rivers came together.

As the flew back the way they had come, Erik Lux indicated, by a series of hand gestures, that they would circle the ranch lands a couple of times, so Tim could appreciate the unique view that their altitude afforded, then head east, towards Square Butte. Erik's final series of gestures were comfortably familiar, reminding Tim Watts of his war days. He, old Watto, was to keep close to Lux's tail, following his every move, while Patricia, flying her bi-plane, would be "in attendance" - keeping an eye on both craft, ready to assist if necessary. Watto Watts couldn't see the German's face. If he could have, it would have been clear to him that Erik Lux planned to take him far, far beyond Patricia's help.

They circled Big Sag ranch lazily, engines droning like insects. Tim drank in the sights, reflecting firstly how different everything looked from the air, and secondly that there was nothing like this in England. He glanced at his watch, nodding as he noted the time. They had plenty of the day left; it was September; dawn broke at six-thirty, and it wouldn't begin getting dark until around nine that evening. It was only two in the afternoon now.

Suddenly, Lux broke off his lazy circling, heading east. Tim Watts followed him, hanging tight to the other Mustang's tail, Patricia a little way behind them in her bi-plane.

Over Square Butte, Lux began to show off. Watching him as he looped, rolled, swooped and dived, Tim Watts had to admit that the German was no amateur – he'd seen pilots like him during the Battle of Britain, full of talent and bravado. Smiling a little, Tim realised he could, for once, admire the skill of this other pilot, in a way that had been denied him during the war. Then, German aces were the enemy, their skill something to be cursed, not applauded. But here, now, it was different. Erik Lux, Tim thought, was a talented pilot, and a friend.

Relaxed now he was back at the controls of a plane, back in the air, Tim Watts matched Erik Lux in every stunt the German pulled, and showed off a few wholly unique antics of his own.

Dropping low, Lux flew west, out over the prairies, then did a wide curve back towards Square Butte, with Tim keeping tight to him, just below his tail, squinting against the harsh glare of the sunlight on the Mustang's windshield.

Suddenly, Lux swooped, making a tight, left turn. Unable to follow quickly enough, Tim realised he was flying far too low, Erik's unexpected turn had left him isolated, heading straight for the hard, unyielding side of Square Butte. There were only seconds left for him to try and avoid disaster – and certain death.

The sweat that coursed over his body was ice cold as he desperately fought to gain height, to pull away from the Butte's summit. He thought he had made it, just, until the sound of metal tearing apart filled his ears. The bottom of the Mustang had collided with the jagged top of Square Butte, and a smear of glycol spattered the windshield, the engine barking a series of disgruntled coughs, indicating to Tim Watts that he was, as they say, in a bit of a state. The plane didn't have long left, and, unless he could float it down, as he was desperately trying to do, neither did he.

As he flew over the open prairie, the Mustang seemed to slow, as though hesitating in the face of its impending demise. Glancing, for some reason, to his left, Tim saw Patricia's bi-plane, almost directly alongside him. Patricia waved her hand in a sharp, upward gesture, which Tim interpreted at once – he'd seen it used during the war. Pushing back the hood of the cockpit, he rose to his feet, and, judging the distance with an expert eye, jumped.

As the small plane rocked, and the wind tried to tear him away and hurl him to the ground, Tim knelt, and clung to the wing literally for dear life.

As Patricia slowed the bi-plane down, Erik Lux flew over them, engines screaming, leaving the bi-plane rocking dangerously in the sudden slipstream. Patricia held the plane as steady as she could, while Lux flew back over them, once more threatening to force the small plane to disaster.

But Patricia was every bit as skilled a pilot as her husband or Tim Watts, and, keeping her nerve admirably, she coasted the tiny craft down onto a grass runway.

As he lay on the plane's wing, panting, his body aching almost beyond endurance, Tim Watts felt an intensity of fear he had not known since his Battle of Britain days. Finally, painfully, he clambered off the wing, standing beside Patricia as she got out of the cockpit. As Erik Lux strode towards them, having landed his own plane, the fear abruptly drained from Tim Watts's body, to be replaced by anger – there was no doubt in his mind that Erik Lux had tried to kill him, and Patricia. What he didn't know was why.

"What the bloody *hell* was that about, man?" he yelled, as Lux approached, all the German's demons suddenly visible, fury flooding his face. Tim felt the hot blood rush to his own features, felt the hardening core of rage inside him.

"You were extremely lucky, Wing Commander – this time at least – no thanks to this...*creature*." Without provocation, seemingly without even the sense that it was in any way wrong, Erik Lux stepped forward, swung his fist hard and fast, striking his wife across the face. As the blood spurted from her nose, and she desperately tried to back away, to protect herself, Lux readied himself for another blow.

Tim grabbed the German by a handful of his shirtfront, jerked him close, and punched him, with the force of all his rage and shock and fear, in the side of his jaw. Lux reeled back into his Mustang, but seemed to come straight back, still swinging. He had lost the element of surprise, though, and blind fury meant his punches were erratic. Tim caught him with a powerful right hook, which nearly lifted Lux off his feet, and saw him slam once more into the side of his plane, blood trickling down his face.

Staggering to his feet, Erik came at him again, and was met with Tim's knee in his face, the Englishman's heavy forearm crashing across the back of his neck. He fell to his knees, gagging, bleeding and struggling for breath. Getting up again, with effort, he launched himself once more at Tim Watts.

Patricia Lux was horrified. So much had happened in the last few minutes. She couldn't even begin to grasp it.

Her husband had tried to kill the man she thought was his friend. It didn't matter that he had been unsuccessful; he had tried to trick Wing Commander Tim Watts into flying into that craggy sentinel that was Square Butte, and now the two men – the two men she had thought were friends – were fighting like wolves at mating-time.

Patricia ran inside, and came out moments later, holding a high-powered rifle and screaming at the two men to stop. She had won first prize at the local ladies' turkey shoot every year for the past five years, and had been the only child of a father who, in his younger days had hunted wolves for a living, and who had not let the fact that she wasn't the male offspring he had hoped for get in the way of him teaching her all the things he would have shared with a son. A rifle was nothing new to Patricia Lux, nor was the idea of using it to kill. Or simply to scare.

The first shot whistled just above the heads of the two men, too accurate in its proximity to have been anything other than a calculated miss. They didn't even glance up as the bullet slammed into the fuselage of her husband's plane. They didn't blink as her second shot kicked up the dirt at their feet.

The third shot, tearing through the sleeve of her husband's shirt as he pinned Tim Watts against the wall of the ranch and swung back for a punch, drew blood, and the men's attention.

"STOP IT! STOP THIS NOW!" Patricia screamed in fury. Wheeling around, Watts forgotten for the moment, Erik Lux charged at his wife. Calmly, she held the rifle level with his approaching midriff, her gaze and hands perfectly steady. Lux stopped in his tracks, shouting in German, a habit of his at times of high emotion. Patricia didn't waver; her gaze and her gun were trained steadily on her husband.

"I want an explanation, Lux. What the hell is wrong with you? You deliberately try and fly me into that Butte, then you try and force your wife's plane, with her in it, to crash! Are you insane, man?"

As he looked up, Erik Lux certainly *seemed* insane, his eyes glowing with an alarming intensity, seeming to be lit with a bizarre sort of...well, dark light, that terrified Watts. He hauled himself to his feet, and spat in the Englishman's face.

"Do you remember 1940, Wing Commander? Do you remember a Messerschmitt, downed off the coast of France? Or were there so many you have forgotten?"

"What are you talking about, man?" Tim Watts was genuinely bewildered; the man must be mad, he thought: he thinks he's a Luftwaffe pilot, come back from the dead.

Erik Lux pulled a wallet from his trouser pocket, and, with surprising gentleness, and tears glinting in the light of the dark fire in his eyes, took out a photograph, and held it in Watts's face.

It was black and white, and showed a German pilot, in full Luftwaffe uniform, standing beside a Messerschmitt ME109, his arm around a young boy dressed in the uniform of the Hitler Youth.

"That was the last time I saw my father. My tenth birthday. He went out on a routine mission a few days later, and never came home. *You* made sure of that – you murdered him. The war is not over, Wing Commander – not for me, and not for you. Collect your belongings, and get the hell off my ranch. You can take my wife with you, if you want – I can't stand the sight of her, now. We'll meet again, Wing Commander – but Vera Lynn won't be singing."

Tim Watts stood there, unable to believe what he was hearing. The sights and sounds and scents of the Battle of Britain came flooding back. He remembered the dogfight, remembered watching the Messerschmitt go down, remembered, a few days later, being told the name of the pilot; Hans Lux. Why hadn't he remembered before? Why hadn't he made the connection when he first met *Erik* Lux?

Tim Watts didn't want to know what demons were inhabiting this man's sick mind, driving him mad, talking to him of vengeance. All he knew was that Erik Lux was dangerous, and that he, Tim Watts, long retired from combat, was facing an enemy he thought he had defeated a long time ago.

Abruptly, and with a filthy look at his wife, Erik Lux turned and walked away. Ignoring Tim Watts, he climbed into the cockpit of his Mustang, and rose skyward, wrapped in a roar of engines.

Patricia watched the plane until it was out of sight, then threw the rifle to the ground and burst into tears.

Tim hurried to her side, and placed his hands on her shoulders. "Come on, old girl. I think a coffee is in order, don't you?"

Mutely, she nodded. Back inside, Tim sat quietly as Patricia talked, trying to make sense of her husband's behaviour. Finally, taking a deep, shaky breath, she looked at him, seeming to be seeing him for the first time.

"I'm so sorry, Tim. Really. I can't apologise enough – Erik…he frightens me, Tim. And to go on about the war like that – I didn't know his father had been killed in the war, you know – I mean, it was all so long ago, and you were just doing your job! Erik shouldn't blame you – if you hadn't shot down his father's plane, another British pilot would have. He shouldn't hate you – he shouldn't have tried to kill you – to kill us." She was shaking, her breathing ragged.

Tim nodded. "But you saved my life, Patricia. I won't forget that, not if I live to be a hundred."

Patricia shook her head, bewildered. "Surely, now, he'll see that he can't go on like this, he'll see how senseless all this anger is? Surely he'll realise that it's best to just move on from the war, from what happened?"

"I don't think he will" Tim said, sadly. "I can understand a ten-year-old child being upset by his father's death, being angry that his father's life was taken from him by another. I can understand a child seeing that other as a murderer, despite the fact that there was a war, that the other man was fighting for his country, just as the child's father was, that the battle could have gone either way. I can understand a child wanting to make someone pay for the death of his father. But...I can't understand an adult still feeling like that, and so passionately. I've known other Germans, since the war – they weren't like Erik." He sighed, his eyes suddenly seeming impossibly sad. "I don't suppose you could give me a lift to the airport? Even if your husband hadn't ordered me off the ranch, I think I'd be leaving now, anyway."

Patricia nodded. "Of course, Tim. And I really am sorry."

Getting up, he patted her arm. "There's no need to be – after all, *you* weren't the one who tried to kill me, as far as I'm aware."

As Tim Watts walked away, to pack his bags and leave Big Sag ranch, Montana, and her life, Patricia suddenly knew, with absolute certainty, that she couldn't stay without him – she couldn't be alone with her husband.

When Tim Watts came out of his room, he wasn't at all surprised to find Patricia waiting for him, with her bags packed also.

"I'm coming with you, to England – I have money, don't worry about that, I can buy my own ticket. I just can't...can't be here when Erik gets back. I can't stay here, with him." Almost as an after thought, she said, "You don't mind, do you?"

Tim shook his head. "Not at all – I have a big house, too big for me, really. You would be most welcome."

"Thank you. I've rung my sister, and told her what's happening. Our parents are away, on a cruise, at the moment – I'll ring them in a few weeks, when they're back." She took a deep breath. "I'm going to apply for a divorce, Tim – Catherine knows a lawyer who does that sort of thing, she doesn't think there'll be a problem with sorting it out from England. I just...I can't stay with him, Tim. The Erik Lux I saw today isn't the man I married. I haven't known that man for a long time."

Wordlessly, Tim Watts put his arm around her. There were no words for this, he reflected. Finally, he picked up his bags, and one of Patricia's.

"Come on, then. It's best we leave now, I think." Smiling, and finding a lighter tone, he said, "I think you'll like England."

CHAPTER SEVEN

Over the next few months, Patricia came to feel at home in Norfolk. Tim showed her the countryside he loved, the many and varied rivers of the county. He took her into the unique market towns, where she was amazed at how different things could be, even when they were only a few miles apart. He took her to the historic areas, and told her about them, his manner easy-going, imparting just as much information as she needed to appreciate what she was seeing, without making a day out seem like a school trip. Together, they walked along the clifftops at Cromer, where Tim had once walked with Joan. Tim Watts felt himself being drawn to Patricia Lux; he found comfort in being with her, and she seemed to enjoy his company, too. Life settled down to simple normality – a welcome relief to both of them after the shocks of Montana.

Shortly before Christmas, Patricia's divorce came through. She was spending the holiday in New York, with her family, while Tim planned to visit Joan's parents, not wanting them to feel the loss of their daughter too much on what would be the anniversary of her death. Not wanting, if he were honest, to feel her loss too much himself, as he still did at times, even with Patricia at his side.

"My mother is going to come with me, back to Montana, in the New Year," Patricia said one evening, as they were finishing supper. "I need to get a few things, sort out my affairs."

Tim nodded, then frowned. "Just your mother? Can't your father go with you, too? I know I would go with my daughter – if I had one – for a thing like that."

Patricia shook her head. "He's got a lot of business commitments – it's just not really practical for him to take the time out. I'll be okay, though."

Tim reached across the table, and took her hand. "You must be dreading it, you poor thing. I wish I could come with you myself."

Patricia kissed him lightly. "Don't worry about me, Tim. I need to do this without you, to…I don't know, prove that I can, I guess."

"I'll be here when you get back, darling."

"I know you will."

She was glad Erik wasn't there. Zeke had met her at the airport.

"Miss Patricia. Mister Erik should be away a coupla days. One o' his planes is faulty, he's took it to be looked at."

"Good. I…I don't think I could do this, if he was here." She glanced at her mother, who sat, expressionless, beside her.

Inside, in the house that had once been the home she had made with her husband, Patricia went from room to room, pausing occasionally to pick up some item she wanted to take with her. Things had been so good here at Big Sag, in the beginning, but all that had changed the day her husband had tried to kill the man he had brought there as his friend. The ranch was home no longer, and she knew that no memories of it would linger with her. She walked around it like a stranger. Then remembered something she had meant to do, while her husband was away.

"Patricia? Are you done here?"

"I...why don't you go and see Merle, in the ranch cottage?" Merle was Zeke's wife, and Patricia knew she would be glad of another woman to chat to.

"Alright, Patricia. But don't be too long. Erik won't stay gone forever – I don't trust him not to've lied about where he's going." As she listened to her mother's footsteps walking away, heard the door slam shut, Patricia sighed. She almost wished she hadn't allowed her mother to accompany her. Some things, she thought, you just had to do alone.

She went to the boot room, a small room built for the holding of outdoor clothing and tools. Unknown to Erik, she had followed him in the past, observed him coming in here after he had left the small room at the back of the first floor that, he said, had been his childhood bedroom, and which he always kept locked. He had never invited Patricia in there, had made it clear that it was out of bounds. Patricia's curiosity was aroused, as was her anxiety, by the fact that her husband was always darkly moody when he had been in that room, sullen and uncommunicative. She noticed he often seemed to be talking to himself in German at such times. Quickly, she searched the pockets of the clothing, tipped up each of the boots. She felt sure the key to that room must be hidden in here somewhere, and she intended to find it, to see what was in that room. Suddenly, Patricia's eyes lit upon a battered, much worn Stetson. She had never seen Erik wear it, and its continued presence was therefore strange. Taking it from its hook, she was rewarded; beneath it, the key hung, gleaming in the dim light. Taking it down, Patricia clutched it in her right hand, feeling guilty as she headed up the stairs. She shrugged the feeling off. She was determined, once and for all, to find out what secret lay behind that door.

Arriving at the door, she hesitated, and almost walked away. Steeling herself, she placed the key in the lock and, with a show of determination, wrenched it round. She heard the lock yield, and the door swung inwards, unoiled hinges screeching. Her pulse quickened, and she glanced around wildly, even though she knew Erik wasn't there. She stepped into the room, where an atmosphere filled with darkness and evil seemed almost palpable. Dismissing the sensation as nothing more than a foolish fancy brought about by the darkness of the curtained room, Patricia groped for the light switch. As light flooded from the bare bulb in the ceiling, her hand went to her mouth, a reaction to the horror she felt as the room, and its contents, were revealed. The room was a shrine to Nazism, a black museum of Fascist memorabilia On every wall was a huge flag bearing the swastika of the Third Reich, walls and shelves were crowded with portraits of Adolph Hitler and other Third Reich leaders. Patricia shivered, the evil in the room rising again, cold and wraith-like. The only furniture in the room was a worn wooden desk and chair, three framed photographs standing on top of the desk. Picking one of them up, Patricia found herself looking at a young boy, no more than ten years old, dressed in a uniform she had never seen before, a swastika flag flying behind him. Something about the boy's face seemed familiar. Staring at it a little harder, Patricia suddenly saw what it was.

"Erik!" she cried, recognising her husband in the boy's features.

"Patricia" said a voice, heavy with menace, from behind her. "What do you think you are doing in here?" Turning round, Patricia Lux found herself looking at her ex-husband, his face filled with rage,

"This is my room, my private place. You have no right to be in here! You shouldn't even be on my property!" His voice was raised, emotion making his German accent more pronounced than usual.

Waving her hands at the room, stamping her feet, Patricia shouted back at him;

"What am *I* doing? What are *you* doing, Erik? World War Two is over! Your beloved bloody *Fuhrer* -" she spat the word out - "is dead. He killed himself because he couldn't deal with losing his wretched bloody war!"

He hit her, then, the connect sounding like a rifle shot in the silence of the room. Blood gushed from her nose. Grabbing her by her long hair, he flung her from the room, slamming the door shut behind her. Leaning against it, panting, he heard her running down the stairs, sobbing. Calming himself, he walked over to the desk, and picked up the photograph his wife had dropped.. Replacing it lovingly on the desk top, he went round to the chair, and sat down. Picking up another of the photographs, he stared at it for a long time. Despite its age, the photograph was a clear picture of his father, standing proudly by the fuselage of his Messerschmitt, holding the hand of the young Erik. It had been his tenth birthday, early in the year of 1940, and he had been to visit his father at his base.

Tears burned the backs of Erik's eyes, but he refused to cry. Pulling open the desk drawer, he removed two items.

The first was his late father's medal, the Iron Cross with oak leaves, presented personally by the Fuhrer.

The second was a small leather diary, embossed with the swastika, and dated 1940. It had been a Christmas present from *mutti*, his mother, in 1939, his first ever diary. He turned the pages to the date of 15th September 1940, the day he had been told of his father's death, and the last entry he had ever made in the diary. He read the words aloud;

Aufweidersehn, Papa. Translating from the German, he read the next word, written in capitals and underlined, in English, as though he were speaking directly to the pilot who had killed his Papa. REVENGE. Beneath this word, first in German and then in English, he added four more words; *The time has come.*

"Ma'am – what in hell happened back there? I tried to stop 'im goin' in, truly I did, but…"

"It's alright, Zeke. It's…over, now. I just want to go home – back to England. I just want to get to the airport, get on a plane, and fly away from all of this."

"Surely, Ma'am." Zeke's voice was soft, shot through with emotion. He felt bad; he should have been there to protect Patricia from that brute of a man. He shouldn't have let Erik Lux get in there, never mind that it was his property. "I'll drive you to the airport now, Ma'am. Sooner you get back to England, the better, I reckon."

Patricia gave a wan smile, and climbed into the truck, where her mother sat, dabbing at her eyes with a handkerchief.

"Why didn't you just come out when I told you to? I knew something like this would happen!"

Patricia looked at her mother, then looked away, making it clear she wasn't going to discuss this.

As Zeke drove them back to the airport, Patricia remembered something she had wanted to ask him.

"I noticed Speedy wasn't in the corral."

"No, Ma'am. Mister Erik rung through a few days back, said that lawyer fella from the edge o' town was comin' over to buy him. Sure sorry ta see him go, a fine bit o' hossflesh, he was. I remember Mister Erik bringing him in that first time."

Patricia remembered, too. In the corral, Erik had tried to lay a rope on the big, black stallion. Speedy had bolted, racing round, bucking, before finally settling as far away from Erik as he could get, snorting and pawing at the ground. Erik had waited, patiently, letting the big animal get used to his scent, had spoken softly, gently, words of love, and of respect. Then he had walked away, leaving the horse to be a horse for a while longer, letting him have his head and his spirit for one more evening. Tears welled up in Patricia's eyes. Speedy was gone, an echo of the fact that the gentle man who had, eventually, tamed him, with nothing more than love and understanding, had also left. Neither of them, she knew, would return. Nor would she.

They had arrived at the airport.

"I'm sure sorry about all of this, Miss Patricia" Zeke said, touching his hat. "Shouldn't have to end like this, should it?"

"No, Zeke. It shouldn't. Take care of yourself."

"You too, Ma'am. I trust that British fella – he knows how to be with a lady, somethin' Mister Erik forgot these past few years, if you'll pardon my boldness."

Patricia nodded, sadly, and got out of the pickup truck, walking away not just from Zeke, but from a major chapter in her life. Her mother followed; Patricia would return to New York for a couple of days, then she would go on to England. Mary Harvey sighed. What had she done, she wondered, that both her daughters decided to up and leave America? Up and leave their family? Patricia knew she would never come back to Montana, would never ride through the wide, open spaces of it again, and for that, in a sudden moment of hot temper, she hated Erik Lux, whose actions had brought about her leaving.

Erik Lux had watched the pickup drive away, hating the woman he had once called his wife. He did not know, now, why he had married her. He had never felt the need of a wife, had seldom even desired the company of other people. He got on better on his own. As soon as the truck was out of sight, he carefully packed up the diary, his photographs, and one of the swastika flags from the wall. He walked out of the room, locking it behind him and putting the key in his pocket. Erik had business in Europe, including travelling to Holland, to make sure the plane his cousin Kurt had found a few months before truly was his father's old Messerschmitt. He almost didn't want to believe that it could be, that his search was finally over. It was, and, apart from the cover-up of the original Luftwaffe markings with dark red paint, and a white stripe down either side – which could easily be resolved, Lux thought – it was in a good state of repair, having been used by the scrapyard's owner, for flying out to other auctions, looking for things he could sell on. A few minutes of haggling, and terms had been agreed for the yard's owner to store the plane securely for a few months, while Erik sought the necessary permissions from both the Netherlands and the UK. Once he had obtained the necessary certificates and agreements from the International Aviation Authority, Erik Lux would collect the plane, and fly it back to England.

Audacious plans were forming in Erik Lux's dark, disturbed mind. The Englishman had killed his father, and taken his wife – granted, the latter was no great loss, except in terms of mere physical attraction, but that wasn't the point. Tim Watts had robbed Erik Lux twice, and had cheated him of restitution once already. Next time, he would not be so lucky. It was time, thought Lux, to settle the score – once and for all. He would have to work hard, would have to plan carefully, but he would succeed. His father's death must be avenged, whatever the cost.

At Heathrow, he passed through customs without a problem; just another American tourist, taking a few weeks' vacation in Great Britain. Once past customs, Erik Lux headed for WH Smith, and the map section. Taking his time, he browsed through the maps detailing London and the Home Counties, as he believed they were called. He selected several maps, including Ordnance Surveys, and paid for his purchases, making small talk with the girl on the checkout, smiling as he walked off. Approaching the taxi rank, he got into a free car, and asked for the Hilton Hotel.

"Right you are, guv'nor. Business, is it? Or pleasure?"

"A little of both, I think – some...pleasurable business, you might say."

Erik Lux had booked his room in advance, and, after showing the confirmation letter the hotel had sent him, was taken up to the 25th floor, and into a room with excellent views, had he been interested in such unimportant things as views.

The first thing he did was to make several telephone calls, mainly enquiring about various airshows in and around London. He was particularly interested in the fact that 1990 would be the 50th anniversary of the Battle of Britain, with a larger-than-ever-before flypast display planned, a display that Lux intended to play a significant part in.

His final call was to book a self-drive hire car, to be collected from Norwich railway station, where he would be arriving the next day, having taken the train from Liverpool Street in the morning.

The station building was impressive, despite the repairs that had been made after the war, when bombs had caused a fair bit of damage, but Lux wasn't here for the sights. He went into the WH Smith at the edge of the concourse, and purchased a couple of local maps, and picked up a leaflet announcing the forthcoming anniversary flypast, marking half a century since the Battle of Britain.

A year ago, Lux had had no thought to how important this event would be to him, how central to his plans it would become. A year ago, he had been thinking of killing Wing Commander Watts in Montana, in a tragic "accident." That had failed, but Erik Lux had not. He had simply moved on to Plan B.

And Plan B, he thought to himself, *could not* fail. He, Erik Lux, would not *allow* it to fail. His father had never failed, and he was, if nothing else, his father's son.

CHAPTER EIGHT

Erik Lux studied the Ordnance Survey maps he had purchased intently, looking for something in particular, something specific to his own, very definite, requirements. He was looking for a remote, but still-functioning, private airfield, out of the way, not too many houses around, secure hangars and a well-kept runway. He paused, finger hovering over a point on the map. Picking up a pen, he circled the name, then turned aside, and picked up one of the local maps. He lay it beside the larger Ordnance Survey, spent a brief moment finding the spot he had circled on the more crowded local map, and studied it in silence. Finally, he smiled to himself, nodded just once, and, taking a notebook and pen, wrote a brief question in his tight, neat handwriting. He glanced at his watch. It was gone six in the evening. His question would have to wait until tomorrow for its answer. Getting up, he picked up both notebook and pen, as carefully as if they had been living creatures, and took them over to the telephone in the corner of his hotel room. He spent several moments arranging them just so, then picked up the receiver.

"Lux, room 595. I was wondering if you would be so good as to deliver a telephone directory to my room? Any time this evening. Thank you – that will be excellent." Replacing the receiver, he allowed himself a broader smile. The time had come, he thought. The time had most definitely come.

Tim Watts stood, looking out of the large windows of the drawing-room, contemplating the bizarre behaviour of Erik Lux. What the hell was wrong with the man? How could he still hold such hatred against Tim for killing his father in a wartime battle where it had been every man for himself, a battle in which slayer and slain could so easily have been the other way around? Tim Watts closed his eyes for a moment, lost in reflections of that long-ago summer. He had felt no hatred for the German pilot he had shot down, no elated feeling of triumph as he had watched the Messerschmitt fall. That had been war, and they had been enemies – it had been a job, nothing more or less than that.

Tim Watts, Watto now only to a handful of men, sighed. He was approaching his seventieth year; was the past of half a century ago to return and haunt what time he had left? Was he, after all he had been through, to face that long-defeated enemy once more? Opening his eyes, Tim wondered how the final battle would be fought. What had Lux got planned for him? Just then, Patricia came into the room. He turned towards her, trying to hide his drawn, concerned face. But she had always been quick to spot the changes in him.

"You seem troubled. What's wrong?"

"It's that ex-husband of yours, I'm afraid. I have a horrible feeling that we're not as free of him as we'd like to be – he's got something up his sleeve, I'm sure of it, and, whatever it is, it won't be pleasant – for any of us."

Patricia rubbed his shoulder, then took his hand.

"Might I suggest we relax, put Erik out of our minds for a while? Dinner in Norwich would be nice. What was the name of that little Italian place we went to a few months ago? Marco's?"

"Yes...fancified spaghetti on toast should buck things up a bit!" Tim laughed, ducking as Patricia threw a playful punch at him. "Let's go –

we can easily be there by seven-thirty, if we leave now. And it's usually quiet during the week – we shouldn't need a reservation."

Although his tone was light, Tim desperately needed the opportunity to relax and unwind. The upcoming 50th anniversary flypast for the Battle of Britain, which would be the last time he would take to the skies, flying his original, World War Two Spitfire, was worrying him, dragging up fear-soaked memories of the War that he'd thought were long dead, and decently buried. Memories, washed in blood and the scent of glycol, of countless dog-fights, fallen comrades. The times, flying home, when you knew loved ones, family, friends, would be hearing, in a newsreader's toneless voice, the dreaded words; "One of our aircraft is missing." There had, of course, been brighter moments, even in the gloom of war, and it was these memories that Tim Watts, with great effort, called to mind; the rush down to the Heart of Oak pub after a scramble, the untrained, raucous voices of hyped-up pilots, navigators and gunners singing along to the tuneless thumping of the pub's old grand piano – *Roll Out the Barrel, Run, Rabbit, Run*, and, later, when the adrenaline had worn off, and alcohol was having its sedative effect on men whose nerves badly needed it, the more nostalgic, mellower songs – *This is a Lovely Way to Spend an Evening, Always* – sung by the pub's blue-eyed beauty, Lana the landlady, accompanied by her husband Ben, confined to a wheelchair by a steel girder crushing his legs at the factory where he'd worked after the end of the first War – Ben had always had a grim laugh about that; you survived the trenches, Ypres, the Somme, and got taken down by a steel girder at work, when you thought you were home and safe. Smiling, Tim recalled how they had all – himself included – flirted, in a completely innocent, harmless way, with the Lovely Lana, as she came to be known. Those times, Tim knew, would stay with him, and all who had survived, forever. They would remember them with fondness, as they remembered fallen colleagues with dignity.

Sitting in the quiet, backstreet restaurant, candles flickering on the table, Tim felt himself relax. Patricia looked wonderful in a pale, dove-grey dress, a single string of pearls at her throat, a black shawl wrapped around her shoulders, to ward off the chill of the evening. Looking at her, Tim felt he could almost see Joan there, dressed up, with a put-on accent, as though she were playing some sort of game. He knew that Joan was happy for him, wherever she was. They had discussed, when it became clear that Joan may well not live to the old age she had dreamed of, the fact that, should Tim meet someone else, later, he should make the best go of it he could, should try and be happy.

"But no one else will be you!" he'd cried, ever the romantic. Joan, always the more practical, down-to-earth one, had patted his hand. "I know, dearest Tim. And that's a good thing. I won't be here, Tim, not forever, and you don't deserve to be lonely." The conversations had been painful at the time, but, now, Tim was glad they had had them.

By the end of the evening, Tim was his old self, laughing with Patricia, looking forward to the Battle of Britain flight, seeing it not as the awakener of old, troubling memories, but as an honourable, decent and dignified memorial to those who didn't make it home, men who, as Tim imagined, would be sitting in the Great Hereafter, watching and approving. All thoughts of Erik Lux were gone from his mind. They returned to the manor, having both enjoyed themselves immensely. The moon was full, floating among a sea of starry jewels in the night sky.

Tim parked the car in the garage, and they both got out, and stood for a long moment, staring at one another. Tim smiled, and walked round to Patricia. With his fingertips, he tilted her head up, then leant over and pressed his lips to hers, his free hand behind her back, pulling her towards him. She responded, leaning against him, pressing her lips to his. As they concluded their kiss, and looked up, still embracing, Patricia smiled. "You know, Tim, I've been wanting you to do that since the day I first set eyes on you."

Erik Lux woke early, as was his habit. As usual, he did not feel particularly refreshed; he seldom slept well, and last night felt he had hardly slept at all. But the reasons were different, this time. Normally it was the white heat of bitter, raging anger, the blinding dark light of insanity, that had him tossing and turning, prey to the very worst kinds of dreams. Last night, though, it had been excitement, anticipation, the sense that, this time, things were going to go his way.

He got up, showered and dressed, and picked up the telephone directory that had been delivered a mere fifteen minutes after he had requested it, the previous evening. Sitting in the one armchair in the hotel bedroom he would be calling home for the next few weeks, he flicked through it, stopping suddenly. A smile split his face; last night's question proved far easier to answer than he had thought. Reaching over to the telephone table, he picked up his notebook and pen, scored three firm lines through the question written on the first page, then, beneath it, wrote a name and number, copied from the directory that rested in his lap. He glanced at his watch. Too early, he thought. Too early for casual enquiries. He decided he would go down for breakfast, would try one of those "full English" things that the hotel seemed to advertise so proudly, perhaps see if he could get hold of a half-decent cup of coffee – the English, he had decided, knew nothing about good coffee – maybe read one of the several papers that were delivered to the hotel each morning, then return to his room and make his phone call – which would, he hoped, dictate how his day was to be spent.

Tim Watts woke slowly, feeling well-rested. Yawning, he stretched, and smiled as Patricia came in, with toast, cereal, Earl Grey tea and that day's *Times* on a tray.

"You must think I'm terribly lazy" he said, catching sight of the time. Patricia merely laughed.

"Not at all – what's the good of retirement, if you can't have a nice long lie-in once in a while?"

Setting the tray down carefully, she climbed into bed beside him, and took his hand.

"Breakfast in bed, read the paper, chat about current affairs, fashion, popular culture and house prices for a while, then get up, and get dressed with a view to doing nothing in particular. How does that sound, darling?"

Tim smiled. "Is there a word that means absolutely delightful, but not quite the done thing at the same time?"

"Yes," Patricia replied at once, "there is; enjoyable."

"Ah, enjoyable. I'll remember that."

"Good morning. Mr Lake, I believe? You won't know me, my name is Erik Lux. I'm looking for an airfield, somewhere a bit quiet, where I can work on a…project, a hobby, if you will, undisturbed, and I noticed your property, at… Elwood? Would it be convenient to come and have a look around this afternoon? I have…very specific requirements, you see, and want to make sure the place I choose is absolutely right. Yes, two o'clock would be fine. I do have a map, but, yes, I think perhaps directions would be helpful." Erik Lux picked up his pen, and began to make notes, his hand travelling rapidly across the paper. "Thank you, Mr Lake. I shall see you this afternoon, at two o'clock."

"This really is a lovely way to spend an afternoon," Tim said to Patricia, as they strolled, hand-in-hand, along the river Thet, where it ran through the town of Thetford, which was named for it. There were other couples around them, doing exactly as they were, and yet, somehow, they felt as though they were the only people there, as though the warm sun glinting on the river, the clear blue sky and the family of swans floating by had been put there just for them. It was a feeling Tim remembered having with Joan, and one Patricia dimly recalled from those distant, early days with Erik, before he had changed. Before she had asked him about Germany, and his father. She shivered, and forced all thoughts of Erik Lux from her mind.

They crossed over the bridge, stopping to gaze over the railings at the sublime, almost surreal, beauty of the river, the willows along the bank, the swans… Patricia turned to Tim.

"Are you happy, darling?"

"Yes," he replied, "I am. I feel as though nothing bad can ever happen, now."

"Good" Patricia replied, squeezing his hand gently.

"Mister Lux, is it?"

The Eagle Will Fly

Erik had stopped at the entrance to a large airfield, an entrance blocked by a red and white pole. He got out of the car.

"Yes."

The man, in his seventies, with wispy white hair and piercingly clear eyes, held out a hand.

"George Lake, owner of Elwood Field. Yer alright to leave the car there, mate – not too many people round this way. Be safe enough."

George hefted the pole aside, not seeming to unlock anything. Catching Erik's look, he grinned.

"Not that sorra place, Mister Lux. It's padlocked at night, see – all them as have planes here have keys, so they can come and go as they like, and the essential workers have got their sets, too." He winked. "Be sure, though, I locks this here barrier down good and proper when the fellas from the insurance comp'ny come around, and I don't tell 'em how many sets of keys is floating around, neither! Far as they're concerned, everyone comes and goes through me. Keeps my premiums down no end."

"But your storage...the hangars..."

"Top-notch kit there, Mister Lux. Ain't gerrin in one o' my sheds unless you gorra bazooka or some such."

"Good. The aircraft I'm working on is...valuable, you see."

"World War Two job, is it? Most anyone who talks about restorin' summat valuable, it's World War Two." George Lake peered at Erik Lux. "You don't look old enough, though."

"I was not, sadly. But my father fought."

"Arr, right. Me, I was up there -" George jabbed a gnarled finger at the sky, as though he might be indicating a tour of duty with the heavenly armies " - Battle o' Britain, all the big showdowns. Sorry- yer German, ain't ya? Lux is a German name? And yer dad – I don't mean to offend yer, or nothin', see?"

"It is quite alright." Erik forced himself to smile. "The war was a long time ago. I...I bear no malice. I am merely an enthusiast for the aircraft of that period."

"Good on yer, mate. Most of us, we never wanted no war, but you gorra do yer duty, ain't ya?"

"Yes, indeed, Mr Lake," Erik replied. *Oh, yes,* he thought, *we have to do our duty. And vengeance is the highest duty.*

George took a pull on a thin, hand-rolled cigarette that was clamped between his yellowed teeth.

"Now, way it is, I opens up weekends, for the public, like. Charge a couple quid at the gate, the misssus does tea and cakes, make a bit more there. Fellas what have planes 'ere, they can open up the sheds, meet people, chat about the planes and what-not, if they fancy it. Got one bloke makes a few bob giving pleasure flights in a little six-seater – nothin' vintage, that, just 'is 'obby, like – but you don't 'ave to be around for that if it ain't your thing. Rest o' the time, it's just me, the missus, and the blokes what've got planes 'ere. No neighbours around, as you can see – right in the middle o' nowhere, 'ere."

"Yes. That is good. I...it unsettles me, too much noise, when I am working, you see?"

"Arr. Coupla blokes like that 'ere. You'll be alright – I don't keep the sheds too close, and people don't bother yer if yer busy. Mebbe say good mornin' and the like, but they'll leave yer be, if they can see that's what yer want."

Erik nodded. "Would it be possible to see one of the hangars? I need to be sure it is large enough not just for the plane, but for myself and perhaps a few others to work around, with our tools and equipment to hand. And I would also like to see your runway, and the landing area."

"Course." George tossed the end of his cigarette to the floor, grinding it out under the heel of his old, dirty boot. "Follow me. I reckon I got just what yer lookin' for, if it's privacy yer want."

Patricia had just come into the drawing room to draw the curtains against the dusk as Tim hung up the phone, a frown on his face.

"What is it, Tim?"

"I'm not sure. I've just had a call from an old mate of mine, George Lake – we were in the RAF together, he's got a bit of an airfield, out at Elwood. Rents out hangars, that sort of thing. Anyway, it seems he had a visit from our favourite German earlier today – said Erik was very interested in renting a hangar for a "project" he was working on, and that he seemed to pay very close attention to the fact that Elwood Field is very isolated."

Patricia frowned. "Does he know about what happened in Montana, this George Lake?"

Tim shook his head. "Absolutely not. We haven't spoken since...since Joan...since Joan passed. He was just calling to see how I was, really. I told him a bit about you, using your maiden name, and he was delighted." Patricia had reverted to calling herself Patricia Harvey as soon as she had arrived back from America, shortly after New Year, wanting no reminders of the man or the life she'd left behind.

"Do you think Erik's up to something, Tim?" she asked, her voice shaking a little.

"I don't know. I mean, he *could* have a perfectly innocent reason for coming all the way over to England, and renting a hangar at a remote airfield. But, somehow, I doubt it."

Patricia watched Tim as he turned and stalked out of the room, his mind already somewhere else. He seemed so tense, these days. She worried about him. Worried about being without him, more than anything. And she, too, worried what Erik Lux was planning, what he was up to.

Back in his hotel room, Erik Lux made two calls, an international call to Holland, and a call to Directory Enquiries, the latter proving necessary as, in a moment of uncharacteristic disorganization, he had neglected to pack his address book. Once more, he jotted something down in his notebook; once more, he turned to his maps, reading them with as much focus and intensity as any priest had ever read the scriptures. He made several marks on the maps themselves, and several pages of notes and diagrams, working late into the evening. Finally, he laid down his pen, and read through the notes he had made, glancing ocassionally at the maps, fixing the locations he had marked firmly in his mind. Then he picked up the telephone directory once more, turning the pages with a calm, concentrated energy until he came to the section he required. A smile spread slowly across his face; the plan that had begun when he had first seen his father's Messerschmitt was taking shape, growing and advancing in detail. There was...preparation to be done, first, though, and, later, he would need expert, outside help.

Expert help. Outside help. Erik Lux sat perfectly still for several minutes, his brain concentrated on the need for expert, outside help, and the finding of that help. Finally, with a sigh, Erik Lux stood up, stretched, and began to get ready for bed. He would be heading to London the next day, but not until later. The people he wanted to meet, as he understood it, were not by habit early risers. Before visiting London – on the way there, more or less – he would pay a visit to a quiet, rural village, where a fellow German lived alone in a large, empty bungalow, and an elderly woman spent her nights awake, in the fog of a half-remembered life, in a private nursing home on the outskirts of the village. He would watch a husband who mourned his still-living wife, and a wife who did not recognise her husband.

In Middle Upton, Tim Watts was pacing around his study, the book he had been trying to concentrate on left, ignored, facedown on the desk. Tim had found that the words were blurring, the sentences not making any sense...he had found himself too restless to read, wound up like a coiled spring with the nervous energy that worrying about what Erik

Lux was up to gave him. And, of course, there was the flypast, too; he couldn't help worrying that he was too old, really, that his skill had gone, that he would make a fool of himself on a momentous, historic occasion, in front of crowds of people – Service personnel, both active and retired, Royals...he couldn't shake the fear that he would do something that left people thinking of the Spitfire they had seen in the skies above London as a joke, a laughable relic of a past that was best forgotten, rather than the thing of beauty and absolute dignity, the symbol of a horror that should be remembered for all time, that it was.

Abruptly, exhausted by this pacing, he flung himself back into the desk-chair, and stared out of the uncurtained window at the dark night beyond, his hands clasped as though in prayer, although he had never been an especially religious man, except for those times when...

He shook himself, got up, marked his place in the book, closed it gently, replaced it with the utmost care on the bookshelf, drew the single curtain across the window, and left, pausing only to turn off the light, and close the door gently, quietly, behind him.

He paused at the door to Patricia's room, which was slightly ajar, as always, and looked in, smiling at her soft face, framed by pillows and bathed in lamplight. She looked so peaceful, lying there asleep, he thought, as, quietly, he stepped out into the hallway, to walk the four or five steps to his own room.

As she heard the soft squeak of the door to Tim's room, Patricia opened her eyes, which were clouded with anxiety. She hadn't slept yet that night, had been kept awake by concern for Tim, by the fretful sounds of his pacing in the study. She hadn't been asleep moments before, when he'd stood in the doorway, seeming almost to draw his strength from her.

She worried because she knew what Erik Lux was capable of, knew that, once he had an idea in his mind, he would stop at nothing until it was completed. If killing Tim were his idea...

CHAPTER NINE.

The day was warm, with a slight breeze, enough sun to let you know it was summer without being overwhelming. Erik Lux rolled down the windows on the hire car, and drew in the scent of an English summer.

He had set off immediately after breakfast, the village he was heading for being some distance from Norwich. A map was open on the passenger seat, various points marked with red circles. In a rucksack on the back seat there was the notebook and pen, and a camera, loaded with a fresh roll of film, a second roll in a side pocket of the rucksack. Occasionally, Lux glanced at the map, but, most of the time, he found he didn't need to. He had always had a certain gift for remembering routes once he had traced them.

As he drove through narrow, winding lanes and sleepy hamlets, he took in the calm, unchanging atmosphere of the places he passed through, the thatched cottages with their neatly-kept gardens, the village greens with their pristine duck ponds, surrounded by graceful willows that somehow understood that it wasn't done to shed their leaves into the still, clear water, the pristine pavements, the well-scrubbed families out for a meaningless walk to nowhere in particular, the perfectly turned out horses with their immaculate riders, the clear, almost musical ringing of a bicycle bell. It was all so unreal, and yet so...beautiful. Lux startled, mentally, at his choice of word, but it was absolutely right. This *was* beautiful, and peaceful, and perfect, and, for a brief moment, he wished he could simply appreciate it, wished his purpose here wasn't dark and dirty and ugly. Shaking his head at his foolishness, he reminded himself that what he was planning, what he would do, *wasn't* ugly; it was, in fact, even more beautiful than these beautiful hamlets, because it was bathed in the transforming glow of *honour*; he was *honouring* Hans Lux's memory by avenging his death, honouring his family by righting the terrible wrong that had been done that day, in the skies above the English coastline.

He came almost unexpectedly to the village he wanted. Glancing over, he checked on the map; yes, this was it. He could see the sign of a pub up ahead, just before what he assumed was the village church. Slowing down a little, flicking on his indicator, he pulled into the pub's car park.

Getting out of the car, he called over to a stocky man who was carrying a barrel towards a door at the bottom of a short flight of stone steps.

"Excuse me – is it alright for me to leave my car here? I plan to return here for lunch, but I would like to have a walk around the village, it is so very pretty, and perhaps see if an...old friend of mine still lives here, first."

"Sure, mate. Nice day for a bit of a walk. Tell you what" the man set the barrel down, and came over to Erik "I know most folks round here. Give me your mate's name, I'll probably be able to tell you if he's still about."

"A German –"

"Old Horst? Horst Block?"

"Yes, that is right. I believe he –"

Ernest Barber

"Married young Rose Fullerton? Pity about her, poor thing."

"She…passed away?"

"No, that'd be a mercy, state she's in. She's in the Home out in near Ravenham – 'bout five or six miles off. Doesn't even know her own husband, these days. Sad when the old folks get like that, really. You can't help thinking death'd be kinder, for them as well as their family, y'know?"

"Indeed. I am…sorry to learn of this. But Horst still lives here?"

"Aye, in that same old bungalow of his, though I don't know why. Too big for him on his own, I've always said, and right at the end of the village – a mile he has to walk when he comes here for his wine of an evening, and his dinner on Sundays, then a mile back. And that little road he lives down – no neighbours to speak of. I mean, like I've said to him, what if he had a fall or took ill? No one'd know. He does have his milk and papers delivered, so you'd think, anything did happen, someone'd notice, but all the same, it's not safe, not now he's on his own there. Anyway, tell him old Joe from the King's Head says hello, won't you?"

"Of course. Thank you, Joe. I shall leave you to your business now, but I am sure I shall be back later – it looks a very nice pub."

"Oh, it is – we do a cracking ploughman's, if it's lunch you're wanting."

"I'll be sure to remember that."

"Catch you later then."

"Yes, Joe – I look forward to it."

Erik smiled as he walked away; it never failed to amaze him how much information the English were willing to give away at the slightest provocation. He had brought his map out of the car with him, and he studied it now, marking the route from the village to Ravenham, which he assumed had been named for the nearby Ravenham Hall Estate. Probably been *part* of the Estate, at one time.

Folding the map into his pocket, he took his camera from the rucksack he had slung across his shoulder, and took a snapshot of the village church; just another tourist, admiring a picture-postcard English village. He strolled around aimlessly for an hour, working on this image by taking more snapshots; the duckpond, a cricket match on the village green, a young policeman talking in an earnest, and most definitely *un*professional, manner with an attractive young woman on a handsome chestnut horse, a row of thatched cottages.

Glancing at his watch, he checked the film loaded in his camera, replaced it in his bag, and set off towards the far end of the village, which, according to the map, was mainly farms, well spread-out, giving way to woodland, with one or two private roads, marked with the faintest of lines, in between.

The road was easy enough to find; five minutes' walk from the last farm, tucked up between a grazing field without any sign of human dwelling, and the wood. The only bungalow was on the edge of the road, as though it wished to distance itself from the three yuppie-type chalets furthur along.

Erik walked past the bungalow, and turned down a dirt track that led into the forest. Once he judged himself safely covered by the trees, he stopped, and waited.

He wasn't waiting long; ten, fifteen minutes later, the side door of the bungalow opened, and an elderly man, dressed in grey trousers and a checked flannel shirt, shuffled out, squinting, and headed over to a flowerbed, where, with obvious stiffness, he crouched down, reaching out a hand to examine a plant. Erik saw the top of the man's head shake, heard a muttered; *"Ach, mein Gott, das ist nicht gutt"*, and knew he had found Horst Block, a man who had served in the Luftwaffe alongside his father, Hans.

As Horst straightened up, still shaking his head, Erik checked the flash was off on his camera, and quickly took a photograph. The old man peered around, perhaps aimlessly, perhaps having caught the *whirr* of the camera's motor, and, seeming to decide it was probably nothing more than someone taking pictures of the wildlife in the wood, shuffled back indoors.

Smiling, Erik waited for a few minutes, then casually walked back the way he had come, not even glancing at the bungalow as he passed.

The ploughman's lunch in the King's Head was, as Joe had promised, excellent, as was the Adnams ale Erik drank with it.

After thanking Joe and settling the bill, Erik got back into his car, and headed out of the village, driving towards Ravenham. He pondered how he would get to see Rose Block, and toyed with the idea of claiming to be a relative of Horst's from Germany, but decided against it; he didn't know if Horst even *had* any relatives still living in Germany, or what he had told the staff at the nursing home. He would play it by ear once he got there, he decided.

By the time he saw the nursing home in the near distance, Erik Lux had decided on his cover story.

"Good afternoon – my name is Wolfgang Klein. I'm afraid I don't have an appointment; I was just passing through the town, you see, and, well...the thing is, I...well, I am having to find a suitable place for my... for my father. He...he is not himself, you see, and, well..."

Erik hoped he was conveying just the right degree of pathetic hopelessness, the right amount of distraction for a busy man with an ailing parent.

The receptionist smiled.

"Would you like to look around, perhaps? Just the grounds, you understand, the gardens and such. You'd need an appointment to see the main house. But I can give you a brochure, and some of the residents will be out in the gardens, taking the air...I'm sure they'd love to have a chat about Westward. Shall I get someone to show you around, Mr Klein?"

"Yes, that would be perfect. This may sound a little strange, but might I perhaps take photographs? Just very general ones, of the outside of the house, the gardens? My father…he gets upset when I bring him to such places, but, at home with me, he likes to look at what he calls 'real' pictures – he means ones – forgive any offence – not taken by a professional photographer for a brochure. He is quite happy, doing this. I think it makes him feel he is in control, that this is his choice, you understand?"

"Of course. And photographs won't be a problem – a lot of the visitors take snaps; it is a rather grand old house."

Erik smiled. "Yes, that is why I stopped. My father, Hans, he can't stand anything modern. He would hate to live in a new place, specifically built as a nursing home."

"Oh, I quite understand – many of our ladies and gentlemen feel the same, Mr Klein. Ah, here we are – Natalie, could you show Mr Klein around outside, perhaps the visiting lounge? He's thinking of sending his father to stay with us, wants to get a feel for the place."

Natalie, a tall, slender brunette, smiled. "Of course, Anna. If you'll just follow me, Mr Klein."

Erik followed her, attempting small talk as they walked, something he was unfamiliar with.

In the large back garden, which had a koi pond with a fountain, well-stocked, fragrant borders, plenty of shade-giving trees, a large patio, and paths of perfectly smooth gravel, a group of elderly people, with uniformed nurses in attendance, were sitting, some in wheelchairs, others on garden furniture, appearing to be doing absolutely nothing.

One of them looked up, scowling at him.

"Who are you? Have you come from the Queen? If you have, you can tell her I don't like her, or her silly little dogs. Why can't she have cats, like decent people? I like cats. I think I had a cat, once. Yes, yes, I did; a funny little thing she was, white, with tabby bits on her ears, and a tabby tail. Lovely little girl. I'd like a cat again, but they're so much work, fur gets everywhere."

Natalie smiled. "Well, Rose, you seem to be feeling better today – very chatty! This is Mr Klein – he comes from Germany, like your hubby does." Turning to Erik, she said, "This is Rose Block – she's not normally this lucid. Very poorly, poor thing."

Rose stared at him, then smiled. "Horst – my darling Horst. You're safe."

"I'm not Horst, Mrs Block."

"Horst. German."

"Yes, I am German, but -"

"Take my picture, Horst – you used always to take my picture."

Erik fought back a smile; luck certainly seemed to be on his side today.

"May I?" he looked at Natalie, apologetic. She smiled.

"Of course. But you'll end up taking all their pictures, I warn you!"

Erik laughed. "That's fine." Natalie took Rose's wheelchair, and moved it to where the light was better. Just as Erik finished taking the photograph, an elderly man hobbled over, moving quickly despite his two walking sticks.

"What she said, about the Queen, young man – that was wicked. Wicked. Still hang traitors, they do. I knew the Queen, once. You take my picture, show it to the Queen, she'll tell you. Head of her private army, I was."

Natalie stepped up, still smiling. "Now, Anthony. You don't have to go telling fibs to get Mr Klein to take your picture – all you had to do was ask him nicely, wasn't it?"

Ninety minutes later, after chatting to several of the residents, and taking many photographs, Erik Lux drove away, with a brochure on the back seat of the car, and a warm sense of satisfaction inside. He had done what he had come to do; now it was on to London.

The Mausoleum was a respectable-looking nightclub. *Too* respectable-looking, Erik thought. He'd seen places like it in Berlin, after the War. Had hung out in them with other black market traders, spending their ill-gotten gains, and adding to the ill-gotten gains of the establishments' owners.

Erik had wandered around the East End for a while, glancing at each pub or club he passed. Walking past the entrance to Shipway Lane, he had seen two police officers smile and shake hands with a slick suited doorman, seen a brief glint of white as their hands parted. *Money, notes, in a white envelope*, he thought, smiling. He'd found what he was looking for.

"That'll be five pounds, sir" the doorman said. Erik handed him a fifty pound note, taking in the fact that the man didn't even blink as he tucked the money into his jacket pocket and handed him a ticket, stamped with that day's date and the club's name.

"And how would you like your change, sir?" murmured the doorman.

"I have a job for your employer" Erik replied, in the same hushed voice.

"Very good, sir. If you'll proceed inside, I'll see if the manager is available to assist you in your enquiry." This was spoken at a normal level, the doorman giving a perfectly plastic smile.

"Your ticket entitles you to one free drink, and ten percent off any meal you order, sir. There is live music tonight, a gaming room through the lounge bar, and…other entertainments upstairs, although there is an extra charge for these. Enjoy your evening at the Mausoleum."

"Oh, I shall, my friend. I shall." Smiling, Erik stepped through the door, his eyes adjusting almost instantly to the low light-level, his senses absorbing the raucous noise of people enjoying themselves, the stench of sweat and alcohol.

He made his way to the bar, and ordered a cognac. He had just begun to drink it when the dimness darkened.

"I'm told you wanted to see me."

Erik looked up. The man who stood behind him was huge; obese, his height, although impressive, not nearly enough to disguise it. His triple chin wobbled, and his heavy-lidded eyes seemed to stare not at Erik Lux, but at some point just past his head. The man was balding, his grey hair thin, wiry, artfully styled. Lux guessed he was in his mid-sixties. The man's accent was pure East End, with a cigar edge.

"Roy Bigley, owner of The Mausoleum, among...other concerns. Shall we go into my office? Leave your drink – I've better stuff for business clients. And I get the feeling we *will* be doing business, Mr..?"

"Lux. Erik Lux. And I hope we shall, Mr Bigley."

"Not here, though. Here's where I get to know you, see if I can work with you, if you can work with me. I like you, I think everything's kosher, I'll give you the name of another gaff, you come there tomorrow, we discuss things in detail, yeah?"

"I am staying at a hotel in Norwich – I'm only in London for this evening."

Roy Bigley chewed on the cigar that he held in the corner of his mouth as he stared at Erik.

"I've got a couple of rooms here, Mr Lux. You can stay overnight, no expense to yourself. *If* I decide to work with you, and *if* you're serious."

"Oh, I am serious, Mr Bigley – trust me on that."

"Trust is a dirty word from strangers, Mr Lux. Follow me."

"So, Mr Lux, what can I do for you?"

They were sitting in Bigley's office, a small backroom, sparsely furnished with a desk, the chair into which Bigley had somehow managed to squeeze himself, and two battered armchairs.

Lux was standing, one hand resting on the back of an armchair. He raised his head as Bigley finished speaking, and looked him straight in the eye.

"I was told that if I wanted a job done well, quickly, with no questions and very little fuss, a job which requires...specialist tools not readily available, you were the man to go to." A cold light came into Lux's eyes, and, finding his confidence, he asked, in a voice that was pure threat; "Was I told correctly, Mr Bigley? Are you that man, or am I wasting my time?"

Bigley's eyes narrowed. "And who told you that, Mr Lux?"

Erik gave a mirthless smile. "Please, Mr Bigley – I know places like this, what they are. Your premises, the...relationship between your door staff and the local constabulary, speak for themselves. As does the fact that money seems to speak very, very loudly here."

For a moment, Lux thought he'd overstepped the mark. Then Bigley began to laugh, his huge body shaking.

"I like your style, Lux. And I think we can make this work."

Bigley tore a sheet of paper from a notepad, picked up a gold fountain pen, and scribbled something on it. He pushed it across the desk to Lux.

"My telephone number. Ring after nine tomorrow morning. You'll get my secretary. She'll be expecting your call. She'll give you a name, an address. You come over there, we'll talk business."

"Why not here?" Lux decided to risk being cocky; Bigley seemed to like that.

The big man heaved himself up, and started to walk towards the door.

"Because this is my hobby, Mr Lux. I don't conduct *business* here, you understand? This is where we relax, enjoy ourselves. Business comes later. Now, if you'll follow me, I'll show you one of the guest rooms I keep for clients who've travelled a fair way to get here. Where's your car, by the way?"

Erik told him where he had left the car, adding that he hadn't paid an overnight charge, as he had expected to be heading back to Norwich. Bigley waved him to silence.

"Give me the keys. I'll have one of my boys pick it up, drive it over." Seeing Erik's face, he laughed. "Don't worry, Mr Lux. My lads are well paid, and I don't hire freelancers; trust me, they don't need to nick a car. Your car'll be there, waiting for you when you get up in the morning, not a scratch on it that wasn't there before, alright? Now, let's make sure your room's acceptable to you, then you can go back downstairs, enjoy yourself. I've told the bar staff that anything you want's on the house."

"You don't have to do that." Erik sensed that Bigley was marking him, making it clear that Lux was in his debt. As if to confirm it, the man bared his teeth. Not smiled, nothing so civilised; he bared his teeth. "I know, Mr Lux. I know. But I've done it, all the same."

The following morning, Erik Lux woke in a room that wasn't his room at the hotel in Norwich. This room was at least twice the size, for a start, and the en-suite bathroom was a proper bathroom, through a proper door, rather than a large cubicle behind a shower curtain. The mattress was clean, with just the right degree of firmness, and the duvet was a thick, good-quality one that, combined with the fine wool blanket, had kept Lux more than warm the previous night. The furniture was ultra-modern, black glass and chrome, the television was a wall-mounted, flatscreen model, with a full satellite package, and the radio was top-spec DAB, with a built-in CD player. There was a well-stocked mini bar, and expensive stationery on the desk under the window. And properly lined, velvet curtains, too.

Erik glanced at his watch. Eight in the morning. He didn't remember what time he had gone to bed, but he had obviously slept well.

He got up, showered, shaved and dressed, and was wondering whether he would be able to get breakfast when there was a knock on the door.

He went over and opened it, to see an attractive young woman standing there, a loaded tray in her hand.

"Mr Bigley asked me to make sure you had a good breakfast, Mr Lux."

"Thank you" he said, only wondering after the girl had left how Roy Bigley had known he was awake.

When he had finished his breakfast, he washed his face and cleaned his teeth, noting as he did so that it was a little after nine. He went over to the desk, where he picked up the piece of paper Roy Bigley had given him the night before. There was a sleek, cordless telephone in the corner of the room, and it was this that Lux used to dial the number Bigley had written down.

"Walthamstow Harleys, Carly speaking."

"Lux."

"Walthamstow Harleys, 33 Main Street, Walthamstow. It should take you no more than an hour."

The receiver was replaced at the other end. After staring at the phone for a minute or so, Erik Lux also hung up, and, picking up his rucksack and straightening the duvet, walked out of the room.

A short, muscular man, dressed in a suit that looked very much like Armani, with collar-length hair of the richest auburn, was waiting outside.

"Mr Lux?" the man held something out, at arm's length. "Your car keys, sir. The vehicle is in the underground carpark to the rear of the establishment. The code to the door is 8151-SO. Have a safe journey."

The man was gone before Lux could thank him.

The motorcycle showroom was situated in one of Walthamstow's more desirable districts. It had been converted from a carpet warehouse during the last yuppification, and boasted an expansive forecourt, which displayed a wide range of machines, from shiny, gleaming new models, through to battle-scarred old-timers, retired, usually amidst many tears and much regret, by their owners, men – and the very occasional woman – for whom the prospect of that last, glorious ride loomed large on the horizon,

The name, in bold red letters on a sign hanging over the entrance, informed potential customers that a Mr Roy Bigley was the sole proprietor.

Erik Lux drove into the customers' car parking area, parking in a spot which had a good view of the premises, which, to his eyes, looked well-maintained, if a little too gleaming for a genuinely legitimate business. He had no doubt that Mr. Bigley was scrupulous about declaring the very last penny of his income from the sale of motorcycles, their parts and accessories, as well as the wet and dry sales from ventures like The Mausoleum, and about filing his various tax returns on time, in the correct format and to the appropriate department.

It was a bright sunny morning, and Lux idly watched two potential customers, helmets and gloves in hands, who prowled across the forecourt, stopping apparently at random to inspect various bikes.

Lux stepped out of his car, aware of the stares of the two men as he crossed the forecourt, and walked purposefully into the showroom, across the expanse of floor to the reception area at the rear. A young woman, perhaps twenty-five, with short, blonde hair, was sitting behind the desk, wearing what Lux guessed to be the staff uniform of red blazer and white blouse. Her name badge told him she was Carly. The smile she had obviously been taught to greet customers with didn't quite make it to her eyes.

"Can I help you, sir?" Her voice was friendly, trying not to be East London, and almost succeeding. Before Lux could reply, Carly continued; "Would you be the gentleman to see Mr Bigley?"

Erik smiled for the first time that day. "That's me." The girl smiled again, the warmth making it to her eyes this time, sparkling in their green glow like sunlight on emeralds.

"Mr Bigley is expecting you; would you like to go up?" she pointed to a staircase to the right of the reception area, marked "Staff Only". Erik thanked her, gave a mock bow, and, a few short steps later, was climbing the staircase. At the top, a sign pointing to the left simply said "OFFICE", and directing the reader down a short corridor. At the end of the corridor was an open door, through which Lux could see the big man sitting at a slightly bigger desk. A goldfish, in a bowl that Lux could have sworn was crystal, occupied the top left hand corner, set a sensible distance from the edge. The goldfish stared at Lux, blinking lazily. The man turned, seeming to be talking to the fish. He sprinkled something – fish food, Lux presumed – into the water, waggled his fat fingers at the outside of the bowl, then looked up. On seeing Lux, the man waved him through, into an office twice the size of Lux's living room.

"Come in, come in. I've been expecting you."

Erik Lux sat down, taking in his surroundings, and the twenty-odd stone man who dominated them, as he did so.

The big man took a cigar from a box on his desk, and, without offering one to Lux, went through the rituals of lighting it. After a couple of long, deep puffs he turned the penetrating gaze of his beady eyes on his visitor.

"I think we can assume it's not bikes and leather you're after, Mr Lux ?"

"No, it is not, Mr Bigley."

"Well, Erik, let's get down to business, shall we? *Your* business. I'm not much for small talk, personally. I told you I can work with you, now you tell me what you want me to do."

Lux licked his lips. He hadn't thought it would be this difficult, this carefully negotiated.

"I have a...rather specialist job. It has a strict deadline, and will require particular skills, and some...tools...that might be...difficult to come by."

The cigar wriggled its way to the corner of Bigley's mouth, a plume of smoke obscuring his eyes for a moment.

"Tell me what it is you want, Mr Lux, and I'll tell you if I can get it for you, when by, and for how much," Bigley replied, his voice betraying no emotion, if, indeed, he even felt any.

Erik Lux told him, precisely and exactly. When he had finished, Bigley looked at him with a furrowed brow, and a growing admiration.

"Well, Mr. Lux. That's a mighty big shopping list, and, if I may be so bold as to say, quite an unusual one, especially as regards the DIY job. That may take a little sorting out – my lads ain't what ya'd call experts at the sort of thing you've described, if you know what I mean?"

"Don't worry about that." From his inside jacket pocket, Lux drew out an envelope, from which he took a photograph and a sheet of paper. Placing the photograph on the desk in front of Bigley, he said; "This man will help you." With a grim smile he continued; "of course, he may need a little...persuading, but I am sure you are used to handling situations like that."

Bigley picked up the coloured photograph. It showed a man who appeared to be in his early seventies, with a good crop of white hair, and cool grey eyes that peered out at the world from beneath busy brows. He was standing in what, to Bigley's untrained eye, was a well-tended garden, and didn't seem to know the picture was being taken. While

The Eagle Will Fly

Bigley studied the photograph, committing the man to a memory famous in certain circles, Lux handed him the piece of paper.

"All the man's details are written on there – his name, address, the name of his wife, and of the nursing home that cares for her."

Bigley nodded without looking up. "Is there a photograph of the wife?" Lux handed him a second photograph, taken from the same envelope as the first, and showing an elderly lady in a wheelchair, a uniformed nurse at her side. Bigley nodded, then picked up the first photograph again, tapping it slowly.

"What's so special about this laddie, then?"

Lux grinned. "From his records, I discovered that he was exceptionally good at his job, a true professional. Just right for my little 'DIY job' "

Bigley stared at Lux. Then he blew cigar smoke straight into the German's eyes. Then he leaned back in his chair, hands folded across his large stomach, and stared at him some more. Finally, he spoke.

"I believe we can do business, Mr Lux. I'll need time to sort out the admin side of it, of course, but we're ahead of ourselves already. I'm not a charity, Mr Lux. I think you know you're asking a lot; I can do it, don't doubt me on that, but it means I've got to ask a lot, too, if you get my drift?"

Lux met Bigley's eyes. "How much?"

Bigley studied Lux. He was a shrewd businessman, and a shrewder crook. He could read people quicker than most of them could breathe, and he knew, for all his bullishness, all his hard-man pretention, that Erik Lux was a complete newcomer to this game, a game in which Roy Bigley was the biggest of the big players.

Bigley thought of a sum, then doubled it.

"Shall we say one million, cash, half up front, half on completion?"

The German didn't flinch. Placing his fingers on the desk as though it were a piano he intended to play, he leaned forward.

"No. I will pay you half what you ask – five hundred thousand pounds, still an exorbitant price, but one I am willing to sacrifice. However, I expect the job I have assigned to you to be carried out just as I have instructed, and without any hitches. I have a strict deadline to meet, and you will enable me to keep it."

Bigley laughed, a low, throaty chuckle. "Trust me, mate – I don't mess up on jobs." To himself, he added "And, if I do, I don't leave anyone alive to yap about it."

Speaking once again to Lux, he continued; "Terms are the same; half now, half when the job's done."

There was no handshake, just the meeting of eyes, the exchange of power between two dark and dangerous souls, and the sure and certain knowledge that a deal had been done. Where the deals were the kind done by men like Roy Bigley, there were never any handshakes.

After agreeing to a time and place for their next meeting, where he would hand the gangster his advance, Lux walked out. Lighting up a fresh cigar, Bigley stared at the glowing tip.

"What's your bleedin' game then, Jerry?" he muttered to himself. Picking up the internal phone that sat on his desk, he barked;

"Carly. Get hold of Mouth. I want him here. Now is good, yesterday would have been better. Got it?"

CHAPTER TEN

Mouth Wilson was Bigley's second in command, being groomed to take over when Roy finally decided he was tired of England, that he fancied somewhere a bit warmer, and not burdened with extradition treaties. In the meantime, he kept the grunts in order, and handled what Bigley liked to call the "admin side of things". They had worked together for nearly twenty years, and, while you'd never call them friends, there was an understanding between them. At forty, Wilson was Bigley's junior by twenty-five years, but deciding which of them was the hardest man would be difficult, if not impossible. All that could be said for certain was that Bigley was the brains of the two, the businessman of the partnership.

As Wilson strode in, an easy gait that assumed power and respect, the atmosphere changed, the kind of change that happens when a big, powerful dog meets a wolf for the first time.

"What's the rush, Biggy?"

Taking a seat without waiting for an invitation, Mouth Wilson revelled in the power he held, the power that allowed him to get away with using the big man's hated nickname to his face. Mouth smoothed his Saville-row suit down over a bulk that was pure muscle, ran a hand through his black hair, barely touched with grey. With his fiery eyes and sheen of expensive tastes, he could be taken for a successful investment banker. His craggy, lined face and shovel-like hands, however, would turn your thoughts to construction, or farming.

Bigley scowled at the man, sensing that the time would come when Mouth, tired of waiting, would challenge his authority, would try and take control of the empire Bigley had devoted his life to building. Bigley resolved, once again, that Mouth wouldn't be successful.

"Ever hear of a fella called Erik Lux?" Bigley asked, head on one side. Mouth shook his head.

"Don't think so. Sounds foreign to me, though. Why, what's he want?"

"He is foreign. A Jerry. And what he wants is something that took even me by surprise. It'll make your eyes water, mate, I'm telling you."

Mouth took a drag on his cigarette, blew out a perfect smoke ring, looked Bigley in the eyes and said, calmly; "I'm listening. Start making 'em water."

So Bigley told him exactly what Lux wanted, leaving out no detail. When he finished, there was silence for a long moment, before Mouth, striking a match to light his second cigarette, said;

"Nutter. He's gorra be a nutter, Biggy."

Bigley shrugged his massive shoulders.

"Perhaps. But money was agreed upon, and the man seems to know what he wants. If we don't screw this up, this could be the biggest score of our careers, mate."

Mouth shook his head. "I dunno. What's his game, this Jerry? It's something massive, innit?"

Bigley smiled.

"I don't much care, me old mucker. Whatever his game is, if he's paying, I'm playing. And so are you." He looked Mouth up and down. "Time to put them posh shoes of yours away, and get yer working boots on." Bigley was smiling as he spoke; he knew he could rely on Wilson to recruit the right boys. He himself would take care of "business", the professional side of things. It would take some hard negotiating with some even harder contacts, contacts outside the borders of England's green and pleasant land, some of them, but he didn't doubt for a moment that he could get what he wanted.

Mouth Wilson left Bigley's office, a frown deepening the furrows on his face. Once seated behind the wheel of his Rover – Bigley always maintained that you should drive an inconspicuous car, something too common to attract attention – he mulled over what his boss had told him. This job would take a fair bit of sorting, but Wilson was a hard nut who lived for challenges. He had carried out more than a few unusual tasks in his time, but from what he had heard from Bigley, this one was in the realms of the truly bizarre. And a lot more sinister. Still, he thought, shrugging his shoulders, a job's a job, and it was time to get on with his part of it. A few names were already running through his mind.

Mouth Wilson lived in an unremarkable terrace in Tottenham, overlooking White Hart Road stadium, home to his beloved Spurs, and it was to this house that he drove now, to change into his "working gear" as Bigley had snidely remarked earlier. Barely twenty minutes later, he emerged, dressed casually in blue Ben Sherman jeans and jumper, and Timberland boots, freshly showered, whistling cheerfully. Your average middle-aged guy, no one special, nothing to draw your attention to him. In public, out shopping or in a restaurant, for example, Wilson was always polite, courteous, respectful. Only those who were very close to him knew the animal that lived, barely leashed, just beneath the surface.

Roy Bigley had been his mentor, and what Mouth Wilson didn't know about the gangland wasn't worth knowing. He had served his time on the streets and in gaol, as Bigley had in his younger days, and, like Bigley, was glad to have survived long enough to get to a position where other people dirtied their hands and took the risks. However, neither Mouth nor Bigley were above stepping back into that world to sort out a problem themselves, when they couldn't find – or trust – anyone else. Wilson was heading for a cafe in Golders Green, cruising through light traffic at a little after 3pm, where he knew he would find Eddie Small, taking a couple of hours' break between his gym sessions. Parking the Rover in a side street, Wilson walked the hundred yards or so to the Full House cafe. As soon as he opened the door, the smell of high-fat foods frying, coffee percolating, and nicotine hit his nostrils. Peering through the pall of cigarette smoke that hung over the whole room, he spotted the man he wanted, sitting alone at a corner table. Wilson brought himself a coffee, and wandered over.

"What's up, Mouth?" Small's physique didn't match his name. Easily clear of six feet, with a lean, hard body, he commanded attention, and Mouth knew that, one day, Eddie Small would be the man who took over from him,

"Cancel everything you've got on for the next couple of weeks. Jobs, women, family – everything. This is coming from the big man himself. We've got a job on."

Eddie didn't want to be a gangster, not really. He told himself that Bigley had taken advantage of him, had conned him into the retained contract he had now. He had a regular job, driving celebrities and the posh set around in top-class limos, a steady girlfriend. But he had borrowed money from one of Bigley's men a few years back, to try and start his own business, in corporate hospitality. It hadn't worked, he hadn't been able to pay his debts, had begged for mercy, and been made an offer by Roy Bigley himself that he couldn't refuse. Now, if the big man said jump, he had to jump.

"When and where?" Eddie Small couldn't keep the sigh from his voice. Somehow, he knew that this would become his life, one day; knew that, one day, he wouldn't have anything left to cancel when a job came in.

The Eagle Will Fly

He didn't want that day to come, but he knew it would, as surely as he knew the sun would rise in the East tomorrow.

"Midnight tomorrow, usual place." With that, Wilson was gone, leaving Eddie Small with a bad feeling in his gut, and the start of a headache.

Back in the Rover, Wilson made his way North, to Ealing and the home of "Doc" Leonard Little, once chief anesthetist at Charing Cross hospital.

Thanks to a little too much coke one day, he had lost his concentration and killed a patient. He was struck off by the General Medical Council, and pretty much struck off from life. He had a habit he could no longer fund, and only the streets had the answer to that.

"Doc" Little had started his tenure on the streets performing backstreet abortions – quite literally; he worked out of a tattoo parlour on one of the worst backstreets in the area. The rise of feminism and the associated rights it brought women had snatched the abortion trade from him, but the tattoo parlour remained, a front for the treatment of wounded gang members. Or the killing of them, if they happened to be off Roy Bigley's Christmas card list.

Wilson strode in without knocking. A girl was stretched out on the black vinyl couch, whimpering. She looked barely old enough to have a working reproductive system, let alone get into the kind of trouble that would drive her to Doc Little, especially when any hospital would have helped her. Doc Little caught Wilson's look of disgust.

"The boyfriend's paying, they both know what's what. They can't go to the hospital because she's underage, right? And he's not. The hospital'd call the cops, and they don't want trouble. Do you, my love?" This last was addressed to the girl, who shook her head. "C'n I go now?" Doc Little nodded. Mouth Wilson held the door open for the girl, then locked it behind her.

"Shut up shop, Doc. The game's on. Tomorrow night, midnight. Be there." As if Leonard had any choice, he thought, as he walked out. Needles always made him nervous.

Next stop Hackney, and the garage of Tony Knox, at twenty-six the youngest man who'd be on this job. Bigley had a policy; no one under twenty five on big jobs.

"Can I help you?" A plump man, in a woolly hat and steel-rimmed glasses, stepped up to Wilson as he entered.

"Tony in?"

"Through the back."

"Thanks." Wilson drew a large denomination note from his pocket, tucked it into the bib pocket of the man's overalls. "I was never here, okay?"

"Y..yes. Of course." The man scurried off, busying himself with a box of spare parts.

Wilson loped through to the rear of the garage, where Knox was working under the bonnet of a maroon Cortina, muttering to himself.

Wilson slapped the bonnet. "Won't start if you keep playing with it, lad."

Startled, Knox shot up, cracking his head on the bonnet.

"Ow. That bloody well hurt. What do you want?"

"You got a kettle, somewhere behind a locked door, maybe?"

As they headed towards a small door marked "Manager", Wilson looked Knox over. He was a scrapper, a terrier; the garage was completely legit, nothing to do with Bigley or any other gang, entirely financed with honestly-earned dough, and Knox was a gangman of his own free will. Violence was his thing, and he got a buzz out of it. Was very, very good at it, too. It was a fight that had drawn him into Bigley's sphere, and his skill with a spanner and screwdriver that kept him there; there were occasions when Bigley needed a car tuned up, or a written-off motor given the engine and credentials of a legit one that had once belonged to an upstanding citizen. Tony Knox was also the best driver bar none in London, and, like most gang bosses, Roy Bigley had occasions where he needed someone who could handle a run.

They faced each other in silence for a long while, neither choosing to sit, before Tony finally spoke.

"What yer got for me, then? Something flash? A Rolls?"

Wilson shook his head. "This is a bit different, Tone. A bit special."

"UFO, then – Bigley's taking over Mars."

They both laughed. "Tomorrow midnight, usual place – you'll find out all you need to know." Wilson glanced at the closed door. "The greaser out there, he keep this place ticking over for a couple of weeks?"

Tony nodded. "But you know I ain't the owner, Mouth, I got money in the place, sure, but Mr. Dextam…"

"Won't be a problem", Wilson growled, his voice all menace now.

Getting up, Wilson glanced at the kettle. He fancied a cuppa, and there was a bloke worked at a scrap yard in Leyton made a killer brew. Usually had some pies and sarnies kicking around, too.

Les Grant was making himself a cup of tea in the staff hut when he saw Wilson's car pull in to the scrubby parking area of the scrap yard, a few cracked paving slabs bordered by mountains of used tyres.

"What the 'ell do 'e want, then?" Les Grant couldn't keep hold of an aitch if you superglued it to his tongue. Setting his mug of tea down on the bench table below the window, he picked up the *Telegraph*, and turned his attention to the crossword.

Les Grant had regrets; the taking of airport property that had seen him sacked from his job as head of security at Heathrow, well-paid, well-pensioned, a job for life. The booze he'd turned to for lack of any other comfort or security. The money he'd borrowed, and couldn't repay. All steps on the slippery slope that led here, to a minimum-wage cover job at one of Bigley's many front businesses, and the life of general dogsbody for the big man.

Wilson came in, deliberately slamming the door. Les glanced up from his paper. "Wilson. I can't think you was suddenly burdened wiv a desire to 'elp me with this 'ere crossword, so why don't you spit it out, eh?"

Wilson slapped him on the back, a little too hard to be as friendly as he tried to make it look.

"Good old Les, straight to the point." Mouth liked Les, and felt sorry for him at times. But that was life; you paid yer money, you took yer choice. You ended up wherever you decided to put yourself. "The old man needs your help. Something a bit special, a welding job. Right up your alley, I reckon. Your missus still around, is she?" Les nodded, wary. "Tell her you've got an away job for a couple of weeks, yeah?" Wilson knew Mrs Grant would understand – she had been one of Bigley's best escort girls, until old age came upon her seven years ago, when she turned thirty. Bigley had liked her, had sensed that a woman would do Grant good, keep him off the sauce for the most part. It wasn't an arranged marriage in the strictest sense of the word, but neither party would have refused Bigley's suggestion. For all that, they were happy, and very much in love still.

Wilson got up to leave. "Tomorrow, midnight. Usual place. Oh, and four across – not sure, but it could be..." he paused, gave a wolfish grin, then leaned forward, whispering, "S, h..." laughing when Les Grant favoured him with a swift kick to the shin.

Wilson had two more recruits to see, but he would leave them for the morning – he knew where to find them. Tonight, he would get his gear together, say goodbye to the woman who satisfied his occasional needs. Goodbye, he thought; strange word, something you'd say if you were moving to Australia, not when you were merely spending a couple of weeks in Essex. Mouth Wilson shivered, and his mind suddenly filled with a swirling grey cloud. His maternal grandmother had been a renowned psychic, and Wilson had an uncanny knack of sensing chaos.

He shook it off, pushed all that mumbo-jumbo to the back of his mind. A job was a job, there to be done well. And if you *didn't* do it well, and Roy Bigley was your employer, God help you – because no one else would.

Although laughably modest by Roy Bigley's standards, Mouth Wilson was always happy to return to his bay-windowed, mid-terrace house. It was his den, the place where, however stressful his day had been, he could lock the world out, relax and unwind. He took pride in the work he'd done on it, knocking the two upstairs bedrooms into one room, and fitting half of that out as a relaxing ensuite, knocking the living and dining rooms together to create a light, spacious lounge/diner, putting in the top-spec kitchen appliances, beech units and granite worktops. Although he knew far better than to tell any of his gangland colleagues, Mouth Wilson enjoyed cooking, found it infinitely restful. If he found himself with nothing to do of an evening, he'd more than likely try to find a television cookery programme to watch, and had a particular soft spot for Delia Smith.

Tonight, though, there would be no alchemy with fresh ingredients, no stainless-steel wizardry. Mouth's mind was on other things – Satin Reeves, his lady of the moment, to be precise. He doubted very much that Satin was her given name, but it suited her. He had been reflecting on his earlier choice of word – goodbye – and realising that it had been the correct choice. Tonight *would* be goodbye. With that uncanny sixth sense he'd inherited from Granny, Mouth Wilson knew that this job marked a turning point, the end of a chapter. It would be pastures new, in every aspect. Strangely, Wilson felt more sorrow at the thought of leaving this house – his home – behind than he did of parting ways with Satin Reeves, and yet he knew he'd have to do both. Knew too that, for a while at least, he would have to drop out of London life, or at least the life of London he knew. He suspected that Bigley was already thinking which country it would be best for a renamed Mouth to lie low in. Deep in his gut, Mouth felt an uneasy stirring, and wondered, fleetingly, if this would be the job he failed.

Pushing all such thoughts from his mind, Wilson headed upstairs, to change into his West End clobber, before catching the Tube to the theatre where Satin worked as a chorus girl, and, he strongly suspected, *worked* the slick, slimy stage-manager. Not that Wilson was jealous – you took what you wanted in this life; sex was a commodity like anything else. He and Satin were both adults, they both knew theirs wasn't going to be a happy-ever-after, roses-round-the-door relationship. What, or who, Satin did when she wasn't with him was her concern, just as Wilson's life when he wasn't with her was his.

Striding out of Piccadilly Circus, he passed a grimy, spotty youth, huddled under a blanket.

"Spare a quid, sir?" Wilson kicked his pace, but the whine persisted. "Please sir. Just the price of a cuppa, sir?"

Spinning round, Wilson grabbed the youth's blanket, got right in his face.

"Get off yer filthy arse, lad, and earn yer money the way the rest of us have to." As he strode off, he heard a harsh, female voice, with a Yorkshire accent, exclaim; "What a horrible bloke! The lad don't mean no 'arm", and a male voice with the same accent say "There ye are, lad. Look after ye self, now, eh?" and the clink of change.

Bloody beggars, thought Wilson. He hated the parasites, wouldn't give them the time of day. He'd never begged from anyone, never would, neither. The third of four children, his mother dying shortly after the birth of his younger sister, Sandra, Mouth Wilson – christened Hank for reasons best known only to his mother – would never say that his childhood had been easy – his father, raising his motherless children as best he could, with the help of the local nurse, was still expected to turn up at the railway yard where he worked every day, and do a good day's graft – but he'd never thought he deserved handouts because of it. Everything he had, he was proud to say, he had worked for, even though he could rarely claim it was earned honestly.

He thought of his brothers. John, the eldest, named for their father, was a factory manager, Dennis was a solicitor in a well-known firm, and quietly hoping to make partner in a few years, while Sandra, whom Mouth still blamed for their mother's death, was running public relations for some company based in Melbourne, Australia. Mouth had had no contact with his family for the past ten years, when his disappointed father had thrown him out of the Kentish Town house where John Wilson senior had lived all his life, but he kept tabs on them. Knowledge, Mouth had learnt early in life, was power, and power was vital in his line of work.

Satin Reeves was not happy. She had arranged to meet Wilson outside the Criterion theatre at 10.45pm, and it was now gone eleven. She tapped her foot, and glared at the group of men, passing on the opposite side of the road, who had wolf-whistled at her.

Seeing Mouth approaching, she refused to smile. "Sod you, Wilson" she muttered. "I'll teach you to treat a lady with a bit more respect." In her heart, though, the twenty-year old Satin really cared for Wilson. He might be old enough to be her dad, but he knew how to make her feel like a woman, knew how to be romantic, not like the spineless kids her age who thought a bunch of cheap flowers and a bottle of naff plonk were all that was needed to get her into their bed.

Satin was no saint; she saw other guys, but it was Mouth Wilson she really wanted, although she'd never tell him so. Let blokes think they're always one wrong step from being shown the door, Satin's mother had told her. That way they don't take advantage.

"Where the hell've you been? I bin waitin' fer ages. I don't much care for standin around freezin' me wotsits off, givin' all the pervs around here their jollies, y'know."

She pouted, planting her tiny, perfectly manicured hands on slender hips. Wilson held out his hands in the universal gesture of supplication.

"Okay, baby. I'm sorry. C'mon – I've booked us a real nice restaurant, proper posh, y'know? Got a brilliant evening planned."

It was gone three the following morning before Wilson got back to Tottenham. The evening had gone well until the very end, the point where he had told Satin it was over, that he was finishing with her. They were snuggled together in her bed, unwinding after what Mouth had to admit had been a fantastic love-making session (he wasn't going to tell her *before* the sex, was he?) when he had sat up, and calmly told her it was over, that he needed to make a new start. One that didn't include her. She had cried. She had begged and pleaded. She had yelled obscenities. She had hit him. She had demanded to know how he expected her to cope without him. He had listened without reaction, got out of bed, got dressed, tossed the remaining notes in his wallet – two fifties, three twenties, a ten and three fives – at her, told her to ask for a pay rise or find another job, and left.

Sitting in his favourite armchair, he poured himself a generous measure of Whyte and Mackay, which he downed in a single swallow. He sat for a long time, just staring at the glass, before heading upstairs, stripping off his expensive clothes, showering, and getting into bed, where he lay with his hands behind his head, staring at the ceiling in the pale light of the coming dawn, and, with a growing unease, thought about upcoming events; the very well-paid, very strange, job, the German who wanted it done, his insistence on secrecy and on perfection. The quiet voice in Wilson's head that told him he should be as far away from this guy's madness as possible.

Tonight, all the players – willing and unwilling – would find out what was going on. It would get rough in the old hall, Wilson knew. But knuckles were fantastic for calming frayed tempers. They'd soon settle down. Fluffing his pillow, he turned over, and fell into a deep sleep.

Walthamstow market was one of London's oldest, if not best known, and it was here that Wilson found his last recruits, the Sampson brothers, Vinnie and Alfie, a little before ten thirty. Mouth Wilson never needed much sleep, nor a lot of time to get "work ready." He'd woken at nine and been out of the house by twenty to ten.

Vinnie, the older of the brothers, spotted him first, and nudged Alfie. "Look what the cat dragged in." Alfie looked over. "Aye, and ain't his mush full of the joys of spring? Maybe he thinks his shoes ain't shiny enough – we could sell him one of them gizmos you bought off that bloke the other day." Vinnie chuckled, drawing himself up to his full six-feet-six, his sharp nose jutting like the beak of a disgruntled parrot as his eyes, pale beneath his mop of thick dark hair, scanned the crowd, focused on Wilson, scanned the crowd again, came back to Wilson.

Alfie, two years younger, at thirty three to Vinnie's thirty-five, was shorter, and altogether less imposing, but he was the seller, the one with the gift of the gab.

"Mornin', Mouth." Alfie was already pulling a box from the stall. "Got just the thing for you here.

"I wouldn't want the crap you two sell if you were giving it away" Wilson snarled, his hangover kicking in. He jerked his head at the Tea Cosy stall next door. "C'mon. I need a cuppa, and we need a chat."

Alfie sloped off to get the teas, while Vinnie chatted aimlessly with Wilson. The conversation stopped as Alfie returned, three cups of tea on a plastic tray, and two hotdogs, spilling onions. Wilson wrinkled his nose, He *hated* hotdogs.

"You got someone who can keep an eye on all this for you for a while?" he said, gesturing at the stall.

"Why?" said the brothers in unison, both sensing they weren't going to like the answer.

"Your draft papers just came through, lads. Midnight tonight, usual place. You'll get your answers then. Be there on time, though. No excuses." Finishing his tea, Wilson strode off.

Watching him go, Alfie shook his head. "Never took to that bloke" he told his brother. "something off about him, sly, unhealthy." Vinnie grimaced. "Ah, he's alright in small doses. Mind you, I wouldn't fall in love with him, if you know what I mean?"

The hall in Bethnall Green could have served any number of legitimate purposes, and, indeed, the snooker hall and social club it advertised itself as seemed innocent enough, as did the small print of "Members Only." No one was to know that the snooker hall and social club was owned by Roy Bigley, or that you had to be one of his "boys" to become a member, just as no one knew that the money registered with tax officials as "membership fees and bar takings" was, in fact, proceeds of less acceptable occupations.

Mouth Wilson strode in at five to midnight, glanced around to make sure everyone was there, then quickly locked the door, sliding the heavy bar across the inside for good measure.

"What's all this crap about, then?" The voice was Eddie Small's. "Packing everything in for the next couple of weeks! We off on a package holiday to Tenerife or something?" Mouth smiled.

"You must be psychic, old son. The budget won't quite stretch to Tenerife, but Mr Bigley here has kindly arranged a nice little stay in Essex for us all." Mouth glanced towards the corner shadows, as though seeing something no one else could. There was an explosion of volume, mostly consisting of expletives aimed against Essex. Alfie Sampson's voice rose above the din.

"That bloody dump? Who's the stopover this time, and why's it need six of us?" The 'stopover' Alfie referred to related to a safehouse owned by Bigley, and used to house those on the run, or who needed to lie low for a bit. The occupant of the safehouse was known by the codename of 'the stopover'.

Roy Bigley suddenly stepped into the room, and was gratified to see the shock registering on his troops' faces.

There was a rustling of restlessness, a noticeable rise in the tension in the room Bigley stepped up, and the room fell silent.

"It's not a stopover, lads. Let's just say it's a bit of a DIY job, and you, gentlemen, have been chosen because of your expert skills." Bigley scanned the room, finally pointing at Les Grant.

"Les, for example, is just the sort of top-notch welder this job needs. Vinnie and his brother, Ford Dagenham's brightest and best electricians, until that unfortunate incident when they thought they'd try their hand at some accountancy work Oh, and the couple of other unfortunate incidents involving the petty cash tin before that. Never let it be said the Mr Bigley doesn't find jobs that fit the natural talents of his staff."

"Cut the crap. What's going down?" Eddie Small again, anger flashing in his eyes. Roy Bigley glanced at Mouth, who was calmly smoking a cigarette.

"Mr Wilson? Perhaps you'd care to explain to these good people?" Roy Bigley made a point of never being the bearer of bad news.

So Wilson told them, and endured the onslaught of verbal abuse and plastic seating that was hurled at him when he finished. Bigley had calmly strolled out through the fire exit moments before Wilson finished speaking, heading for Poorly, the closest thing Roy Bigley had to a friend, or family, who was waiting out the back with the Rolls Royce, almost as if he'd known what was likely to happen.

"Let's go, shall we?" Bigley said, getting into the car. Poorly Manthorpe smiled at him. "Your place or mine, boss?" Bigley returned the smile. "Wherever takes your fancy, Mr Manthorpe. Wherever takes your fancy."

Back in the hall, things were heating up. Mouth Wilson hadn't expected any jumpers, but Eddie Small was on his feet.

"Bollocks to you, Wilson" he spat "I ain't going."

Mouth stepped forward, body tensing into a fighter's stance. "Oh, you're going, Eddie. If it's the last job you do, you're going."

"Why?" sneered Eddie "because the fat man says so?"

Wilson slammed his fist into the side of Eddie's face, a movement so quick no one even saw it happen. Only the blood trickling down to stain the collar of Eddie Small's shirt told that it had.

"No," Wilson growled. "Because *I* say so." Mouth Wilson and Eddie Small squared off to one another, both ready for a scrap, both dripping aggression and testosterone. As Eddie raised his fists to land a blow, Mouth punched him in the kidneys, then again in the solar plexus, a rapid one-two combination that would have drawn a round of applause from Mohammad Ali himself. As Eddie fell to the floor like a wilting sunflower, Les Grant got to his feet. Wilson swung round, ready for him, but the quiet crossword addict wasn't looking for a ruck. Instead, he simply helped Eddie Small to his feet, and stared hard at Wilson.

"That was uncalled for. You should have just let him walk, if that's what he wants. None of us want this, Mouth. We may be tradesmen, we may once have been the best in our fields, but what do you think we know, any of us, about the crap you've just been muttering about?"

"Don't worry," Wilson told him "you're going to have someone to teach you all about that." Turning away, he waved off the torrent of questions.

"That's yer lot for now. Les, you get the van tomorrow, Mr Small there'll be your first pick up. Tony, put your alarm on – I know what a lazy git you are. Last pick ups are Vinnie and Alfie. You'll all be on the A12 before breakfast, and I'll meet you at the holiday camp."

Wilson noticed that Doc Little was still seated, nervously clasping and unclasping his hands.

"Problem, Doc?"

"Well, not exactly…it's just what you said, about Eddie and Vinnie and the rest, about their being expert tradesmen."

"Yeah?" Wilson barked, waiting.

"Well, I'm hardly a tradesman, am I? I don't even know how to change the oil in my car. I don't really see how I'm the sort of man you need."

Wilson stepped forward, motioning the Doc to his feet and jabbing a finger into his chest.

"Oh, I'll need you, Doc. Medicine's a specialism, ain't it? There'll be something for you to do, don't you worry." Wilson turned, and crossed to the same door Bigley had used earlier. As he switched off the lights, he called over his shoulder; "Goodnight, Doctor. I'll see you in the morning."

CHAPTER ELEVEN

George Lake's old airfield up at Elwood might have seen better days, might be a bit dilapidated and run down, but it was a legitimate concern, and Lake himself was one of the most law-abiding citizens you could hope to meet. He wouldn't tolerate anything shady. Had he been able to glimpse the thoughts in Erik Lux's dark mind, he would have had kittens, but that wouldn't have stopped him from escorting Mister Lux, his plane and his monthly rent off the premises pretty sharpish, with George Lake's trusty twelve-bore stuck up his backside, just for emphasis.

It was a bright, warm day, a week after his visit to London, and Lux was flying back to Elwood from Holland, in his father's Messcheschmitt. He had gone out on the early morning ferry from Harwich, and the plane's former owner had met him at the terminal, driving him from there to a small, private airfield a few miles away. From there, Erik had launched the plane he had desired for so long, heading, finally, for home in it. George and his wife were away, visiting family for the day, so Lux knew the airfield would be undisturbed. He had told Lake that the plane he had purchased to work on was being delivered as soon as he had received confirmation that he could collect it, but he hadn't told him he would be flying it back – that might have sounded a little suspicious, especially, Lux thought, when combined with the fact that he had told Lake he would have to be doing a lot of work on the plane. No. It made more sense to let George Lake think the plane was still coming over on a trailer.

"Just tell 'em to park up at the gate – boxed up on a trailer, is she? - me and the wife can't be there, then – only relations, like, but it's more'n my life's worth to try & gerrout of it. The wife's family, see? You just haul back that pole – like I said before, I don't hardly lock the place down, 'cept for the sheds – and have 'em back right up, close as yer like. I ain't worried about the grass, long as they keeps away from the flight area, like."

"You're certain it is acceptable for me to let them onto your property, Mr Lake? I'm sure I could reschedule the delivery."

"No, Mr Lux – you're a good sort, I reckon. I trusts yer."

Erik Lux had smiled. A good sort, someone who could be trusted, had been exactly the image he had worked on presenting to George Lake. He was glad to see he had pulled it off.

"You'll have to come and see her, Mr Lake, when I've had a chance to smarten her up a little."

George Lake's face lit up. "I'll be sure to, Mr Lux – never looses the love of sumat like planes, do yer? An' I don't recall as I've ever seen a Messerschmitt in as good nick as you describes."

In truth, Lux didn't want anyone else around his plane, but he sensed that George Lake was the sort of person who wouldn't be suspicious of anyone who welcomed him in to their world, especially when that world involved vintage aircraft. And Erik Lux knew it was very, very important to keep George Lake from becoming suspicious.

"There you are, my beautiful All safe and sound." Erik caressed the plane's flank, gazing at her as a youth might gaze at his first love

"Oh, we will have some fun together, you and I." Erik Lux was already anticipating the enjoyment he would have from in his plane – which, he was sure, was nothing like the innocent George Lake was imagining.

As soon as he had finished checking the plane over, and had locked the hangar securely behind him, Lux headed to the airfield office, where he placed a call to a London number.

"I have the scaffolding. Have you sourced the materials yet?"

"They're on order."

"I am working to a deadline."

"I know that. The materials are on order. Trust me on that."

"And what about the...labourer I recommended to you?"

"One of my people should be contacting him later. And another will be paying a visit to his friend, make sure she won't throw the proverbial spanner in the works."

"I do not want to have to go elsewhere to get this job finished on schedule."

"You won't."

The last two words were spoken harshly, and Lux was left in no doubt that they were intended as a threat, not a promise. If he took issue with the speed Roy Bigley was working at, if he tried to walk away, it would be the last thing he did. And his audacious plan wouldn't even get off the ground. He couldn't let that happen.

"Of course not. I'm sorry. This is a big job, and I need it to be done well. I'm nervous, that is all."

"Don't be. I'm taking care of everything, you understand? Are you still staying at that hotel, in Norfolk?"

"Yes – I'm looking for a cottage or something, though, just to rent for a few months. I have heard that the village of Middle Upton is rather pleasant."

A chuckle came over the line. "And it just so happens I've a property only a couple of miles from there, in a village called Elwood, due to fall vacant very shortly. *Very* shortly, if you see what I mean?"

Lux smiled. Obviously, the existing tenant had done something to upset his landlord. And he got the feeling it wasn't subletting, or excessive noise. The voice on the end of the line continued

"I'll send you out a key, shall I? You should get it day after tomorrow. Move in whenever you like after that. I'd get it to you sooner, but I've got some...clearing up to do at the property."

"I understand. And as to the rent –"

"What rent, Mr Lux? It's only for a few months, you say? Consider yourself my...caretaker, until I either find a buyer for the property, or a more permanent tenant. You happy with that arrangement?"

"Well, yes, yes, of course. It seems very fair. I am delighted with your proposal, Mr Bigley."

"I thought you would be. And don't worry – you'll get your materials in good time. I give you my word."

Lux decided to take a trip into Thetford – he needed to buy some paint, and new brushes, to restore the markings on his father's plane. He got into the Volvo, and drove away from Elwood, enjoying the pleasant drive through the countryside.

Arriving in the town, he parked in a small carpark. Walking into the town centre, he looked at the shops around him, but could not see a hardware store among them. Spotting a group of people at a bus stop, he went up to them;

"Excuse me – do any of you know where I might find a good quality hardware store?" A middle-aged man directed him to Primrose Hardware

The Eagle Will Fly

- "Got everything, they have", and, thanking him, Lux headed off, following the directions he'd been given.

A short while and friendly chat with the sales assistant later, Lux walked out of Primrose Hardware, carrying tins of paint, sandpaper, paintbrushes, and an assortment of other equipment that would be used in his work on the Messerschmitt.

A few days later, as he was preparing a simple supper in his new accommodation – a small, but perfectly adequate, cottage just down the lane from the church in Elwood, and a short drive from Elwood airfield – the telephone rang. Erik Lux answered it, to be given just three words;

"Wapping Docks, midnight."

As he replaced the receiver, Lux thought how cliched a midnight rendezvous was; how cliched, in fact, Roy Bigley's whole operation was. He didn't realise that this was the secret to Bigley's success; neither the police, nor other criminals, took seriously someone who looked and acted so much *like* a gangster. A costly mistake when dealing with someone like Roy Bigley and his gang.

It was a full moon that night, the brilliant white light shining on the slick black tarmac as Lux made his way to the docks, in an old Volvo he had seen for sale by the side of the road. The owner had come out as he slowed his pace to look the car over, seeing its potential for his scheme, and the deal had been done in under twenty minutes. Having purchased the car, Lux had transferred what amounted to several thousand pounds from an account he had kept open in Montana, and split it between two branches of Barclays Bank, one in Bury St. Edmunds, the other in London. He could easily drive into Bury St. Edmunds, then take the train to London, and he didn't want to arouse suspicion by making an exceptionally large deposit or withdrawal at one branch.

Lux arrived at the dockside at one minute to midnight. Two minutes later, a low hum broke the waterfront silence, and a sleek motorboat loomed up out of the darkness. Two figures jumped onto the wharf, and two boxes, metal, oblong and obviously heavy, were hauled from the boat into the boot of Lux's Volvo. As soon as the boot slammed shut, the figures were back in the boat, turning it around, and gliding back into the night. It occurred to Lux that this all seemed a bit surreal, as though he were merely dreaming. But then he remembered the money he had handed over to a gangster, in the office of a motorcycle showroom, and it began to seem very real indeed.

Lux was about to get back behind the wheel of the Volvo when a pair of powerful headlights lit up the area like floodlights on a football pitch. As the lights went out, Lux heard two car doors slam, and saw the shadows of two men, silhouettes against the light of the full moon, walking over to him.

There was no mistaking the fat one, even in this poor light; it was Roy Bigley. The man with him, who was burly, but in a fit, powerful, well-kept way, Lux had never seen before.

Bigley chuckled as he stepped in front of Lux.

"You see, Mr Lux - I didn't let you down, now, did I? By the way-" he gestured to the burly man beside him, whom, Erik noticed, now had a memorably broken nose - "this here is Mr Mouth Wilson – a mouthy sort of bloke, if you see what I mean?" Bigley chuckled again. "Mr Wilson will be taking charge of your little project – I'm a busy man, you see. Can't be everywhere, all the time. Got to delegate."

Lux had been surprised, seeing Bigley there, to say nothing of his rather menacing-looking companion. But he sensed it would be best to act as though nothing could surprise him.

"As you say, Mr Bigley, you have kept your word. It was nice of you to be here to, err, to...well, to greet me, but I should be getting away; I suspect *my* journey is longer than your own?"

Roy Bigley held up his hands. "There has been a...slight change of plans, Mr Lux, a change of plans which involves a little detour."

Erik shivered. Was this a trap he had walked into? What kind of game were these gangsters playing?

"I do not understand, Mr Bigley. What change in the plans? What is this detour you mention to me?"

Seeing the alarm on his customer's face, Roy Bigley laughed outright. "It's alright, Mr Lux. As you mentioned, it would be rather...difficult, shall we say, for my men to come and go from that airfield you're at out in Elwood. Too many people, too many questions. Why should we have to take that risk, if I can take the gear direct to the rendezvous my lads use, where your little job is to be carried out?"

"But why did you not tell me in the first place?" Lux protested. "Why not come here yourselves, collect the goods yourselves, deliver them yourselves to wherever this rendezvous you speak of is?"

Bigley chuckled once more. "Better you be caught with the goods than us, Mr Lux, if the Old Bill's snouts had been waiting to see who was doing the pick up." The fat man chuckled again, then, turning to his second-in-command, said; "Be on your way, Mouth. Poorly will drop me off where I'm going, then he'll come down to the farm, pick you up and drop you back into town." He touched the back of his hand to his forehead. "Have a safe journey, Mr Lux, and sleep well." Still chuckling, the vast expanse of flesh that was Roy Bigley waddled back to the Rolls Royce, which had been waiting, engine purring, the whole time.

Erik Lux couldn't have known that, in a couple of days, he would get a very unexpected visit at Elwood – his supposed sanctuary - from a very unwelcome guest.

The following day dawned bright and clear, and Erik decided to have a day off from working on the Messerschmitt – he couldn't do anything else until he heard from Bigley that the next part of the plan had come off. He decided to go for a drive through Middle Upton, to sit in a layby a little way past an impressive Georgian manor house, and wait for an hour or two – another, recently acquired, habit of his.

He had been watching the Manor House for several days, observing the comings and goings. He had found a convenient lay-by, within sight of the Manor's main entrance, where he could watch without arousing suspicion.

This morning, Patricia pulled out onto the main road and turned left, meaning she was heading for Thetford. Adjusting his dark glasses and black Beanie hat, Erik Lux pulled out, following her at a distance of two cars behind.

Patricia had taken this route before, and Erik now knew the road quite well. When the country road ran straight for several miles, he swung round the two cars ahead of him, pulling in behind his ex-wife's vehicle, bumping the rear bumper with a blare of the Volvo's horn. He saw Patricia startle and look in her rearview mirror. Keeping his hand on the Volvo's horn Erik pulled out and sped up, drawing alongside Patricia's Toyota. He pushed back the dark glasses, allowing her a clear view of his face.

Her mouth gaped in horror as she recognised him. Gripping the Toyota's steering wheel, her whole body froze in fear; she felt a sickening thud as Lux rammed her car, trying to force her onto the grass verge. Patricia pressed her foot down hard on the accelerator, trying desperately to get away from him, but he kept level with her, forcing her to the very edge of the road. All around them, other drivers were blaring their horns – they were approaching a blind bend.

Suddenly, a Land Rover came round the bend, hurtling towards the two speeding vehicles. Seeing the danger, Lux reacted instantly, managing, by some miracle, to squeeze the Volvo between the Toyota and the Land Rover, without incurring too much damage. Patricia swerved, and brought the Toyota to a skidding stop, her body shaking uncontrollably.

The Land Rover had also stopped, and the driver, clearly shaken, had jumped out, and was hurrying over to Patricia's car.

"Are you alright, miss?" he called.

"Yes" Patricia replied, "yes, thank you – I'm fine, thank you. I'm alright. Please – please, leave me. I'll be perfectly alright in a minute or two."

"Well...if you say so, miss," the driver of the Land Rover said. "If you ask me, though, that bloody lunatic of a driver ought to be reported.

I've half a mind to do it myself. Well, if you're sure you're alright – take care, won't you?"

"Yes – thank you."

Once she had stopped shaking, and felt in control again, Patricia turned around and drove back to the Manor. Parking on the drive, she rushed into the house, running straight into Tim, who was just on his way out.

"That was a quick visit to Thetford, old girl," he said, smiling. The smile froze when he looked at Patricia, and saw the state she was in.

"Tim...Tim...oh, Tim, darling – get me a drink, please", she cried, sobbing hard, her whole body shaking.

"Of course, my darling – but you must tell me what has happened."

As Patricia drank her gin and tonic, she told Tim of the events on the road to Thetford. His expression shifted several times, settling into something cold, hard and unrecognisable.

"That bloody swine! I've a good idea where he's stationed himself – I'm going over there to have it out with him once and for all."

"Oh, Tim, please don't! Not right now, Tim – please, stay here with me – I'm so terribly frightened." Putting his arm around Patricia, Tim kissed her gently.

"I won't leave you, old girl. Nothing could make me leave you."

As he held her, Tim Watts recalled the phone call he had had a fortnight or so previously, from his old friend George Lake. He would call him, would see if he couldn't get a guided tour of Elwood Field, and perhaps meet its newest tenant Tomorrow, he thought, hugging Patricia tightly. Tomorrow, he would go out to Elwood, would stand up to Erik Lux, show the man that he wasn't afraid of him, make it clear to Lux that he was to leave him and Patricia alone.

He would go tomorrow. Today, Patricia needed him.

CHAPTER TWELVE

Horst Block was an unassuming man who lived in an unassuming house, a detached 1950's redbrick, with a grey-tiled roof, set in a large plot, enclosed on three sides by a sturdy pine fence. Horst enjoyed gardening, and the front lawn of his property was neatly mown once every six weeks during spring and summer, his borders were rife with colourful blooms, and the garden as a whole had that look of contented order familiar to places that are not merely tended to, but loved. The house itself was located in a small village, and looked out onto open countryside, where Horst would walk for an hour once a week, on a Sunday afternoon, aside from his walks to the local pub, for a pint of beer on a Saturday night, and a roast dinner on a Sunday afternoon. The village had, unusually, not been built in order to "create" an immediate community, and Horst's nearest neighbour was half a mile away, a fact which had made the surveillance that both Horst Block and his house had been under for several days a lot easier than it might otherwise have been.

The night they came for him was ideal; the rain meaning that even the hardiest dog walkers weren't paying attention to anything other than getting home as quickly as possible. The village was not on the way to anywhere worth going, and so there was no road traffic at all. No moon or stars broke through the blackness, and the sheets of rain that had been falling steadily since early evening were accompanied by a fierce wind that ripped through the open fields and rattled the fence around the Horst property. Inside, it was warm, a log fire giving off a cosy blaze in the living room. The elderly occupant glanced up at the wall clock, and, with a sigh, set down the book he was reading. Time for his regular nightcap, he thought, and then to bed. As he wandered around the spacious, modern kitchen, he listened to the gathering storm outside. Shaking his head, he reflected that it would be very unpleasant for anyone unfortunate enough to be out in this weather, and was grateful that he was indoors, warm and safe. Horst loved this place, the pride and joy of both himself and his wife, Rose. As he prepared his nightly cocoa, memories came flooding back to him.

He remembered the first time he had been invited into Rose's modest council house, not long after the war had ended, and he had decided to stay in Norfolk, the county in which he had been held as a German prisoner of war. The cocoa Rose had made for them both went cold as they held each other and kissed in her tiny kitchen, the young German knowing that this was indeed love, and that, foreigner and enemy though he was, it was this English Rose he wanted to marry. They had talked long into many a night about what the future might hold for such as they, before deciding to take the risk of finding out.

Now, many years later, Horst's seventy-year old face cracked into a smile. Everything had turned out so well for them, the people who knew Rose accepting him once they saw how very much in love with her he was. A few people hadn't been kind, but even their cruel words couldn't shatter the protective barrier of love that surrounded Horst and his wife. Abruptly, though, reality hit him, and he stopped smiling. His beloved English Rose was not here anymore, and had not been for several months. She had been taken very ill two years ago, and rushed to hospital, where cancer was diagnosed. A few months later, she began showing signs of dementia. Horst, beside himself with grief at the thought of losing her, had kept her at home, caring for her with a lover's devotion until it was no longer possible. The chemotherapy had ceased having all but the most minor effect on the cancer, and the dementia was drawing her away from reality, and from him, daily. Now, when he visited her, although he would hold her hand and talk to her for hours at a time, he knew she was barely aware of his presence, and that she saw him as a stranger.

Sighing, he picked up his cocoa and retraced his steps. Sitting down once more, he picked up the television remote, clicking to BBC1 just in time to hear the presenter announce that this was the ten o'clock news.

Suddenly, there came the piercing sound of the front doorbell. Frowning, Horst turned down the volume on the television, and went out into the hall, wondering who on earth could be calling at this time of night. Peering through the frosted glass of the front door, he could make out no more than a dark shadow, a hood pulled well over the person's head. Probably some poor soul whose car had broken down, Horst thought, unlocking the door, feeling concerned for whoever it was, ready to help if he could. A gust of wind and rain hit him as he pulled the door open. The first thing he noticed was that he couldn't see his visitor's face. The next thing was the large, dark-coloured car pulled across his drive.

Horst opened his mouth to ask what the stranger wanted, but found a hand forced against it, and himself pushed back into the hall. As if on cue, he heard the slamming of car doors, and two other men rushed into the house, slamming the front door behind them. One wore a donkey jacket, the other, younger, a baseball cap.

"Are you Horst Block?" The question was barked by the first man, the one who had rung the doorbell. Horst nodded.

"Please, what is happening? What do you want? I have no money, no valuables – the television, the radio, that is all. Take them. I won't make trouble for you. They are old – I am old…" a dirty, terrifying laugh cut him off.

"*You* are the valuables, old man, though God knows why." It was one of the other two men, the one in the donkey jacket, who spoke.

Horst felt a sudden chill, and knew instinctively that these men were dangerous. The man in the cap and donkey jacket pushed him roughly back into the living room, shoving him back into the chair he had vacated in order to answer the door.

Gripping the arms of the chair, Horst thrust out his whiskered chin, and demanded to know what was going on.

"Shut your mouth, Kraut. I ask the questions, get it?" Cap and donkey jacket glared at him. Horst began to rise from his chair.

"I am calling for the police – you have no right to be here..." he was silenced by a stinging blow to his face, delivered by the man dressed in the donkey jacket, whose name was Ed Small. The man who had rung the doorbell, Doc Little, stood silently in a corner. Removing his baseball cap, Tony Knox sat down on the arm of the chair.

"Listen to me, Kraut. You just answer our questions, do what we tell you, and we'll go easy on you, right? Muck as around, and you'll get hurt. Badly hurt. Understand?"

Horst was shaking. "My wife will have woken by now..." he began, hoping to scare off the men. Tony Knox barked with laughter.

"No, she won't – we know where your wife is, Mr Block. She may well be in bed, but she's not in this house." Horst began to shake more violently. How could these men know Rose wasn't there?

Before he could ask, Tony Knox barked a question at him,

"You get your milk delivered, old man?"

"Y..yes," Horst stammered "three times a week, Mondays, Wednesdays and Fridays." Knox thrust a notepad and pen at him.

"You're going away for a while, cancelling the milk until further notice, okay? Write another note for the postman, telling him the same thing, and that he's to keep any parcels, anything that needs a signature, at the post office for you. Got it?"

Horst, too tired to fight, merely nodded.

"Good. Doc, do your thing."

The man who had rung the doorbell came over, carrying a black leather pouch. Unzipping it, he drew out a syringe and a small vial of amber liquid. Inserting a needle into the syringe, the man drew a full measure the substance, and, while the other two held the old German down, pressed the needle into the skin of his left arm, and pushed down the plunger on the syringe.

Horst Block screamed, then went very still.

Doc Little pulled the needle out, wrapped it in a dirty handkerchief, and stuffed it into his black leather bag..

"He should sleep for about eight hours, maybe longer."

"Good." Knox jerked his head towards the stairs. "Find his room, pack him some clothes, something warm – don't want him coming down with pneumonia now, do we?"

Within fifteen minutes, the men were bundling Horst into the back of their BMW, having locked up his house and pinned two notes, one to the milkman, the other to the postman, to the front door. Just as they were about to leave, Tony Knox got out of the car, and sprinted back to the bungalow. Once inside, he darted into the living room, and switched the television off; everyone had forgotten it was still on. He was back out, back behind the wheel of the car, in less than three minutes.

Doc Little and Eddie Small sat either side of Horst in the back of the car. Doc Little glanced over at him; he was breathing easily.

Tony Knox swung the car round, heading towards London and the A140. They were heading not for the capital, however, but an isolated farm in the middle of rural Essex.

Erik Lux hadn't bothered with breakfast, choosing instead to drive straight to the airfield that morning, having been woken by a call from Bigley, reassuring him that the last part of what the gangster called "the admin side" of their plan had been dealt with successfully.

Walking over to his hangar, Erik Lux was stopped in his tracks by the sight of George Lake talking to Tim Watts.

Panic grabbed at Lux's throat. What was the Englishman doing here? He surely couldn't know what he was planning? His mind raced as he tried to reassure himself that he had never mentioned Tim Watt's name, or Patricia's, in his dealings with Bigley. Of course! That time when he had spoken of wanting to live in Middle Upton, when Bigley had offered him the cottage. Bigley had laughed; he must have worked out that Lux's plan had something to do with someone in Middle Upton... how had he found out it was Tim Watts?

Erik Lux suddenly realised George Lake had been speaking to him.

"...to meet an old friend of mine, Wing Commander Timothy Watts. Tim, this is -"

"We've met," Tim said, his voice icy, his stare hard. He didn't elaborate. Without extending his hand, he said to Lux, "So, this is where you keep your little toy, is it?"

"Yes, indeed, Wing Commander" Lux said, smiling. "Perhaps you would like to see it?"

"I've seen it, you recall, Herr Lux – but I would like another look at it." Erik noted the 'Herr' in Tim's harsh response. "My pleasure, Wing Commander."

Tim Watts knew the German was up to something, but he couldn't for the life of him thing what. Having a closer look at the Messerschmitt might tell him.

He walked around the aircraft, noting its gleaming paintwork and the expertly-restored body.

"What are your intentions, ... Erik?" Tim nearly spat as he spoke the German's Christian name. "What are your plans for it, I mean?"

"Put it on show, I thought" George Lake butted in.

"Yes" Tim nodded "why not do that, Erik?"

"Oh, it will go on show, when the time is right. I hope you will be there when it does, Wing Commander. I wouldn't want you to miss it."

With a shrug of dismissal, Tim turned to George. "If you've got that spare part I came for, George, I'll be on my way – bit of a hectic day ahead of me today." George nodded, and began to walk off. With a curt nod to Lux, Tim Watts followed him.

"Just a moment, Wing Commander." Tim turned back to Lux. "There is something I would like you to know about the Messerschmitt, my 'little toy', as you call it – it is the same one flown by my father, Hans Lux, during the Battle of Britain. The same one that, in that battle, in August 1940, was shot down, and landed in a French field. As you can see, Wing Commander, it is back to its former glory. A pity the same can't be said for the pilot, don't you think?"

Tim noted the menace in Lux's voice as he spoke, and abruptly turned away.

CHAPTER THIRTEEN

The whispering purr of the Bentley's engine was heaven to Poorly's ears. He was out of the Smoke, on a delicate, discreet mission for his old friend and boss. Driving down a quiet, rural lane, he reflected on his past. Did he have any regrets? No, he told himself. Okay, so he'd served time, a fact which had led to his parents throwing him out at seventeen, but that no longer bothered him. It was, after all, a long time ago now, and, Poorly thought, his present life was more than comfortable.

A confirmed bachelor, he collected rare antiques and lived in the kind of large, luxury house anyone would be envious of. For the most part he had only himself to please, and earned a good wage at a job he loved, one he was very, very good at. From the day he had first met Roy Bigley, the two had clicked, and, while having no ambitions to leadership, Poorly was the gangster's brightest and most loyal footsoldier. He was also the only person Roy Bigley had ever called a friend.

Slowing the Bentley, he paused at a crossroads, consulting the maps spread over the passenger seat. Taking the right hand turn, he cruised through a small hamlet of thatched cottages, pausing once more, just past the last cottage, to consult his maps again. About a mile on, he saw the sign he was looking for; *WESTWARD: Private Nursing Home.* With a smile, he turned down a short, gravelled driveway, flanked by shrubs, flower gardens and neatly kept lawns.

A large gravel turnaround area had been created in front of the house, a three-storey greystone in the Georgian style. A workman's van stood to the left of the parking area. Parking away from the van, facing the house, Poorly got out of the Bentley, and looked around.

It looked as if the place was having a make-over; scaffolding covered the front of the house, with two scruffy, stocky blokes working up the top, and a third standing at the bottom, smoking and staring idly into space.

The heavy oak door of the house stood open, a wide corridor stretching beyond it. Poorly stood and watched for a moment, observing people criss-crossing the hallway at regular intervals, headed for the rooms on either side, most in nurse's uniforms.

Taking out his wallet, he removed the photograph his boss had given him.

It depicted a woman in her early seventies, sitting in a wheelchair with a uniformed nurse at her side, and had evidently been taken in the grounds of the nursing home.

The woman's hair was pure white, swept back from a long, thin face, hollow cheeks giving her a gaunt look. It was a colour photograph, taken on a bright, sunny day, but even the colour and brightness of a photograph couldn't hide the fact that the woman was very ill indeed.

Placing the photograph back in his wallet, and folding his wallet back into his pocket, Poorly pressed the button on the Bentley's key fob that would secure the car, and walked up the short flight of stone steps to the main entrance. A welcome mat lay across the entrance, a printed, laminated sign, pinned to the wall above a small brass bell, said **PLEASE RING FOR ASSISTANCE.** He rang the bell, which brought an immediate response.

A brunette in her late thirties appeared from the gloom of the corridor, the smile she offered him seeming to come from behind an iron curtain of professionalism. Her uniform of green and white stripes, with its white collar, was crisp and clean.

"Watch yourself with this one," thought Poorly, flashing his own smile.

"Can I help you, sir?" the nurse asked, her voice confirming Poorly's initial image of an iron curtain.

Clearing his throat, conjuring his best David Niven voice, a voice which should have melted even the coolest ice maiden, he said;

"Well, yes, I believe you can. I am a very good friend and near neighbour of Mr and Mrs Horst Block." Silence prevailed. Unmelted, the ice maiden inclined her head, waiting for him to continue.

"I believe Mrs Block is a resident here?" The woman's black eyes scanned his face,

"And *I* don't believe I've met *you* before, Mr - ?"

"Oh, of course, how very rude of me!" Poorly offered her his hand, introducing himself as Mr Cedric Vaughn Washbrooke, resident of Ravenham Hall.

The woman was unimpressed. "What is the purpose of your visit?" she asked, her tone bluntly direct. Poorly felt himself begin to sweat; this cow was giving him the jitters. Getting a grip of himself, he continued;

"I'm here on behalf of my friend, Horst – Mr Block, Mrs Block's husband. Really, I'm just doing the 'good neighbour' act, if you see what I mean?" The look on the woman's face told him she didn't. He continued anyway.

"You see, it's like this; Horst – Mr Block – won't be in to visit his wife for a while. You see, he has a ninety-three year old aunt living in Augsburg, and she has been taken ill. *Very* ill, I'm afraid." He paused, allowing the meaning of his words to sink in. "Augsburg – it's in Germany", he said, needlessly.

"I am well aware of where the city is, Mr Washbrooke. What I am not so aware of is why Mr Block couldn't have told us this himself?"

"Well, you see, the call came rather suddenly – there was no time. The old lady is nearing the end, I'm afraid, and Horst felt it was his duty to be there. He packed the very moment he received the news, and is on his way to Germany as we speak. I happened to see him getting into a taxi, you see, heading for the airport, and, well, that's how he came to ask me if I could tell you what has happened, and perhaps pop in on his dear wife."

The starch in the nurse's voice came across when she spoke.

"It's not like Mr Block to go off, whatever the circumstances, without informing me, or coming in to see his wife himself."

Poorly rubbed his hands. "Well, you see, he was in *such* a rush, and *so* upset – I gather he had been rather fond of his aunt in his youth, you see." He was feeling more confident now.

Frowning, the nurse stepped back into the corridor.

"This way, Mr Washbrooke – *what* did you say your first name was?"

"Cedric. Cedric Vaughn." Poorly let the name roll off his tongue, as though emphasising its importance.

Giving him a look that made it clear she was unimpressed, the nurse led him halfway down the corridor, and into a room with a brass plaque bearing the words *Head Charge Nurse* screwed onto the door.

It was a small room, with a tall, narrow window. A desk and chair took up a good third of the space, with filing cabinets, bookcases and a sofa fighting over the rest of it. Sitting in the straight-backed chair behind the desk, she indicated that Poorly should take a seat on the sofa. Instead, he remained standing, and produced a white envelope from his top pocket, which he placed on the desktop.

"Horst asked me to give you this – he felt it would explain everything."

The nurse opened the envelope, and read through its contents carefully, only once pausing to give her guest a quick glance.

Putting the letter down, she looked up.

"Well, Mr Washbrooke – *Cedric Vaughn* – that all seems very straightforward." Poorly noted that she made no effort to conceal her sarcasm as she said his assumed name, and he wondered what that might mean. She continued;

"Nevertheless, I find it very strange that Mr Block did not telephone me before flying off to his sick aunt – in Augsburg. A fine city, I believe. No doubt your neighbour has spoken to you about it?"

"Oh yes, Sister. He spoke very fondly of it."

She folded her arms confidently, giving him a long, hard stare.

"I know Augsburg well, you see – I holidayed there a few years ago. A pleasure – the city has some wonderful sights. Did you know, for example, about the Pelachturm?"

"An eleventh-century watertower" Poorly replied coolly. "I believe Horst told me it is something like 230ft tall, and has a 35-bell glockenspiel inside, that chimes daily at noon?"

A good thing, Poorly thought, that he was so conscientious about research. At school, he had been unique in actually enjoying homework, and even now would make sure he found out everything he could about every aspect of any cover story – one of the many reasons Roy Bigley liked him so much. He knew bugger-all about bloody Augsburg, but he damn well knew how to read a guidebook.

He accepted the previous offer of the sofa, and casually chatted about the city's other charms – charms he had been entirely innocent of up until the previous evening, some of which the iron lady herself seemed not to know.

Finally, when he felt he had shaken her enough, he calmly requested to see Mrs Block.

She stiffened, glaring at him once more.

"As I'm sure you are aware, Mrs Block is suffering from severe senile dementia, as well as recovering from very intensive treatment for cancer?"

"Yes, Sister. Of course I am aware of that – I shan't stay too long, or upset the good lady, if I can help it."

The nurse took him back into the corridor, and led him to a room furthur along. Pausing at the door, she turned to him;

"You do realise she won't recognise you? She barely recognises her husband most days." Poorly nodded. "Yes, Horst mentioned that. Very difficult. No, Sister, I don't expect anything from Mrs Block – I just want to make sure I carry out her husband's wishes, really. I myself am on my way out of the country, as it happens – leaving for Australia. This place is sort of on the way to the airport, you see. So I don't have a lot of time – I really just want to be able to tell Horst I looked in on her, if he asks."

The nurse opened the door, and Poorly stepped in. A woman sat in a wheelchair, staring with unseeing eyes out of the window.

"Hello, Rose, love. It's Cedric – Horst asked me to come and see you, he's had to go away for a little while, you see." With one hand, Poorly turned the wheelchair to face him. It was the same woman he had seen in the photograph, although in life she looked even older.

"Who are you?" she asked, her voice quavering. "Who is this Horst you're talking about?" Growing agitated, she flapped a frail arm at him. "I don't know anyone called Horst! I don't like you – go away!"

"Alright, Rose. Goodbye. I'll tell Horst I've seen you – he'll be back in a couple of weeks or so. You might be feeling a bit better by then, eh?"

Stepping out of the room, he shut the door.

"Thank you, Sister. As you say, she doesn't know me. Very sad, this bloody dementia. Oh, well, must rush if I don't want to miss my flight." Smiling to himself, Poorly walked briskly away, knowing that the *real* Cedric Vaughn Washbrooke was indeed leaving for Australia that very day, and would be catching a Quantas Airlines flight in a matter of hours.

After the stranger had left, Sister Doris Maitland sat down with a cup of coffee, and, between sips, re-read the letter he had left her. It was short and to the point;

Dear Sister Maitland;

By the time you read this, I shall be in Germany, visiting a dear relative, the sister of my mother, who has been taken very ill, and is unlikely to survive. Somehow, it did not seem right to tell you this on the telephone, and, as this is an emergency which necessitates my immediate departure, I have no other way of letting you know.

I am entrusting this letter to a good friend of mine, who has promised to deliver it in person.

I trust yourself and your staff with my wife's care, and hope to return as soon as is possible.

Yours

Horst Block.

Doris Maitland stared thoughtfully at the letter. Although rather smug, the man had been courteous and polite – why was something troubling her about him? Reflecting on their conversation, she thought she knew what it was; the fact that, after she had mentioned the Pelachturm, he had felt the need to spend the next ten minutes listing every other attraction of Augsburg, as if he felt he had to convince her that Mr Block had indeed spoken to him about the place. Looking back, the whole thing seemed rehearsed, as though he had been remembering an entry in a guidebook. She came to a decision. Picking up the telephone on her desk, she rang the number for Horst Block's home, and listened to the continuous ringing of a telephone that was obviously going to go unanswered. She replaced the receiver, then immediately picked it up again. Dialling directory enquiries, she asked for the number of a Mr Cedric Vaughn Washbrooke, of Ravenham Hall. On being put through, it was a butler who answered her call, and informed her, in smooth, cultured tones, that his master had left for Heathrow, and would be away on business in Australia for several months; if it was urgent, he could provide her with the number of his master's hotel there? Doris Maitland thanked him, explaining that it wasn't urgent enough to trouble Mr Washbrooke with while he was abroad, as it really required him to be in England anyway. Replacing the receiver, she felt relaxed, and was relieved that she could now carry on her duties without concern.

Back in Middle Upton, Tim discussed his meeting with Erik Lux with Patricia.

"He's a madman! He wants my hide, doesn't give a damn that the war ended years ago!"

"What do you think he will do?" asked Patricia, concern filling her voice.

Tim poured himself a large whisky and handed her a glass of her favourite wine.

"I don't know – but it will involve that bloody aeroplane!"

Patricia gazed at him for a long moment, then stood up and took his hand.

"Let's go for a ride, Tim – it's a lovely afternoon out there. We should enjoy it, instead of sitting here, worrying about Erik."

Tim smiled. "I think that's an excellent idea. I'll go and get the horses ready."

Back at Elwood, Erik taxied the Messerschmitt out of the hangar, and over towards the flight area. He had completed the routine work on the plane, and planned to take advantage of the clear skies to test-fly it.

The Eagle Will Fly

The roar of the engines as he took off was music to his ears. As he gained height, he could see George Lake and his wife waving to him in the friendly way of fellow flying enthusiasts. He waved back. No reason not to be friendly. He knew exactly where he was heading, and, once he'd reached a good altitude, headed there with single-minded determination. He had always wondered what the pretty village of Middle Upton, and its Manor House, looked like from the air. He relaxed as he gained height; being airborne always made him feel good. He checked the compass. He was on course. He wondered if Patricia was still living at the Manor, with the Englishman. Lux did not regret the ending of his and Patricia's marriage – in reality, it had been over for years, and they had been man and wife in name only. In recent years, Patricia had spent most of her time in New York, returning to Montana only for a few weeks in the summer, when the weather was good for riding and flying. Below him, the unmistakable steeple of Middle Upton's church came into view, then he saw the thatched village pub, with its hanging sign, and, beyond it, something that could be a market garden. Circling round over the village, he spotted the Manor House, surrounded by meadows, a copse of trees in the near distance. Lux banked the Messerschmitt, dropping altitude, just missing the top of the church steeple as he turned back through the village, skimming the rooftops of the market garden greenhouses – he could almost hear the glass shatter. Turning once more towards the manor, keeping low, skimming the hedgerows, he suddenly spotted two people on horseback, crossing one of the meadows and heading towards what appeared to be a stable block at the rear of the main house. As he flew nearer, Erik recognised Tim Watts as one of the riders. As the second came into view, he saw clearly that it was Patricia. With a grim, half-amused smile, Lux dropped the plane still further, the 109's engines screaming in protest. As the horses panicked, and tried to bolt, Tim looked up with alarm, noticing the plane's markings, the ominous black cross and yellow nose cone. He took quick stock of the situation. The pilot could only be Lux, and he could only want one thing. Shouting to Patricia, Tim gestured to the stables. As soon as she was ahead of him, he dug his heels into his horse's sides, making for safety whilst desperately trying to shield Patricia, in case Lux decided to go after her as well as him. His thoughts were racing as he tried to anticipate what the madman German would do next. They reached the stables just as the Messerschmitt screamed over the roof above them.

Tim leapt off his mount. "Stay there!" he shouted to Patricia, dashing out of the stables, through the back door of the house and into the kitchen. Running hell for leather, he raced into the gun room, snatched up his high-powered rifle from the rack, and was back out in the yard as Lux came screaming over on the return flight. Spotting Tim, Lux wrenched the Messerschmitt into a roll, levelled out sharply, then went into another roll, all the while dodging the bullets that Tim, boiling over with anger and shock, was firing at him.

Tim knew that shooting at Lux was a waste of time. Throwing his gun down, he went back to the stables, back to Patricia.

Erik laughed to himself as he climbed higher in the summer sky. "You thought that was frightening, Wing Commander? Wait until you see what I have planned." By now, Roy Bigley's men should be putting the next stage of his plan into action. Bigley had made it clear he didn't like the idea of Lux being at the farm;

"You're my client, Mr Lux, and I prefer to keep the clients away from the lads. But, as you're paying me rather a lot of money, I suppose the occasional visit wouldn't be too unreasonable."

CHAPTER FOURTEEN

Lost Horse Farm. The very name of the place could be a story itself. A remote, desolate place, in the middle of nowhere, it could only be approached by a narrow, rutted, mile-long track.

The farm house was showing its age, and in desperate need of renovation; the thatched roof was full of holes, with reeds hanging loose in many places. The exterior, once painted a brilliant white, had faded to a dull, dirty grey, spotted with yellow-green mildew. Of the original seven hundred acres that had once belonged to the farm, in its early, proud days, only forty now remained, mostly woodland and marshes. A six-feet high electric fence bordered the whole of the property, and two guards were permanently based there, along with four Rottweilers. Owned by Roy Bigley, Lost Horse Farm was better-known in the underworld as "the Stopover", a place to hide out and change one's appearance and documentation when on the run from the Old Bill, before continuing to sanctuaries on foreign soil, such as Spain, Switzerland or South America. For some, though, it would be a permanent stopover. Those who had crossed Roy Bigley, or displeased him in some way, were brought here for a brief and bloody interrogation before being discreetly deposited somewhere in the Thames Estuary, with plenty of cement for company.

To the rear of the farm was a cluster of outbuildings, in the centre of which was a large barn, built in the Dutch style, in red brick with a black tiled roof. This barn was to be playing a major part in the very strange show that would soon be going on at Lost Horse Farm. It was here that Roy Bigley's crew would learn how to fit and load a Messerschmitt's canons in less than twenty minutes, and here, safe from prying eyes, where no one was going to become suspicious at a lot of men coming and going with heavy-duty tools, that the guns that had been delivered to Wapping Docks were being stored. Erik Lux, Mouth reflected, had been well on the ball when he'd mentioned to Bigley that he was uncertain about the suitability of the gang working on the plane at Elwood. But, naturally, the German did not want that particular plane to be damaged by amateurs as they learned how to load heavy cannon, how to strip wing panels. How, essentially, to make such a plane warworthy. But the gang needed *something* to practice on. Fortunately, they were Roy Bigley's gang, and Roy Bigley was very good at taking care of problems. In his world, this one was minor, so small as to be laughable, the solution found in what seemed like moments.

From a scrapyard in Kent, which specialised in vintage aircraft and machinery, the forlorn-looking wreckage of a Messerschmitt ME109 had been rescued, and transported in bits and pieces to the farm, where Mouth Wilson's motley team of ex-tradesmen would attempt to assemble it to a point where the dilapidated wreckage was strong enough to take the weight of the machine guns and cannons that would be loaded repeatedly, in order for the crew to gain the utmost precision in their task, and be ready for the day when it was done for real, on the other Messerschmitt ME109, owned by Erik Lux and flown in the Battle of Britain by his father, Hans Lux.

Wilson's crew were completely new to this kind of work; they needed a good teacher to get them up to scratch.

Ex Luftwaffe Flight Sergeant Horst Block was to be that teacher. With the life of his ailing wife under threat, he would have no choice but to comply.

Mouth Wilson stood in the middle of the now-empty barn, imagining it as it would be in a couple of days, resounding to the sounds of frantic hammering and sawing, the shouting and swearing of men hard at work. A hive of activity.

When Horst Block awoke, he found himself in a small, windowless room. He ached all over, and felt very cold.

He tried to make sense of where he was, tried to comprehend how he could have got there. Slowly, it all came back to him, the three men, forcing their way into his house late at night, the one they had called "Doc" injecting him with something.

The room was damp, and smelled of stale cigarette smoke. The bright yellow duvet that covered him seemed brighter than the forty-watt bulb that hung under a frayed, grubby shade.

He began to shout in German, the way he had when he had first been taken prisoner many years ago.

As if in answer to his shouting, he heard footsteps, then a key turning in the lock on the other side of the door to this room.

The door swung open, and two of the three men from the night before entered. The one they had called Doc was one of them, the youth in the baseball cap the other.

Tony Knox kicked the door shut, and indicated with a jerk of his head that the old man should get up, and sit on one of the chairs that were scattered haphazardly around the room. Horst complied, but obviously not quick enough for the bully-boy's liking. Knox grabbed him by the shoulders, dragged him across the room and pushed him roughly into a chair.

"Messcherschmitts, old man. Remember what they look like, how the guns work?"

Horst nodded, bewildered by the question.

"Good. The Doc here's going to stay with you. I'll get you some grub – nothing if not a good host, me."

"Wait. I do not want breakfast – only an explanation." Horst's voice was strong, his confidence returning as he sensed that these men needed him alive.

Tony Knox paused, shrugged.

"Our boss'll be coming to see you a little later, Kraut. For some reason he wants a Messerschmitt built, and he reckons you can show him how it's done. Now, I'm going to get you some grub. I'd suggest you eat it, you'll get nuffink else."

The young man stalked out, slamming the door behind him. There was silence for a long while, then Doc came quietly to Horst's side.

"Are you alright?"

Horst looked at him, seeing something in the man's eyes.

"You do not want this, do you?" He asked. The man didn't answer for a moment. Then, quietly, he said; "I don't get a choice. My advice? Answer questions truthfully, do as you're told, don't fight the others."

"And I will be safe then?" Horst sneered. He knew he wouldn't – he had been in the war, had known people in the Gestapo, back in Germany. You didn't leave witnesses alive, however compliant they were.

The large Dutch barn, painted a once-garish, now faded red, was set well back from the farmhouse itself, in a wide clearing surrounded by natural woodland and scrub.

The main house consisted of the ground floor, which comprised a large living room, a cloakroom, a modern kitchen, a second reception room, used for storage at the moment, a utility room and a single-storey annexe to the rear, where Horst Block was being held prisoner, and the top floor, comprising of a long, wide dormitory, filled with bunk beds, which had evidently once been two rooms, a bathroom, and two regular bedrooms, comfortably furnished. Although Mouth Wilson had often stayed here when it got too hot, in a metaphorical sense, in London, Roy Bigley, although the owner of the farm, had never had occasion to spend more than a few hours there.

Now the three main players, Bigley, Wilson and Lux, were engaged in deep discussion in the living room. Lux was questioning Bigley. It was clear that the gangster wasn't happy with him being at the farm, but Lux had reminded Bigley of the handsome sum of money that he had been paid, making it clear he would stay out of the way of the workmen, that he only wanted to speak to the men in charge. Bigley had suggested they meet at the showroom, but Lux had insisted on the farm. He had to know, he had told Bigley, where his work was being carried out.

"This crew you have put together, you think they are efficient?"

Roy Bigley removed the cigar from his mouth, blew smoke out in front of him, watched it spiral and disappear.

"They've got the know-how and the tools for the job, Mr Lux. How efficient they are is down to their instructor, and that man, if I recall, was your choice."

"And I have chosen well," replied Lux, his voice betraying no emotion, "he was one of my country's best craftsmen, before the war."

"The war was a long time ago, and your craftsman is old now" Wilson reminded him "he may have forgotten his craft – it can happen to any of us."

"Not to us Germans – we do not lose anything." Lux stuck his chin out, aggressive. Wilson, lighting a cigarette, calmly stated; "You lost the war, remember?"

Lux stiffened, and crossed over to the window where he stood, staring out, hands behind his back.

"*My* war, Mr Wilson, has not yet been fought, never mind lost. And when it *is* fought, I shall win." He turned to face them. "I wish to see Herr Block now."

Bigley nodded to Wilson.

"Go and fetch him. Join as at the barn."

Horst was marched into the barn, Vinnie Sampson and Ed Small on either side of him. As he was led through the huge barn doors, he saw, scattered about, the remnants and parts belonging to a very poor-looking aeroplane, a mere shell sitting in the middle of the barn, that could once have been a Messerschmitt 109, the pride of the Luftwaffe. On seeing Horst being brought into the barn, Lux walked over to him. Snapping his heels together, he thrust out his arm in the Nazi salute.

"*Heil, Hitler!*" he barked. Horst stared at him in shocked amazement, keeping his hands resolutely by his sides, a prickling chill coming over him. Horst, like most Germans, had fought because he had been told to, because he feared the punishment that would come to those who refused. What could be possessing this man to behave as though they were once more in the 1930s, at the height of the power of the Third Reich?

Lux took his arm, and, with an expansive gesture, indicated the plane and its parts.

"The Luftwaffe will rise again, Herr Block. The war will be won for the glory of Germany, the glory of the Fuhrer." He spoke in English, wanting the other men who stood about the barn to understand.

In German, Lux explained what he wanted, and why, his eyes alive with a chilling fire. Also in German, Block began shouting, shaking his head and looking as though he would punch the other man. In a flurry of harsh words and sharp gestures, the conversation seemed to be concluded. Everything fell silent.

Mouth Wilson stepped between the two men.

"Everything alright, Herr Lux? Your craftsman seemed to accept your instructions with some vigour – or *did* he accept them? I don't know German that well, so it was kind of difficult to tell."

Lux glared first at Block, then at Wilson. "He will do as I have said" he growled. Horst Block shook his head.

"You are all crazy-mad! All of you! I am leaving now – this is madness!"

"Hear, hear!" called Tony Knox, as Eddie Small clapped his hands and Vinnie Sampson whistled approval. Knox continued;

"This is a madhouse, alright, and I don't intend hanging around for the next ten days playing Meccano with some Nazi fantasist."

Bigley stepped forward.

"You will stay, Tony." He looked around the barn. "All of you will stay. You work for me, remember? And this is the best paid job you'll ever have. You'll stay."

The barn fell silent, all of them knowing they wouldn't walk out on Bigley, not now he'd made their position clear as crystal.

But Horst Block wasn't finished yet.

"Neine, neine! No – I will not stay. Shit on all of you! I am leaving now! Crazy-mad, all of you!"

Block headed for the barn doors, the wide expanse of Essex countryside beyond them. Mouth Wilson grabbed hold of his arm. Gently, he pulled him back. Quietly, he said;

"Just a moment. There's something I want you to see, Herr Block. Then, if you still want to leave, you can leave. I'll get Tony there to run you home, come with you myself to make sure he doesn't do anything daft. Okay? Just five minutes, a quick look. That's all." Block nodded, and Wilson led him to the centre of the barn, to the shell of the Messerschmitt. Pinned to the fuselage was a colour photograph, depicting a white haired woman in her late sixties, smiling at the camera.

Horst Block fell to his knees, his head down.

"My wife" he murmured, then, in German, *"Meinen frau."* Raising his head, he looked at Wilson. "Please – please do not harm my wife. *Bitte, Herr Wilson! Abfahren sie!* Leave her!"

"Will you do as you're told?"

"Yes – only do not harm my wife!"

Wilson shrugged.

"You do what we want, she doesn't get hurt."

Back in the annexe, Horst Block reflected on the day's events. The insanity of the thing was beyond belief – they were all crazy, of that he was certain, and the other German, he was the craziest of the lot. But, for Rose's sake, he would have to go along with this madness. With a sigh of regret, his thoughts turned to the Germany of his childhood, to memories that were not tainted with the evil of Hitler's increasing insanity. Germany had been a good place, once, before Nazism took hold, and replaced the brightness with the dark, stinking spectre of evil. No one Horst knew at the time had wanted it. His father had muttered darkly about how no one wanted the Jews dead, their businesses just needed to be monitored more closely, that was all. Perhaps some of the foreigners, those who did not work so hard, should be encouraged to return to their own countries. Not from malice, of course, but because Germany could not support everyone. There wasn't an endless supply of money, after all.

In the damp, dark annexe, on a farm in the middle of nowhere, Horst Block found himself inexplicably remembering the Berlin Olympics, remembering how he, his mother and his aunt had listened to the broadcast of the various events over an old, crackling radio – the same radio over which they would hear the news that Germany was at war. Horst Block, although neither a member of the Nazi party, nor particularly interested in politics in general, had signed up, as had many of his friends and fellow Germans, because it was what you did when your country was at war, and because they were already hearing rumours of what was happening to others who refused, to the socialists, the pacifists, the homosexuals. They did not want to be labelled as any of these things. They hadn't wanted war, most of them, but war had come and found them anyway.

Horst Block reflected on his life so far. Born in Augsburg, southwest Bavaria, in 1920, to parents who were neither rich nor poor, but hard-working and devoted to their son, he had had a happy childhood, roaming the streets of the city, especially during the Festive times, for which Augsburg rivalled even Munich, wandering through Bavaria's forests, playing with his friends in the rivers, the Lech and the Wertach, that met in Augsburg. Horst Block enjoyed school, and proved himself especially apt at mathematics, science and engineering. By the time he left school, eager to work and make his own money, Emil Messerschmitt had chosen Augsburg as the headquarters for the building of the much-feted warplane he had designed, the 109, named for the designer. Horst Block, like many other young Bavarians, went to work in the Messerschmitt factory and aerodrome complex, where he proved himself every bit as apt at practical engineering as he had been at the theory he had studied in school. Over time, Horst learned his trade well, soon becoming a leading expert in the field of aeronautical engineering, and a personal friend of Emil Messerschmitt himself.

As he drifted into an uneasy sleep, Horst Block found himself thinking about the German, Erik Lux, and wondering what kind of madness held the man. He looked too young to have fought in the war, and yet he was a passionate, living, breathing Nazi, more committed than many who had served the Party faithfully in the years immediately before the war. Horst Block knew nothing good could come of such insanity, and his last thought, before sleep claimed him, was to wonder just how bad this thing was going to be.

In his dreams, Horst was back in the prisoner of war camp, a dreary place, set in bleak, featureless countryside. It had been winter, bitterly cold, with snow laying thick on the ground. The place had reeked of misery, degradation, defeat and shame, all overlaid with the smell of overcooked vegetables. Even now, Horst could not stand the smell of boiled cabbage. The camp had housed Luftwaffe personnel, and some men from Rommel's Afrika Corps. While some were jovial, glad to be away from the fighting, many simply looked broken, and defeated. Horst had been neither of these. Instead, as he paced the length of the razor wire fence, he was in love. It had been 1944 when Horst Block, serving over the Russian Front, had been shot down, captured, and made a prisoner of war. At first, he had been sent to an internment and assessment camp in Yorkshire, on the edge of the moors, then, that winter, along with several of his German comrades, he had been transferred to Edgegreen Labour Camp, situated in a small, picturesque village on the Norfolk Broads. The prisoners had not been welcomed by the locals. They had arrived at the start of the sugarbeet season, and the farmers had seen a way to get their crop harvested on the cheap, by giving the work to the inmates of the camp rather than the locals, as they normally would. It had been like this with all the harvests since Edgegreen had first been set up, so the local hostility was understandable. The work was back breaking, and Horst always found himself looking forward to the rest breaks mid-morning and mid-afternoon. He was not the only one who found the work hard, and most of the other men were in their early twenties, as he was, some only in their teens, all relatively fit and healthy.

During these breaks, Horst would carve statues of small animals on old pieces of wood that he found lying about him, usually sitting apart from the other prisoners. It was during one of these breaks that a young woman rode past, a young girl strapped into a rear seat on her pushbike. Horst had noticed her before, on other days, and had often wished he could talk to her. On this particular day, the road surface was slick with rain, mud from the fields adding to the dangerous conditions. Suddenly, a large motor vehicle came roaring along the road, travelling far too fast. The driver was too close as he went to overtake the woman, and forced her to swerve into the grass verge. Both woman and child landed in a heap, the child screaming with fright. Horst was on his feet instantly, rushing to their aid. Although his grasp of the English language was limited, he was able to communicate with her enough to ask if she was alright, if the child were hurt. Reservedly, wary of this foreigner, this

German, she nodded her head, once, mumbling a curt "thank you" as she got to her feet and rode off. A few days later, Horst saw the woman riding along the road again, and stepped out in front of her, waving her down. Hesitantly, rather puzzled, she stopped, and got off of her bicycle. Horst held out his hand. Clutched in it was a small, wooden doll, in the style of the toys he remembered from Bavaria. He nodded to the doll, then to the child. Understanding, the woman took it from him with a shy, nervous smile. Horst pointed at himself, then at the doll, and said, hesitantly, in heavily-accented German, "I make." The woman's smile widened. "Yourself? You made this all by yourself?" Horst did not fully understand her words, but he nodded, smiling. The woman handed the doll to the little girl, pointing at Horst. "Say thank you to the nice man." The girl smiled, clutched the doll to her chest, and shook her head, waving at him. He laughed, and waved as the woman got back on her bicycle, and continued on her way. Over the next few weeks, one of the more friendly guards taught Horst a few phrases of English. The woman would often stop now, and talk with Horst, further increasing his knowledge of the language. In the summer of 1945, Horst Block was made a trustee, and was allowed time away from the camp. He would always spend it with the woman, walking in the lanes around Edgegreen, talking to her, telling her about his youth in Augsburg, in Bavaria, and his work, before the war, in the Messerschmitt factory. Eventually, she asked him into her small council cottage for tea. She had already told him her name was Rose Fullerton, and that the little girl was Amy, her three year-old daughter. She had not been married to Amy's father, she explained, although they were engaged. He had been killed in the war, she explained, and, although she had been upset by his death, she did not hate Germans because of it.

"After all," she had said "I am sure there are German women in my situation, their men killed by an English soldier. It isn't good to hate people when they are just doing as they are told." Horst – whose name Amy pronounced as Orsie – became fond of the woman and her child, and would sometimes dream of giving them back some of the life that had been taken from them.

In 1946 Horst was repatriated to Germany, and, had to leave Rose and young Amy, although they exchanged addresses, and both fulfilled their promises to keep in touch. In 1949, Horst returned to England, and, six months later, married Rose Fullerton. Lack of work in Norfolk forced a move to Hatfield, where, despite his German origins, Horst got a job at an aircraft factory as an engineer, the same kind of work he had done at the Messerschmitt factory in Augsburg before the war. Their final move, some twenty-odd years later, after Horst had taken early retirement in order to fulfil his dream of running his own business, was to the outskirts of Diss. Horst set up a small hardware store in the town, which he ran very successfully, until Rose was taken ill with cancer. Selling the business, he cared for her at home, lovingly, for as long as he could, before, at the urging of Amy, he realised that it was no longer practical, that the time had come to put her into a nursing home. Two years later, Amy had announced she was moving to America, and a few weeks later, Horst, who had known the joy and love of a family for many years, found himself alone.

The next day was madness, beginning early. All day, the huge barn rang to the competing noises of electric saws whining, hammers whacking against metal and wood, gruff voices arguing, swearing, complaining, and Horst Block yelling out instructions. The air sweltered in the heat of blow torches and frayed tempers, the smell of oil and high emotions providing a kind of anti-aromatherapy. There was grease and sawdust everywhere, and people were forever walking into one another, or tripping over things.

Every day was chaos, but it was on the fourth day that things nearly got out of hand. Horst had called them lazy, had told them to get on with the job. Horst had then shouted at them all, furiously, in German. They had laughed, cruelly, to cover their lack of understanding.

Tony Knox, pointing at a drawing of a Messerschmitt that Lux had pinned to the wall, had said;

"Gawd, this is like *Flight of the Phoenix* – all we need is Jimmy flaming Stewart!" The others had burst into raucous laughter, and Horst had muttered that it wasn't a joke, they should start to take this seriously – which had resulted in his second shouting match of the day, this time in English, and with Tony Knox.

Later, for a reason he could not recall, he had thrown a heavy spanner at Eddie Small, narrowly missing him. The man had lost his temper, had hit him, drawing blood. A full-scale fight had ensued, during which somebody – possibly Tony Knox, Horst didn't remember – had pointed at the scaffolding that held the body of the Messerschmitt, and said;

"Let's end this bloody war now – let's lynch the Kraut." A cheer had gone up, someone had tossed Knox a rope. Horst Block had been terrified – these men wouldn't think twice about killing him; he already sensed all of them had killed before, and that some killed for a living. He scurried to the scaffolding, climbing to the platform for safety.

Mouth Wilson had been the one to stop it, striding over with his shotgun.

"Oi! Enough, you lot. Playtime's over. Let's get back to work, yeah?"

"No way, mate!" Knox had yelled, and the pack had closed in on Horst Block. Without thinking, Wilson threw the shotgun up to Block, who caught it, and held it over them, barrels facing the baying mob.

Everything fell silent. You could have heard a pin drop. Mouth Wilson wondered if he'd done the right thing, or been bloody stupid. The silent tension was suddenly shattered by an explosion of shotgun fire. Pellets ricocheted off the roof. Everyone ducked, scrambling for cover.

It fell silent again, but no one moved. Block pointed the gun at Lux, who had arrived on one of his rare visits, and was now cowering in a corner, his hands above his head. Wilson waited, wondering what would happen next. Abruptly, spitting out something in German, Horst Block tossed the gun down to Wilson, who gave a wolfish grin, set the gun down and clapped his hands.

"Come on, you lot. Back to work. And show some respect to our international friends, yeah? Herr Block is only doing his job, and Herr Lux is bankrolling this madness."

As the activity resumed, Wilson gave a grim smile. Somehow, he doubted there would be any more trouble.

Wilson wasn't quite right about there being no further trouble. A couple of days later, when tempers were once again fraying, Horst was pacing around the barn, clearly agitated, muttering to himself in German.

"Acht, warum? Warum? Warum ist Ich hier?" was the only phrase Mouth Wilson caught. Suddenly, Horst Block collapsed, gasping for breath and drenched in a cold sweat. He lay on the ground, his face grey, still asking, in German, why he was there, although no one understood.

"Doc!" Wilson shouted, gesturing to Block. "Gerrova here. This is your department."

Doc Little went over to Horst Block, and knelt beside him. Taking the man's wrist, he felt his pulse, and shook his head.

"Doesn't look good, Mouth. Not a heart attack, I think – angina – but he needs to go to hospital."

"No!" Wilson barked. "No hospital. No one leaves here!"

Horst was frantically trying to speak, struggling for breath, gripping his chest. Grabbing Doc's sleeve he managed, with extreme effort, to say something.

"I...I don't understand, Mr Block. Can you say it in English?"

Horst gasped, pressed a hand to his chest. "Pocket. Pills. Pills...in...pocket."

He was clearly in pain now. Doc Little hurriedly searched through his pockets, finally coming up with a small brown bottle. Unscrewing the lid, he shook out a couple of pills, and handed them to Horst, who, with effort, swallowed them.

It was an anxious few minutes as everyone in the barn waited to see if the pills would have any effect. Eventually, Horst's colour returned, and he sat up. Doc Little helped him to his feet.

Mouth Wilson came over, concern in his eyes.

"You okay?" Horst nodded. Mouth turned to the Doc. "Get him out of here. He needs to rest. You lot -" he turned to his crew "- don't you have work to do?"

As his crew got back to the job in hand, muttering between themselves, and shooting dark looks at the retreating form of Horst Block, Mouth Wilson sighed. The sooner this job was over, he thought, the better.

CHAPTER FIFTEEN

One morning, while Erik Lux was working on his Messerschmitt, George Lake cornered him, startling the German as he spoke.

"Why'n't you put that plane of yours in an airshow, Erik?" The old Englishman's country accent, splitting the dark mists of Lux's thoughts, nearly caused the latter to injure himself. Fortunately, Erik Lux had learnt at an early age to control his reactions.

"Forgive me, Mr Lake. I was...absorbed in my work. I did not hear you."

"I said, wharrabout showing off that plane of yours? I've gorra couple of vintage ladies I'm sending out to an airshow in Bedfordshire. Place called Long Hill. What do yer reckon?" George inclined his head toward the Messerschmitt. "Yer done a good job on 'er, comin' up a treat, she is. Pity ter keep 'er hidden away, I says."

Erik paused, his mind racing. Putting the plane on public view, being open about it, would surely give Tim Watts cause to doubt that the same plane was the centre of a plot against his life?

He told George Lake he would think about it. "I cannot promise I will be there – I need to be sure everything is perfect with the plane, you see. Details that trouble no one else, I notice. Then, I cannot be happy. It is my nature, to be…obsessive about such things."

"Ar, well. Tha's the German, innit? Allus said to the missus, yer want summat doin' proper, gerra German to do it. Take pride in yer work, doncha, way our young 'uns don't no more."

"Indeed, Mr Lake. Although –" and here Erik Lux thought back to that visit to Berlin with his cousin Kurt - "it seems even in Germany young people are becoming careless. They think they will all work with machines, that all they will have to do is press some buttons and a robot will do their work for them!"

"Yer ain't far wrong, Mister Lux. No, it's a sad state of affairs, when people ain't prepared to do an honest day's work, when they don't take pride in it."

"Indeed." Lux was thinking of the showdown he had planned, of his orchestration of Tim Watts' demise. He knew he couldn't have worked harder, couldn't be planning to take more pride in it. He was, he realised, satisfied. Happy. For the first time in his life, he felt comfortable being Erik Lux.

By lunchtime, Lux sensed he was simply making work; the Messerschmitt was as ready as it would ever be until the next stage in the plan came to fruition, and he was wasting time fiddling about with it. Storing his tools safely, and taking care to lock the hangar behind him, he returned to his cottage.

Back at the cottage, he went upstairs, and retrieved a briefcase from under his bed. Taking it back down to the kitchen, he sat at the large oak table, taking in for the first time the gleaming wooden floor and the shiny, modern appliances – shiny, modern appliances that seemed at odds with the rather old-fashioned stripped pine cabinets and worktops, and the large, unashamedly rural, Aga. Shrugging his shoulders, Erik made himself a cup of coffee, and began to examine the maps he had brought when he had arrived in England this time around. It seemed like a lifetime ago, now. As he studied the networks of tiny coloured lines, took in the strange names of unfamiliar places, Erik Lux found it hard to believe there had ever been a time he hadn't known Roy Bigley, hadn't been planning the murder of the man who had killed his father. It was as though all his years of adulthood had been wiped out, and he had gone straight from that ten-year-old boy hearing of his father's death to the bitter, vengeful man, fixated on murder that he was today. Briefly, and entirely unexpectedly, he wondered if Bigley ever felt like this about his life, if he ever wondered about the time – Lux assumed there had been a time – before the big man had become London's – and possibly England's – most feared gangland boss.

George Lake's talk of airshows had given Lux an idea. He knew he would not be going to the display at Long Hill, but he did want to show off his plane, in a manner of speaking. He had an idea of how he would do that, but it needed Bigley's consent. And some planning on his part. He wanted, in his own way, to shout at the world before he took down Tim Watts. Elwood was not the right place for what he had in mind, but he was certain that *finding* the right place wouldn't be too difficult, not from what he'd seen so far of rural Norfolk.

Erik Lux was soon driving through the winding lanes that comprised much of the Norfolk countryside, referring, every now and again, to a map that highlighted the sites of World War Two airfields.

Shortly before dusk, Lux found what he was looking for; a disused airfield, turned back to agricultural use, that had gone to seed since, he assumed, the last lot of farmers had failed to diversify quickly enough for the relentless march of capitalism. The place was a few scrubby acres of rough heathland, bordered by trees. There appeared to be no fence, so, getting out of his car, Lux strolled forward.

What had evidently been the runway was still in place, although the tarmac was cracked, and barely visible through a gardener's nightmare of nettles, and the control tower, minus the glass from its windows, the lock from its door, most of its paintwork and a few bricks, still stood.

This was what he wanted, Lux thought, nodding to himself as he prowled over it. According to his map, this was Hunton Airfield, less than 19 miles from Elwood, though it might as well have been a million miles away.

Lux returned to his cottage, where he spent the rest of the evening consulting maps and making notes. At about four a.m, too late, he knew, for the nightmares to trouble him, he gave up the fight with his eyelids, and went to bed. At seven a.m, he was awake once more, eager to face the day. Restless, half-wild, he filled his time with a pre-breakfast jog, his usual light breakfast of scrambled egg on toast with a cup of coffee, a shower, reading the newspaper that had been being delivered since he got there, and, from all the evidence, in the interval between the previous occupant leaving and himself arriving, completing all of the crossword apart from three down and seventeen across.

At nine a.m, he got up from the kitchen table, and headed for the living room, where he picked up the telephone, and dialled a number he had come to know by heart.

"I'm sorry, sir, Mr Bigley doesn't usually come in to the office before eleven, unless he has meetings there. Shall I have him return your call?"

"As soon as he gets in. It's Erik Lux, the number -"

"Mr Bigley knows how to reach you, Mr Lux. I'll tell him you called."

At a quarter past twelve, the telephone at the cottage rang.

On the other end of the line, Roy Bigley hid his surprise at Erik Lux's request. He was curious, to be sure, but he knew that, in business, and in *his* business in particular, it didn't pay to allow your curiosity to get out of your own skull. Gangsters like Bigley were the kings of their jungles – and curiosity and cats had never made easy bedfellows.

"Well, Erik. You're the client. If that's what you want, that's what you get...for a price, of course."

Erik Lux sighed. "But of course, Mr Bigley. Do you think I am, perhaps, a thief? That I would rob you, would take the bread from your children's mouths?"

Bigley, who had no family beyond the inner circle of his most loyal henchmen, laughed. "I dunno what the hell you are, Mr Lux, or what your game is, and I don't much care. If you're paying, I'm playing."

"I am glad to hear that, Mr Bigley. I would hate for us to have a...falling out."

On his end of the line, Bigley scowled. What went through his mind was; *Whatever you are, Kraut, you're not a player. Not one of us. You talk a tough game, boy, but in the end, talk's cheap, and it's just that – talk. You ain't nothing, Mr Lux, except out of your depth. You wanted to run with the big dogs, and found yourself playing with wolves.* Roy Bigley had known many people like Lux, people who got cocky on the basis of a mere acquaintance. The acquaintance didn't last much past the time it took Roy Bigley to deposit their final, large, amount of cash in his offshore bank account.

CHAPTER SIXTEEN

It was 3am, a morning in early July, and Erik Lux arrived at Elwood, ready to move his plan forward.

He parked his car at the barrier, heaved it aside, and walked over the field to the hangars. Unlocking his own, he swung wide the doors. The dawn moon gleamed against the ME109, which was highlighted by the promise of a coming sunrise. Erik Lux crossed to the large maintenance hangar, and repeated the procedure. He ducked inside and, a few seconds later, the rumble of the towing tractor could be heard.

Lux drove the tractor out of the shed, and over to his own hangar, where, backing it up, he fastened chains between tractor and plane, and towed the latter over to the runway. He freed the plane, wound up the chains, and returned the tractor to the maintenance shed, which he took care to lock securely behind him.

Minutes later, the dawn air was filled with the roar of the Messerschmitt's engine as Erik Lux took it up into the misty, morning air of a Norfolk sky.

It was a short trip to the old, abandoned field at Hunton. Lux swung the Messerschmitt in low over the trees, and, as he cleared them, spotted a dark van parked at the edge of the runway. He gave a sigh of relief. The men were here, waiting for him, as he had arranged. This was to be the first practice run, where Bigley's gang would do for real, on his father's plane, what they had been practising on the mocked-up shell at Lost Horse Farm.

Lux taxied to the end of the old runway, jolting over cracks, putting on the brakes just before the twisted form of an abandoned pushchair which seemed to serve to mark a boundary between the airfield and a field of wheat, which, from the richness of its sheaves, was ready for harvesting. In the time it had taken him to bring his plane down and to a stop, the van had turned around, facing out of the field, with its rear doors open. Two metal crates, heavy, to judge by the effort employed by the men carrying them, were taken from the back of the van, set down on the grass beside the runway, and opened up to reveal the machine guns. The crates were lowered onto a tarpaulin that covered most of the ground that side of the runway, and boxes of ammunition were placed, with a care that told of a level of fear, beside them. The ammunition seemed no less heavy than the guns. Lux smiled. All was as it should be.

Mouth Wilson got out of the van, gesturing to someone to follow him. The thin, stooped figure of Horst Block emerged, his whole expression conveying exactly what he thought of this whole venture. When he saw Erik, he spat, and snarled something in harsh German. Erik made a gesture that, while not used in England, was unmistakable to the Englishmen in its intent. Horst spat again, and turned away, muttering, and bringing the index finger of his left hand to his temple, in the German sign which was used to signal someone was a few slices short of a loaf. Mouth clapped his hands, and jerked his head at Horst.

"Get on with it, then. We haven't got all day – clock's ticking, Mr Block."

With a bitter shrug of his shoulders, Horst Block raised his arm, set a stopwatch, and began shouting orders at the six men who swarmed over the Messerschmitt, removing wing panels, fitting machine guns, and loading the heavy canons. The driver stayed behind the wheel, looking for all the world as if there was nothing unusual in transporting machine guns to a deserted airfield in the early hours of the morning. Perhaps, in his life, there wasn't. Both Lux and Wilson also stood by with stopwatches. The men worked like demons, as though they were trying to break some sort of record. Which, in a way, they were; their own. Horst continued to bellow instructions, then stopped, giving a curt nod. As the men stepped back from the plane, he flung up a hand.

"Twenty-three minutes. Not good enough. I thought we had almost got this right. Imbeciles."

"I'm sure the lads are just a bit nervous, Mr Block." Mouth Wilson turned to Lux. "Alright if they have another go?"

Erik looked at his own watch, and shook his head. "I need to test the guns, before people start to wake up, and become curious. I intend to be back here before first light. There is no time. I suggest you return to Lost Horse Farm, and work harder on getting things *right*. Do I need to remind you of the money I have paid to your boss, precisely so that things are done *exactly* as I requested?"

Wilson shook his head. "No, Mr Lux. You don't. Trust me, it'll be down to nineteen minutes on the day – I give you my word on that. We'd done it in twenty, back at the farm. I reckon it's just nerves, like I said. It'll be alright on the day."

"It had better be. On the day, I will have no time to waste."

Erik Lux decided to head for the coast between Cromer and Wells, a beautiful, deserted stretch he had walked along many times. He felt a low, happy buzz in his stomach, and a feeling of euphoria in his brain, as he thought about the guns the Messerschmitt carried, fully loaded. It had cost him an extra five grand to get Bigley to agree to his men transporting the ammunition - "I tend to leave that sort of thing to the gentlemen who supply me with heavy firepower, Mr Lux" - but he had got the gangster to co-operate. Erik Lux was no racist, but he didn't like the thought of Asians – for Bigley had told him the ammunition was coming from Karachi, where they mysteriously managed to get hold of such things the way the English could get hold of Smarties – working on his plane, and possibly attempting to hijack his plan, his revenge mission, for their own ends. Not, of course, that he felt they would do so because they were Asians, it was just...well, it just *was*. That was how he felt, and he wasn't about to apologise for it. He smiled as he gained height, knowing he would blast the calm of the North Sea to pieces this morning, would make a lot of noise, whilst being very careful not to accidentally kill someone, or damage anything. If he got high enough, he reckoned, the North Sea was more than wide enough for what he wanted to do.

Once over the North Sea, Erik Lux opened the Messerschmitt up to its full capacity.

Moonlight shone on the black sea as the plane skimmed the waves, engines screaming. Lux began to put the veteran machine through its paces, diving, rolling, twisting and turning like some glorious, out of control bird. Finally, as he skimmed low over the roiling surf, the body of his plane almost touching the water, he wrenched it upwards, engines screaming. All he could see was the sky, a blur rushing past him, space whirling across his vision. All he could feel was exhilaration As soon as the sea was nothing more than a splash of black on the grey canvas of the early morning coast, Lux straightened up, and flew hard and fast towards the clifftops, and the forest of pines beyond them. Midway through his flight, he pressed the button that opened up the guns, the sound of the firepower rushing forward echoing in his head. In the distance, far, far below him, he saw the briefest of splashes as his shells hit home. There was another round of ammunition in the black van that had arrived at the airfield that morning, and Lux was glad he had ordered the second box, although it had made a sizeable dent in his finances.

Allowing the plane to drop a little, but not too much, he raced for the cliffs, skimming the tops of the trees before banking left, and heading back to Hunton.

Back at Hunton airfield, the men sat on the ground around the van, swigging from flasks or bottles, some reading magazines, others smoking. Horst Block was sleeping in the back of the van, whose driver had joined the men on the ground, and was flicking through a pornographic magazine, without much apparent enthusiasm. Tony Knox, the most talented driver in London, according to himself, decided he would have to get a better quality of material on the day, when, as he had been now, he would be doing nothing but sitting in the van, waiting, ready to get out of there like a bat out of hell when it was all over.

In the midst of the activity, no one had noticed the gold Vauxhall Cresta that had been parked at the edge of the woods. Its owner, one Percy Brown, poacher, had been up and about since a little after midnight, having chosen to hunt a little further afield than usual, at least until things cooled down around his home village of Elwood. There'd been that dust-up a couple of months ago with Moore, who farmed out of the Old Hall estate, then, just the previous week, Larry Hemmingway, gamekeeper at Lodge Farm, had returned home, late and rather the worse for wear, from a session in the pub. By the time Percy was clambering over the fence, Hemmingway ought to have been sound asleep, dozing off the effects of too much ale. But he wasn't, and Percy had felt the business end of a shotgun being rammed up his scrawny backside, had heard a belligerent, drunken voice demand to know what the bloody hell he thought he was playing at? Percy Brown reckoned he'd got lucky, and also that it didn't pay to play your luck too long. So he'd got the car out of the garage, and trundled off to pastures new.

He'd just tossed a couple of brace of pheasants into the boot of the Vauxhall, to join the half dozen rabbits already in there, and was mentally working out the price he could get from Johnny Wicks, Elwood's butcher, when the sky started to hum with the roar of a powerful engine, and an aeroplane came down, and landed on the old runway.

Edging out from the wood, shotgun cradled against his chest, Percy ducked behind a large oak, and, mouth gaping in astonishment, had watched what had transpired, rubbing his chin all the while.

"I's sin that thar plane sumwheres, I reckun. Sin them markins. Now, Percy, bor, where've yew sin the little birdie, eh?" Suddenly, it came to him. "Thar'll be that Jerry's plane, ower at George Lake's place, I reckun. Now, wot yew up to, bor, wiv them fellas o' yers? Don't look like nothin' good, tha's for sure, my lad."

Suddenly, the roar of engines came again, and the Messerschmitt was airborne. Cocking his head, Percy Brown followed it with watery gaze until it disappeared into the early morning.

In his bungalow on Cliff Road Farm, Barney Williams had been jolted from a sound sleep by what sounded like...guns? Getting out of bed, he grabbed his shotgun, which he kept fully loaded beside him, and, barechested and barefoot, headed for the bedroom window, which overlooked the yard where his equipment was kept.

He'd been worrying for a few days now, ever since Gerry Jacobs, who farmed over Wisbech way, had had one of his tractors nicked. Went down to do the morning milking, to see two fellas driving a brand new John Deere out of the yard. One of 'em had had a shotgun with him. Only having gone out for the milking, Gerry'd had nothing. Like he said, you didn't take people on with them odds.

So, Barney went prepared. If there was anyone out there, in the yard, he'd see them. And he reckoned he could take them out from the bedroom, if he got the right angle through the window. Didn't much care it was illegal; taking his property was illegal, too, last he'd checked.

As he drew back the curtain, he heard the roar of a gun again, and saw a flash of light, far out to sea. In the bed behind him, his wife stirred.

"Barney? Barney Williams, whatever are you at, now?"

"Thought someone was at the tractors" he said, lowering the curtain "but they e'nt. Summat bloody strange goin' on, though."

"Well, strange or not, it's nowt to do with us. Back to bed with you, Barney Williams – and mind you put that shotgun somewhere safe, before you do us both an injury."

"Why'd'you reckon there'd be flames over the North Sea, this time of the morning, then, woman, if it e'nt nothing to do with us? Or nowt important, what's the same thing? Eh?"

"Flames over the sea? Get away with you, Barney Williams. Your fancy's running away with you, man."

"I'm tellin' you what I seen. I've a mind to call the Old Bill."

"Later, Barne. Get some sleep. We'll have to be up in a couple of hours as it is."

Barney Williams reluctantly climbed back into bed, but not before deciding that he was going to ring the police first thing – well, first thing after he'd fed the goats, chickens and pigs, and collected the eggs. And had a wash and his breakfast.

Suddenly, he heard a sound that he recognised from many years ago, when he'd been a lad on a farm out by Dover, working with other lads too young for the Army, and the women whose menfolk were doing their duty. It was the unmistakable roar of an ME109, and the bugger was flying damn low, from the sound of it.

"You hear that, woman? Messerschmitt."

"Right. Get to sleep with you, Barney Williams."

"It is, I'm tellin' you. What's it doin' out 'ere, that's what I'd like to know."

"The War's long over, Barne. I 'spect they let the Germans fly where they like, us bein' in Europe, like."

"Bugger Europe" Barney muttered.

"You don't upset yourself, now, Barney Williams. Remember what the doctor said about your indigestion?"

"Bugger the doctors" Barney muttered, and fell into a fitful sleep, to dream of a world without tax officials, the Government, doctors, and the European Union – in that order – in the three hours he had left before his day would begin.

Back at Hunton airfield, Percy was still crouched behind the oak tree, watching the men who had come in the black van. They didn't appear to be in a hurry to go anywhere, seemed almost like they were waiting for something else to happen.

Jock, his black Labrador, whined, and Percy knelt closer, soothing him with his hand and his voice.

"Easy, bor. Thar's summat funny goin' on out thar, an' I don't reckun we wants to git caught up in it."

Percy Brown settled down to wait. He couldn't do anything else. He wouldn't be able to get off the airfield without being seen, and something told him it was far better that the men didn't know he was there. The morning sun was brighter now, and, while the Vauxhall was partially hidden by a gorse bush, anyone glancing over in that direction would be sure to spot it. Percy was losing patience; did he dare to try and get away without being seen? Could be he was getting himself all worked up over nothing, could be they were actors, making one of them films for the television, though he couldn't see any cameras. Just as he was deciding to make a run for it, the sound of engines split the air, and a small black dot appeared on the horizon, heading for the airfield.

"Well, blarst me if the bugger ain't comin' back", Percy muttered, hunching down.

Erik Lux taxied the plane to the end of the runway, as he had before, then turned it around, so that it was ready for take-off again. Percy watched as the men by the van got to their feet, swarming over the aircraft, dismantling the armaments, stowing everything in the van, and throwing the tarpaulin that had been spread on the ground over the lot. The doors of the van banged shut, and, with a howl of gears, Tony Knox sped away from the airfield. Percy rubbed his chin. "Now, if I aint dreamin', them looked a bit like machine guns," he muttered to himself, feeling a shiver run through his old frame. Hunkering down, he watched as the van drove away, watched as the Messerschmitt rose into the sky like some omen-bearing bird.

Erik Lux was already manoeuvring the Messerschmitt down the runway before the van was out of the gates. Old Percy Brown watched it take off for a second time that morning. Once the engine noise had died away, everything seemed unnaturally silent, and the birds that sang sounded too loud, almost false in their cheeriness. Percy decided now was as good a time as any to get out in a hurry – them buggers might come back. He tossed his shotgun onto the backseat of the Vauxhall, and motioned for Jock to jump into the front beside him, then quickly backed the Vauxhall round, and headed for home. Whatever had been going on, he decided, it was nowt to do with him. He would go back to his cottage at Elwood, have himself a good, full English breakfast - sausages, bacon, eggs, mushrooms, fried bread, a grilled tomato – and a mug of strong, sweet tea. A widower these past five years, Percy Brown took pride in looking after himself, and he'd been brought up to believe that a good breakfast should always be the first priority of the day.

As the old Vauxhall headed along the country lanes, Percy thought about it with affection. It was coming up to its twenty-first birthday, starting to show its age, but good enough to get Percy Brown where he wanted to go of a night.

Percy had intended to go straight back to his cottage, but, as he drove along the road that led past George Lake's place, he decided to make a stop.

"That Jerry might be back, might be able to suss out what's goin' on" he explained to Jock, who merely whined, as if to try and suggest that this wasn't a good idea. But curiosity was getting the better of Percy, as he recalled the local gossip that the Jerry never let anyone other than George Lake look at his plane, kept it locked down tight, while all the other pilots couldn't wait to show off their planes. Never took it to a show, neither, so they said, which Percy thought was odd. Surely the point of a plane like that was to show it off, let other people admire it?

Erik Lux had taxied the plane back into the hangar, and was walking around it, running his hand along the fuselage with a feeling of pride.

The flight over the North Sea had been exhilarating, and soon, very soon, the gunfire would ring out for real. He let his eyes rest on the fantastic, beautiful machine, imagining the part it would play in a dramatic scene that would be unfolding in the very near future. Rubbing his hands down his black courdoury jeans, Erik Lux strode out of the hangar, his brown Oxford brogues barely making a sound. He paused to lock the hangar securely behind him, then carried on towards his Volvo.

Percy Brown had parked his Vauxhall at the entrance to the airfield, from where he'd been watching the grey Volvo, parked near the hangars, that he knew from things old George had said belonged to the German. Suddenly, the man himself came into view. Percy patted Jock's head.

"Best be getting away from 'im, I reckun." Too late, he realised Lux had noticed the Vauxhall, had turned to look straight at its driver. He seemed to hesitate, not quite long enough for Percy to do anything. Feeling suddenly cold, Percy wondered if Lux had spotted him at Hunton. He decided to get out of the car, and walk onto the field, casual-like. Jock followed at his heels.

"Mornin' mistah. Nice bit of kit yer got yerself – I jist come by to pick up some eggs old George was leavin' out fer me, saw yer take it in that hangar, thar."

The German's face stayed blank. Percy cleared his throat. "I come over from Hunton way – was it yew I sin, flyin' low ower that way? Beautiful little bird, I thought to meself at the time. Don't see too many like 'er, see. Real beauty when yew brung 'er inta -" Percy stopped, realising what he had just said. He had not only admitted to being at Hunton, he had told the German he had been at the old airfield when he had landed. Which meant he had seen the men in the van. Percy cursed himself. Why couldn't he have just carried on with the tale of driving over from Hunton, seeing the plane in the sky as he drove?

"So, Mr Brown – you saw my plane this morning." George Lake had pointed Percy Brown out to Erik Lux one morning, when the poacher had been taking a shortcut across the field. "I wonder what else you saw?"

Percy tried to evade the question, prattling on about how he'd been after rabbits, he could get a good price for them from Johnny Wicks, only them woods belonged to Jack Wright, out at Mill Farm, so he wouldn't say anything, about the German or the plane, see...

Lux interrupted him. "I said, what else did you see?"

Suddenly, Jock began to growl, his hackles rising. Percy put a hand on the Labrador's collar to restrain him. "He int too good when he don't know yew, mistah," he said, trying to force a smile.

Lux was having none of it. "Answer my question, Mr Brown. What else did you see this morning?" Lux's tone was abrupt, harsh.

"Yew don't talk ter me like that, mistah!" Percy bellowed. "I sin wot yew was up to – No Good, thass wot I sin. Yessir, I knows all about your sort..."

Suddenly, Jock leapt forward, pulling his master with him. As Percy lost his grip on Jock's collar, the dog started barking furiously at Erik Lux, who kicked out at him with his foot. As though that act unleashed something in Lux, he lost control of himself. Grabbing Percy by his shirtfront, he began to shake the old poacher like a ragdoll. He didn't notice Percy's cap falling off, jolted from the old man's head by the force of the shaking.

"What did you say?"

"I sin everythin', an' I'll be reportin' yew ter young Pike, the local bobby, yew see if I don't!" Lux snarled something, then howled in pain as Jock bit him. He lost his grip on Percy, who weakly called to the Labrador to follow him as he got to his feet and headed for his Vauxhall while Lux was swearing and rubbing his leg. But the German was too quick, and, seeing what the old man was up to, swiftly got between him and his car. With an effort, Percy went to try and headbutt Lux in the stomach, but he was no match for the German, who pushed him to the ground as though he'd been nothing more than an irritating terrier.

Panting with rage, Lux made to get to his feet, planning to walk away, but his hand suddenly fell on a large, jagged stone. Seeing Percy trying to struggle up, something flipped in Lux's head, and he went beserk, smashing the stone into the poacher's head over and over again, oblivious to the barking and bites of Jock, still desperately trying to defend his master. Suddenly, the old man went very still, and slumped back, limp.

Lux seemed to come to his senses. Dropping the stone, he got up, and started to back away. Jock was barking louder now – someone would hear him. Picking up the stone almost on autopilot, Lux threw it at the dog. It caught the Labrador on the rear, and he shot off between the buildings, evidently sensing that, with nothing to be done for his master, self-preservation was in order. Lux watched him go, then, suddenly, realised something - the car, old Percy's Vauxhall. Hurrying across the field, Lux jumped into the Vauxhall Cresta, grateful that the old poacher had left the keys in the ignition, and drove the vehicle deeper into the woods. Getting out, he hurriedly pulled some brush, scrub and loose leaves over the car. Taking a few steps back, he nodded. The car wouldn't be seen, at least not for a fair while. Not unless someone were deliberately looking for it, and there was no reason why anyone would be.

Lux knew what he had to do next. Hurrying to the general maintenance shed, he ducked in through a side door, and came out with a sheet of tarpaulin, which he hastily wrapped Percy Brown's body in, rolling it up as though it were carpet. When he lifted his gruesome bundle, Lux found that the old man weighed next to nothing. He put the tarpaulin-wrapped body in the boot of the Volvo. Sweating, he looked around for the dog, but it was nowhere in sight, a fact he was glad of. He was just about to slam the boot closed when he realised he would need a shovel – he hadn't seen one in the general maintenance shed, and remembered George saying one had gone missing. There were other sheds on the airfield, any of them might contain a shovel. Lux went through all the sheds he had keys for, but no luck. He began to panic. Suddenly, he remembered; there was a shovel back at his cottage. He had bought it himself, intending to cement his image as a normal, unremarkable person by working in the garden at weekends, when he wasn't working on his plane.

Lux hadn't noticed Jock creep out of hiding, and jump into the boot of the Volvo. He'd been too caught up in looking for a shovel. He didn't notice the dog now, as he slammed the boot closed and got into the car, to make the ten minute drive to the cottage. None of the good citizens of Elwood was up and about yet.

Parking the Volvo by the cottage's front gate, Lux quickly made his way to the shed where he kept his tools, found what he was looking for, and retraced his steps back to the Volvo. Just as he had opened the back door to put the shovel in, Lux was stopped in his tracks by a voice.

"Up and about early this morning, aren't we? Can't say as I blame you, though, nothing like listening to the birdsong, taking in the morning air before everyone else gets up and fills it with exhaust fumes."

Looking up, Lux found himself face to face with a young police constable, sitting astride a pushbike.

"Oh, yes, constable. You're absolutely right. I have an early morning appointment in Norwich – a meeting with a...friend, who has travelled overnight from Edinburgh. I am meeting them at the station."

"Well, you'll not be wanting to take that shovel with you, will you, sir? Not unless you and your friend are gardeners, and Norwich seems an awful long way to go for a couple of quid off a pensioner."

Police Constable Raymond Pike laughed as he said this, the twinkle in his eyes showing genuine amusement.

"Ah, no – I am dropping it round to a friend on the way – he does not sleep, you see, and he telephoned me very early, very upset. He had gone out to work in his garden, which sometimes helps with his insomnia, and found the handle of his own shovel to be broken. I literally have to pass his house on my way, so I offered to drop my own round to him." Lux tossed the shovel onto the backseat, in what he hoped was a casual manner. He headed round to the driver's door.

"If that is all, Constable...?"

But Ray Pike was evidently in a chatty mood. "You the chap who's got that Messerschmitt out at George Lake's place, sir?"

"Yes, Constable. And now, if you'll excuse me, I really must be off..."

"I'd like to see her up close, sometime, sir. Looks mighty fine when she's in the air. Wonderful beast."

Lux got into the driver's seat, wanting nothing more than to be away from this nosy policeman.

"Anytime you are over at Elwood, Constable, I will happily show you my aircraft." With that, he sped away.

Police Constable Pike watched the Volvo disappear with a puzzled frown. He'd seen the chap around the village, but never had reason to speak to him before now. Something in what he'd said didn't quite add up, and, being a policeman, Pike didn't like it when things didn't quite add up. He tried to work out why the German would lie about where he was going, what he was doing. Perhaps he was sneaking off to see a ladyfriend, a ladyfriend who wasn't, strictly speaking, available. Perhaps she was going to use the shovel to do in her husband, and then run off into the sunset with the German.

Grinning with that thought, Constable Pike peddled away, wondering what other queer creatures were out and about this morning.

Lux drove quickly. It was nearly six in the morning, and this was a rural area. The farmers and their workers would soon be up and about, making their way to their various places of labour. He couldn't risk too many people seeing his Volvo – which would stand out at this time of day, in this place, by virtue of not being an agricultural vehicle or a Land Rover – as one of them might well remember it, and comment on it.

He didn't need anything else to go wrong with his carefully laid plan. He was heading back to Hunton – the only place he could risk burying Percy Brown's body. It would mean he'd probably have to change his plans, which would mean he'd probably have to pay Bigley even more money, but that was that. Only at Hunton could he get rid of the body, and his connection to it.

CHAPTER SEVENTEEN.

Erik Lux parked the Volvo slightly to the right hand side of the front of the old control tower. Getting out, he looked around, his eyes narrowed, scanning every possible horizon. He had been observed without his awareness once; he would not be again. He stood completely still for several minutes, listening to the absence of humanity, trying to ascertain that it was, indeed, a true absence.

Finally satisfied, he went round to the back of the Volvo, pausing once again before opening the boot.

He was nearly knocked over by a large, muscular black shape, a shape which leapt from the dark recess at the back of the boot, and, after slamming into him with the force of a freight train, shot off into the woods. For a moment, Lux couldn't think what it could be. Then he realised.

"*Das dammerund hund*!" he shouted, followed by some far harsher German words, all cursing the dog, and turned to go after it, before catching himself. Why risk someone seeing him? And how could he even think about leaving the Volvo out in the open while he ran off after some mutt that couldn't tell anyone what had happened, even if it knew itself, which Lux, who had never rated the intelligence of dogs, was inclined to doubt. He decided to ignore the dog. It could probably take care of itself, he reasoned; most animals could. And besides, even though the woods were quite clearly identified as being private property, he knew a poacher or courting couple would pass through soon enough, and take pity on a hungry, frightened dog. The British were like that with animals, Erik had learnt. They would probably leave an infant to perish of the cold, would certainly kill that infant's father, given half the chance, but they would never neglect an animal, or leave one to the mercy of the wild that was, essentially, its home.

It didn't take Lux long to clear a small patch of ground, and dig a shallow grave. It took him even less time to dump Percy Brown's body into the hole he had dug, and shovel the loose earth back over it.

He stowed the shovel back in the Volvo, and drove off the airfield, decided that he would, after all, drive to Norwich – he didn't want to risk running in to PC Pike again, and at a time that was far too early still for him to have made it to Norwich and back.

As he drove along country lanes which gradually widened as they neared the main roads, Lux noted the number of farm vehicles – pick up trucks, Land Rovers, tractors and combine harvesters – that were out and about now. He had left, he deduced, at exactly the right time. He could easily be taken by these country men for nightwatchman at one of the nature reserves, or larger estates, returning home. Or a commuter, perhaps, heading to the station to catch a train to his office in London – a place as distant to most of them, Erik sneered to himself, as Atlantis.

Erik Lux did not look back as he drove away. Had he done so, he might have glimpsed a black dog, slinking out of the woods, sniffing first the air, then the ground, then trotting, nose-to-dirt, to the exact spot where, so very recently, a human body had been hastily interred.

But Erik Lux did not look back, and so he did not see Jock return to Hunton airfield via the woods into which he'd disappeared earlier. He didn't see him search for, and find, his master's scent. He didn't see him begin to furiously dig at the loose soil that Erik had hastily flung back over the body. He didn't see Jock take the edge of the tarpaulin in his teeth, and pull it back to reveal his master's cold, dead face.

Erik Lux did, however, hear Jock's mournful howl, though he didn't realise what he was hearing. The sound was other-worldly, and seemed to echo through eternity. Erik nearly lost control from the shock, and his nerves kept jangling long after he had travelled beyond range of the noise.

"What the hell was that?" he muttered, shaking, gulping the breaths he knew would calm him. But Erik Lux's question went unanswered.

"You did *what?* Are you out of your tiny mind, Mr Lux? Who the *hell* authorised *you* to kill anyone? Eh? I could've taken care of this old boy for you – I mean, a *poacher?* Wouldn't've cost hardly anything to get him to keep his yap shut about what he'd seen at Hunton, would it? I mean, it ain't like he's got much of a living going, flogging dead bunnies to the local butcher, is it? There'd've been something he wanted that he couldn't afford, believe you me."

"I'm sorry, Mr Bigley. I just didn't think -"

"No. Exactly, Mr Lux. You *just didn't think*. If you'd've thought, you'd've got a message to me, asked me to take care of the problem for you. If you'd've thought, you'd've realised you're way, way out of your depth. No, *don't* argue with me. You're not out of you're depth? Fine. You tell me what our next step is. You tell me what we're gonna do now."

Erik looked bemused. "We will proceed -"

Bigley's fist slammed down on the desk, nearly bouncing the goldfish out of its crystal bowl. The fish went still for a moment, then resumed its lazy swimming, as though such near-death experiences were a regular feature of being Roy Bigley's pet. "Dammit, man! *We can't continue using Hunton airfield anymore!* The body'll be discovered in no time – you see if it ain't – and Old Bill're going to be all over the place. And, since you was in a flap, you'll have left evidence behind. Typical bloody amateur. No, Mr Lux, you're a stupid, thick-headed puppy, and you've made a bloody mess that me and my boys have got to clear up. I don't like clearing up other people's messes, Mr Lux. That's not why I went into this business."

"I'm sorry, Mr Bigley."

"So you keep saying. I don't see much evidence of it, though."

Erik Lux had come prepared. He took a thick bundle of notes from a pocket on the inside of his jacket.

"It is all I can get at the moment. All my other money is still in the transfer system between America and England." Lux laid the roll of notes on the desk. Bigley made no move to pick it up.

"This ain't a discount or down payment, Mr Lux. This is extra, on top of what you owe me, gorrit?"

Lux merely nodded. Bigley exhaled cigar smoke, and picked up the bundle of notes, thumbing through it.

"A grand, for the trouble I'm going to for you? Bloody 'ell, this recession's affectin' us all, innit?" He tossed the cash into an open safe, which he then kicked shut with a well-shod foot.

"Now, Mr Lux. Perhaps you'd like to have a *professional* explain where we go from here?"

Again, Lux simply nodded.

"Sensible boy. Right..."

Freddie Croft turned the combine in through the entrance to old Hunton airfield; it was easier, no gate to stop and open, and closer to the 100-acre barley field that he was responsible for harvesting that day. It'd probably take him until lunchtime, he reckoned, then the gypos from the encampment down the way would be allowed to pick whatever the combine had discarded, to take back for their horses, or whatever they used it for. There'd always been gleaners, but they'd never had an invitation before. Jack White reckoned if you let the gypos take stuff, they wouldn't nick it off you. Sally Croft had snorted at this, telling her husband that his boss was too soft by half, that that sort of nonsense was what a fancy degree in "Agricultural Husbandry" from a posh London university got you. And what did young Jack want with a degree anyway, Sally had demanded? His father had never needed one, nor his grandfather before him. Waste of time and money, that's all his degree was, if you asked her. Freddie had long ago realised it was pointless explaining to his wife that no one *was* asking her. You got her opinion anyway. Pulling the combine up to a stop, Freddie jumped down, and headed over to the old control tower, to attend to a call of nature. He had been raised by Quaker parents, and, unlike most of the other farm hands, did not like relieving himself in full view of anyone who might happen along. It was as he was zipping up his trousers that he saw recently-disturbed earth. Curious, he went over to investigate further. Freddie Croft was country born and bred, as were his parents, his wife, and her parents, and both sets of ancestors as far back as could be traced. He had seen his fair share of death, some of it brutal, bloody, and come upon its victim too soon. But the sight of the grey face, the blood, and the terrified rictus of the mouth saw this hardened country man lose his breakfast As he straightened up, wiping his mouth with the back of his hand, Freddie Croft was already pulling a mobile phone out of his pocket and punching in a number.

"Boss? It's Freddie. I think you'd better get the Old Bill down to Hunton airfield – I've just found a body."

As she got off the bus that ran between Elwood and Thetford with her weekly grocery shop, Molly Stubbs, widow of the parish of Elwood for the past three years, and next door neighbour to Percy Brown, was surprised to see Jock sitting at the door to Percy's cottage. Surprised to *still* see him; the Labrador had been there when she'd left that morning, and it wasn't like Percy to leave Jock on his own, outside, half the day. Molly went into her own cottage, put her shopping away, and then went over to her neighbour's pausing to pat Jock, who suddenly started to whine, a thing that was most unlike him.

"Poor boy. Has nasty Percy locked you out? Hmm? Molly will have words with him, don't you worry."

She banged on the door, calling Percy's name. When there was no response, she tried the door. It was locked. Now that was very strange; Percy only ever locked his door when he went out poaching, and Jock always went with him, then. Nervously, Molly Stubbs went round the back of the cottage, and repeated her performance at the back door, with the same result. She was worried, now. Percy was old – older than herself, and she'd be seventy-two next month. Anything could've happened to him out there, wandering all over the place the way he did. She'd told him he shouldn't, not since his Maude wasn't there to notice if he wasn't back when he should've been, but men were always so stubborn, in Molly's view. Her Tom had been the same, refusing to see the doctor about the pains he kept getting that turned out to be cancer. Returning to her cottage, Jock following her like his very life depended on it, Molly Stubbs decided to phone the local police. Young Ray Pike wouldn't mind having a bit of a cycle round, she felt sure. Just to make sure Percy hadn't had a turn, and was lying in a ditch somewhere. They'd probably pass each other, she thought, have a good laugh about silly females who panicked at the least little thing.

"Now, Constable Pike, that *is* unusual, wouldn't you say? First, a report of early-morning gunfire out to sea, then a call saying an unidentified, but recently murdered, body has been found, appearing to be that of a male in his late seventies, *then* you get a call saying that a seventy-five-year-old man isn't answering his door, and his dog's been left outside all morning, which isn't like him at all. Wouldn't you call that unusual, Constable?"

Detective Inspector Simon Foxley, of Thetford CID, didn't mean to intimidate the young constable, it was just that, at the larger station in Thetford, there was generally a lot more banter, which, over the years, had proved a useful way to find unexpected solutions.

But Police Constable Ray Pike wasn't used to those kind of games.

"I...I suppose so, Sir."

"You know this Stubbs woman? She given to over-reacting?"

"Well...no, Sir. I wouldn't say she was, like. She's a country family, Sir – we tend to keep level heads on our shoulders, like."

"Hm. And this old farmer, out Cromer way?"

"Not my patch, Sir, but Murphy – he works that part of the world – reckons he's sound enough, bit paranoid that someone'll pinch his tractor, but then there was a spate of tractor thefts out Lincoln way not so long ago. And his missus keeps him in line. The farmer, I mean, Sir."

"And Percy Brown? You know him? I'd like to spare the lady having to identify that mess, if we can."

"Oh, yes, Sir. Everyone around here knows Percy."

Silently, Foxley held up a photograph. Dropping his head, Ray Pike whispered; "*Knew* him. Everyone around here knew Percy." Raising his head, he said, loudly and clearly, "That's Percy Brown, Sir."

"Very good. We'll have to have it official, call his doctor in – I assume he had one?"

"He'd've gone to Doc Greenwood, Sir, where we all go."

"Get him here. This is murder, Pike, and I want the investigation done absolutely by the book, is that clear?"

"Yes, Sir."

As the police went about the village, asking polite questions, making discreet inquiries, Erik Lux watched them from the bedroom window of his cottage by the church, opposite the village pond. He had panicked, he knew that now. The old man could have been harmless enough, would probably never have mentioned anything of what he'd seen. This could upset all his plans – the big day was tomorrow. He had waited so long to avenge the murder of his father, nothing was going to stop him now. He needed to meet with Bigley. The gangster was only aware of Lux's requirements, not the end purpose. He could put two and two together, of course, but Lux knew, when you paid big money, it was to someone whose part in your scheme would never come to light. He suspected all that Bigley was interested in was covering himself should anything go wrong, and collecting his payments on time.

Lux went downstairs, and headed out. Getting into the Volvo, he reversed out into the village lane. As he passed a row of cottages, he took note of the two suited men, evidently plain clothes police, knocking on one of the doors. He had seen them earlier, from his bedroom window. They would knock on his door, soon enough. When there was no response, they would go away, but he knew they would be back. Hopefully, though, by then it would be too late.

Inevitably, word of Percy Brown's murder got out, and, inevitably, rumours began to fly around. He'd been caught by big Larry Hemmingway, gamekeeper out at the Lodge – everyone knew Larry'd been threatened with the sack by the muckety-mucks who owned the place, reckoned he was a waste of a good weekly paycheque and a nice little cottage, with potential for a holiday let, in the grounds. He'd come across Percy at the pheasants, and – wallop!

No, it wasn't Hemmingway; it was old Frank Moore, what farmed out of Old Hall. Remember, he'd had that set-to with Percy before, been up in court for it...

No, it was nothing to do with Percy's poaching. Charlie Stubbs, (him as was the brother of Tommy Stubbs, what was married to Molly Smith as was, till the ciggies got him) had caught Percy having a bit of the other with his dead brother's wife, and hadn't liked it one little bit.

No, it weren't like that, it were Molly 'erself what done Percy in, when he come on a bit funny with 'er.

No, no – 'twas definitely Frank Moore. He's alus had a temper, he has...

And so on, and so on, while, ignoring all of it, Thetford Constabulary took over the reins of the investigation, under the command of Detective Inspector Simon Foxley. Barely an hour after Percy Brown's body had been found, Foxley was standing at the front of a large room, a potted plant in one corner, badly in need of watering, beside a full-size flip chart, a red permanent marker in his hand. Police officers, both uniformed and CID, sat at clean, white tables, notebooks in hand, occasionally, quietly, sipping hot, well-sweetened drinks. Wide windows, gleaming from a recent cleaning, held no interest for them. Their collective attention was focused on Foxley, on the flipchart, on the photographs of Percy Brown, the two maps of the area in which he'd been found, one professional, purchased from the Tourist Information centre, the other hand-drawn, that were pinned up on a white board that took up most of the far room. They listened to the dry details of Percy Brown's demise, watched as Foxley made notes on the flipchart. Occasionally, he would point to one of them, bark an order as to what their role in the investigation was to be. The clock, of a type familiar to anyone who has ever sat in a cold school examination hall, not knowing the answers to any of the questions in front of them, ticked loudly, but no one noticed it. The passing of time was not a distraction they could afford to notice – not when someone had been murdered on their patch.

Finally, Foxley put the cap back on his permanent marker with a loud *click*. "Right, that's it, lads. You all know what you're doing, yes?" A chorus of "Yes, Guv" echoed through the room. Papers shuffled, people coughed, the air rang to the soft sounds of paper coffee cups landing in bins, and the might of the Thetford Constabulary filed out of the room, to begin the tasks associated with murder – the making of discreet enquiries, following-up of hopeful and hopeless leads, knocking on doors, asking questions to the curious, the slightly shifty, the guilty-of-something-else-entirely, the genuinely helpful, and the downright obstructive, putting up posters and all the other quiet, generally unobserved, parts of their job that they had to do when murder had been committed. Someone was guilty, and it was their job to see that person brought to justice.

In the office above the motorcycle showroom, the large table was covered with a map detailing the road network around London. The goldfish, moved to make space for the map, as well as the notepad and selection of pens, watched from the windowsill. Or, rather, watched from its bowl, which was in the windowsill.

"Now, Mr Lux...here's how we're going to sort out your mess, see? How we're gonna keep this bloody mad show of yours on the road. Cos I know it's tomorrow, I know ye're worried we ain't going to make it – and I *know* that, as long as I'm in charge here, nothing – but *nothing* can go wrong. You hear me, Mr Lux?"

"Yes."

"Good. You keep on hearing me, and we'll be fine and dandy. Now, as I said, we can't continue with the plan to use the airfield at Hunton, for obvious reasons – although even I wasn't expecting the body to be found that quick. And, if you'd've even asked me for help once you'd offed the guy, it wouldn't've been – so myself and Mr Wilson here put our pretty little heads together, had a think, and came up with a workable alternative. Workable, that is, if you're as good a pilot as you think you are, Mr Lux?"

"There is none living who is better" Erik replied, his accent strengthened by insulted pride. Roy Bigley grinned.

"Good. So, you can land a plane on a road, then? On..." the gangster's chubby fingers danced over the map, before landing on a coloured line marked with an asterix "...the A1, for example? Just before the Mill Hill roundabout?"

Lux stared at Bigley. Then he stared at Mouth Wilson. Then he stared back at Bigley.

"But...the traffic..."

"Will be taken care of. Mr Wilson knows some...gentlemen who can provide us with a realistic police presence, including blocking off the road with official vans and the like, without the hassles of there actually needing to be an incident for them to block the road off *for*, if you follow me?"

"But -"

"No buts, Mr Lux. Ask me no questions, I'll tell you no lies. Just accept that these guys are going to get your nuts out of a clamp, Mr Lux. A clamp of your own making, might I remind you. *And* will need payment for their services."

Lux sighed. "But what else, Mr Bigley?"

Bigley glared at Lux, and jabbed a chubby finger into the German's face. "You don't get the kind of war games you want for free, Mr Lux – especially not when I have to keep changing the game cos you've thrown away the bloody rule book. You don't want to pay? Your scheme doesn't happen, and you never see the outside of this room again, we clear?"

Lux didn't answer.

"I said, are we clear, Mr Lux?"

"Yes, Mr Bigley."

"Good. Now, listen, and I'll tell you what we're going to do."

Lux listened, no expression on his face. When Bigley finished, Lux asked only one question;

"Can you do all of that, in the time we have?"

"Mr Lux, I'm Roy Bigley – I can do anything I bloody want."

Hunton airfield was swarming with Forensics officers in their alien-looking garb of blue suits and purple gloves. Bags were carefully unfolded from pockets, seemingly insignificant things – twigs, empty Coke cans, scraps of paper – were tweezered up, and placed in the bags with the utmost care.

Suddenly, a shout went up; "Guv! Over here!"

Foxley hurried over to where one of the team, a young woman, was holding up a clear plastic bag which seemed to contain a tissue.

"There's blood on this, Guv. Recent, from the looks of it."

"Log it, DC Kelly. I suppose it is possible that some unfortunate passer-by happened to be standing in the exact same spot where a shallow grave was dug, and had a nosebleed, but, somehow, I doubt it very much. Let's hope Chummy got some of Mr Brown's blood on him when he was burying him, so we've got a definite link between our victim and his killer."

Something was worrying Foxley, but he couldn't quite put his finger on it. It was something about the airfield, about Hunton...

"Are we sure he was killed here, Guv?"

Foxley turned, and found himself in the disconcerting position of looking up at one of the uniformed PCs from Thetford, Tony Cliveson, easily six-feet-four or five, and big with it. The officer's face was flushed from his exertions, and his brown eyes were squinting in thought, which was evidently an unusual activity for him.

"Why do you say that, Tony?" for some reason, Tony Cliveson brought out the protective, paternal streak in Foxley. For all his height and bulk, there was something about him that told you he'd been hurt one too many times in his life, that he was close to breaking.

"Well...I dunno...it's just...you'd expect things to be mucked up more, wouldn't you? More blood, like. I mean, I've seen what was done to the old boy...had to be a rock, stone, something like that. Be covered in blood. Nothing like that here, and no place something like that could've been before it was picked up, neither."

"Bloody, hell, Tony, I think you're right. I think he was killed somewhere else, and brought here. The ground's so bloody dry... You lot!" he clapped his hands, waited until all his officers had stopped what they were doing, and had turned to look at him, then continued. "PC Cliveson has noticed something very important -"

"What, that it's nearly lunchtime?" someone shouted, to much laughter. The blush that flushed Cliveson's cheeks, and the way he dropped his gaze, didn't escape Foxley's notice.

"No. What PC Cliveson noticed, that none of the rest of you clever sods has, is that *there hasn't been a bloody murder committed here!* No blood, no signs of a struggle, nothing that could've been a weapon. Our boy killed Percy Brown somewhere else, ladies and gentlemen, and brought him here. That means a car. That means asking questions of anyone and everyone who was within spitting distance of this place in the early hours of this morning. Go on, get off with you!" As the men and women turned away, muttering loudly amongst themselves, Foxley lay a hand on Tony Cliveson's beefy shoulder.

"Good spot, big fella. I'll not forget it was you who noticed that Brown couldn't have been killed here, trust me on that, right?"

"Guv."

"I said, *trust me.*"

Cliveson nodded. In his experience, the only promises that existed were the ones that got broken. He was nothing. He knew he didn't have a future in the Force, didn't want one, either, really. When the time came, Foxley would credit himself, or a chosen favourite, with the observation. Tony Cliveson didn't mind, not really. He was used to it.

As the vehicles drove away, Foxley wondered where Percy Brown *had* been killed, and why he'd been taken to Hunton. Somehow, he sensed it was something to do with airfields and planes – perhaps the memory of that old farmer over at Cromer, telling him a Messerschmitt had been firing into the North Sea in the early hours of this morning... Foxley turned to Tony Cliveson, whom he'd asked to drive him back to Thetford nick.

"How far're we from the coast here, you reckon?"

The big officer glanced at him, just once. "Not far. Could probably drive it in half an hour, less if you did a blue-light run."

"What about flying?"

"Flying, Guv? Well...less than ten minutes, I'd say."

"So...twenty minutes out and back...any idea how much fuel an ME109 carries?"

"Not much, Guv. If they're anything like the Spitfires, they were fired up with just enough to do their job, turn around and head for home. Wouldn't be able to be out long."

"Twenty minutes out and back...but he's got his guns to fire off, hasn't he? And you wouldn't go straight into that, would you? No...you'd put your plane through her paces, you were in that frame of mind. You'd want to push it to the limit. You're getting off on *not knowing*. A maverick pilot, Tony. That's what I reckon we're looking for."

Tony Cliveson shook his head. "Needle in a haystack, Guv. Most of 'em're just big kids inside."

Foxley looked at him, and something about the Inspector's gaze chilled Tony to the core.

"Not this boy. He's a *little* kid inside. A little kid who's gone and got very, very angry about something. And done something very, very bad. He'll be looking for someone to help him, trying to find Mummy or Daddy."

Tony Cliveson frowned. "You saying he's mental, Guv?"

"No." Foxley knew what he was about to say was the truth. "I'm saying he's *disturbed*. He'll seem entirely sane to you or I, will *be* entirely sane, apart from something, one little thing, that didn't get wired quite right when he was growing up. A switch that trips the madman."

In Roy Bigley's office at the motorcycle showroom in Walthamstow, a group of men were sitting around Bigley's desk, the goldfish blinking at them from its bowl, which had been moved to a filing cabinet, maps, notepads and pens spread out across the desk's surface, takeaway food cartons, empty drinks cans and mugs of cooling tea and coffee littered the whole room. The blinds were drawn, and the lights were low. On the main map, which was pinned to the wall, several spots were marked with thick black *X*'s; Apex Corner, the roundabout at Mill Hill, and

Romford. A red felt-tipped pen had made a thick line along Watford Way, stopping a few hundred yards past the roundabout. A blue dot marked the point where the line ended. Wilson tapped the blue dot with a ballpoint pen. "This is where he's going to touch down. Then the show starts, and there won't be a moment to lose. Mr Bigley?"

Roy Bigley jabbed a finger towards one of the maps. "A1, heading to the Mill Hill roundabout. Mouth, where're the cars?" Mouth Wilson, shoving a handful of crisps into his mouth, sauntered over to the filing cabinet. Crouching down, he tugged open the bottom drawer, and took out a shoebox, which he brought over to the table.

Still standing, he took the lid off the shoebox, and started bringing toy vehicles out – police cars, vans and motorcycles. He set them to the side of the map, on the edge of the desk, then looked around the table.

"We all watching? Good." He picked up several of the toy motorcycles, placing them onto the map.

"You lads -" Mouth gestured at a group of men who sat off in a huddle of their own, dressed in motorbike leathers, helmets on the floor at their feet " - you'll be blocking everything off. When it's all over..." Mouth pushed the motorbikes over "... hellfire, yeah? Gonna be pretty damn spectacular."

One of the bikers looked agitated. "Why've we gotta burn the bikes?"

Mouth glared at him. "Saves me a job. And, before you ask, no, we can't keep 'em – that's the kind of stupid mistake that gets people caught, keeping a vehicle that's been used in a job. You don't want to do time, do you?" The bikers were silent. Mouth carried on, placing more vehicles at different points on the map, moving them around.

"...then, Mr Lux comes into play, using the code name Red Eagle..." Wilson picked up a toy aeroplane, flying it low over the map "... *neeowwn*...comes down, nice and smooth, right onto the road...Tony, you drive the van -" Wilson pushed a plain toy van swiftly across the map, bringing it alongside the aeroplane "- right up to Mr Lux's plane. In real life, you're going to be just back from his wing, right, and when he flies off, you drive the van under his wing, get the hell out of there as quick as you can, right? I'll be in the van with you, Tony, on the radio, under the codename Foxhunter One. Bikers, you're going to be Bloodhounds One, Two and Three."

"Radio?" Vinnie Sampson interrupted. Mouth smiled.

"Yeah. Figured you and your brother could sort us one of them out. You can, right?"

"Sure. 'Course, Mouth. No problems."

"Good. Tony, you clear on what you're doing?"

Tony Knox nodded, taking a drag from his cigarette.

"Lads?" The bikers nodded, sullen in their corner.

"Right…details. Pay attention, fellas. I'm only saying this once…"

An hour or so later, Mouth Wilson sat back down. "Everyone clear on what they're doing out there?" There were nods, murmurs of assent. "Right. Good. Vinnie, Alfie, you stay here – Mr Bigley's had a little idea that he wants you two to work on for him. The rest of you, get the hell out of here, and keep your heads down, right?"

CHAPTER EIGHTEEN.

Erik Lux had returned from his visit to Roy Bigley to find a card on the mat in the hallway of the cottage.

SIR/MADAM;

THETFORD CID ATTEMPTED TO SPEAK WITH YOU TODAY, REGARDING A LOCAL INCIDENT. PLEASE CONTACT DETECTIVE INSPECTOR FOXLEY ON...

This was followed by the crest of Thetford Constabulary, a telephone number, fax number and address. Lux threw the card into the bin in the corner of the living room. He wouldn't be around long enough to worry about not getting in touch with the police. Tomorrow, the final, glorious part of his plan would be enacted, and his father's death would finally be avenged. He really couldn't care less about Thetford CID, or Inspector Foxley. Roy Bigley had assured him that the British police were idiots, who couldn't investigate their way out of a wet paper bag. They were handy for getting the time, or directions, but not much else. Having noted that they did not seem to carry firearms of any description, Erik Lux was inclined to agree with the gangster's conclusion.

He smiled as he recalled the wording of the card; "A local incident". As though the brutal murder of an innocent old poacher were nothing for the community to trouble itself about, on a par, perhaps, with hooligans congregating on the cricket field, or people not clearing up after their dogs.

Dogs... Lux had had a niggling worry about that bloody Labrador all day, couldn't shake the feeling that he'd played it wrong in letting it get away. Too late now, though. Tomorrow was it, the big day, the final showdown. Too full of nervous energy to sleep, Erik Lux decided to go for a drive. As he cruised down the lane, he tuned the car radio in to Classic FM. Wagner, the Fuhrer's favourite composer. He smiled. He had always loved the classics, a common enough thing in Germany, but something that set him apart even more than his accent when he'd got to Montana. Briefly, he thought of those endless blue skies, skies that contrasted so very well with the pale, dusty colour of the land, and the pink-and-grey sculptures of the surrounding mountains...he thought of Square Butte, and snarled as he remembered how very close he had come, then. Had it not been for his bitch of a wife – ex-wife, now – he would not be nearly bankrupt, would not be beholden to a man like Roy Bigley, would not be at the mercy of this man's gangmembers, and their dubious skills. If only, if only... he noticed that the Wagner piece had ended, and switched to cassette. The car was filled with the pure sound of a young girl's singing. The singer was Nicole, and the song was A Little Peace, which had had the dubious honour of winning the 1982 Eurovision song contest, Erik believed. He had never followed the contest, seeing it for what it was – stage-managed trash that celebrated political wrangling rather than talent – but, since the time he had first heard it, he had liked this song. And it was very apt. Soon, very soon, there would be a little peace for him, a little respite from the demons that had tormented him all these years.

The following morning, Simon Foxley was talking to the two CID officers who'd done door-to-door in Elwood the previous day.

"You say one lad hasn't got back to us?" he barked. Fifteen people, in all, had been out when the constables had knocked round Elwood, most of them at work, although they had had a call from a Miss Agnes Jones, who announced that she was popping in to a Mr Drewery's cottage once a day, to collect his post, water his plants and have a dust around if needed, while the said Mr Drewery was away visiting friends in, she believed, Ibiza – or at least that's what she *thought* he'd said, though why a nice young man like Mr Drewery would want to go *there* was beyond her – where he'd been for the past three days, facts which were being checked at that very moment.

"Yes, Guv."

"And what did you say his name was, again?"

"A Mr Lux, Guv. A Mr Erik Lux."

"Lux?" Foxley barked "what kind of a name's that?"

"He's German, Guv." All heads turned as PC Pike spoke. "Well, American-German," he continued. "Y'know, got that accent of theirs, but sometimes you hear him say *haff* instead of *have*, or something. Not been in the village long."

Raymond Pike spoke as though not being in the village long was in itself an arrestable offence. Which, Foxley mused, it probably was in this part of Norfolk.

"You know him, then?"

"Well, not as such...I mean, I spoke to him yesterday mor -" Pike broke off, realising what he was saying. "Guv, I thought something was off at the time, but couldn't say what – the chap was putting a shovel into his car! Gave me some cock and bull story about how he was meeting a friend from Edinburgh off the early train into Norwich, and *another* friend had asked him to lend him a shovel, so's he could cure his insomnia with a bout of early-morning digging. *And* he's got a plane, Guv – Tony told me in the canteen you reckon there's a plane involved."

There were murmurs of excitement, now. Foxley rose, and went to say something, but was cut off by the ringing of the telephone. A WPC answered it.

"Thetford CID Incident Room, WPC Hall speaking. Mr Lake...yes, go on...yes...yes...no, sir, you've not wasted our time at all." Her eyes shining, she held the phone out to her governer, a slight nodding of her head indicating that she felt he should talk to this particular caller. "It's a Mr Lake, Sir. He owns the old airfield, out at Elwood."

Foxley strode over and took the phone. "Detective Inspector Foxley speaking. How can I help you, Mr Lake?"

On the other end of the line, George Lake took a deep breath. "Maybe it's the other way around, Detective Inspector – maybe I can help you." He paused, took another breath, deeper than the first, then continued. "You see, I've just found old Percy's cap up on the airfield. I...I thought the old boy was trespassing – he knows he's not meant to be on the airfield unless it's open to the public – so I went looking for him." Lake's silence was longer this time, and he coughed, as though beginning to regret the telephone call.

"Go on, Mr Lake." It was all Foxley could do to keep from shouting.

George Lake coughed, took a deep breath, coughed again, and, finally, continued. "I...I found his car, Detective Inspector. Hidden, like. I...I hadn't heard what had happened before..."

Thanking George Lake for his call, assuring him that it wasn't a waste of Thetford Constabulary's time, Foxley replaced the receiver, and turned to Pike.

"Where did you say this Lux chap keeps his plane, Constable?"

Pike's eyes were shining with excitement. "I didn't, Guv. But it's George Lake's place – it's Elwood airfield."

Foxley pressed his fingers to his lips, deep in thought, thinking and re-thinking, trying to put things into perspective. Firstly, the old poacher – a harmless soul, by all accounts, if a bit of nuisance to the gamekeepers and farmers in the area – gets himself murdered. Second, some old farmer had claimed to have heard Messerschmitt engines and cannon fire over the North Sea, in the early hours of the morning. Thirdly, the place where Percy Brown's body had been found, Hunton, was another World War Two connection, an airfield last used as a base during that conflict half a century or so ago, and yet it had quickly become apparent that he had not been killed there. Once they had established that Percy Brown's body had been moved, the question remained as to where he had been killed. Perhaps, shortly, they would have an answer.

Foxley turned, clapping his hands to call the room to silence.

"Right", he said, addressing them all "I reckon a visit to Mr Lake's place out at Elwood is in order. DS Monument, you're with me. You too, WPC Hall. Cliveson, you're the driver – let's get going."

It was the 13th of September, 1990, and, at Lost Horse Farm, all work came to an abrupt halt at twelve noon, when Mouth Wilson had consulted his wristwatch, then shouted; "That's it, lads. Tools down. No more pretending. Pack up, and get some rest before tomorrow." As if, somehow, it had heard Mouth Wilson's shout from forty miles away, and was echoing him, Big Ben rang out the midday hour. Tomorrow, at almost exactly the same time, this monumental icon of the City of London, along with the other monumental, iconoclastic images, crafted in brick and stone, glass and steel, that made the London landscape real, would be shaken to its very foundations by the wrath and vengeance instigated at Lost Horse Farm.

The last practice run at Lost Horse Farm, the last fitting and loading of the guns to the Messerschmitt, had been conducted in a strange, woeful silence. There were no cheers, no back-slapping, no bawdy jokes. Every mind of the assembled gang of shady characters, both the eager and the reluctant, had been focused on the coming day, and the real test that lay ahead of them. Tomorrow, the skills they had been taught by an old German, a former prisoner-of-war, would be proved or would fail in the skies above the capital. God help them if they failed. If they got this wrong, it would result in what Bigley liked to call a Double-D outcome; Danger and Death. If you were lucky, you could run, with Danger following at a disadvantage, and escape Death. But, usually, if you were dealing with Roy Bigley, you weren't lucky.

On that last practice run, they'd managed to strip off the wing panels, fit the guns, replace the wing panels, load the guns and have everything secure and out of the way in eighteen-and-three-quarter minutes. Allowing for nerves and tension on the day, the job should be done in the nineteen minutes Erik Lux had specified. Alfie and Vinnie Sampson, once the highest-rating electricians Ford Dagenham had ever known, had set up the two-way radio link between a Toyota van, which would be done up to look like a security van, and codenamed Foxhunter Gold, which would be loaded with the guns and tools for the job, and Lux's Messerschmitt, in the early hours of the morning at Elwood Airfield. They had also wired it in such a way that Jock Jackson, in his Sikorsky helicopter, with its custom-built bomb hatch and hopper, courtesy of Roy Bigley, could communicate with the van as well, should he need to.

Detective Inspector Simon Foxley was in the yard at Elwood airfield, accompanied by his Sergeant, Ian Monument. WPC Hall was making notes, while Tony Cliveson watched the proceedings from the driver's seat of an unmarked car. George Lake was saying what a rum old do it all was.

"I can't believe anyone'd have it in for old Percy, Detective Inspector."

"Well, someone certainly did, Mr Lake, and they made a damn good job of it, too", Foxley replied.

"You said you'd not seen Percy Brown in the woods or the lanes for a few days" Sergeant Monument said, continuing a previous line of questioning. "Does that mean, Mr Lake, that you saw him elsewhere? Somewhere, perhaps, he wouldn't normally go?"

"He'd come onto the airfield. He never did that, usually, see, but he wanted to get a look at that Jerry plane."

Foxley's ears pricked up. "What Jerry plane would this be, Mr Lake?"

George Lake put the police officers in the picture. "Bloke comes to me a few months back, saying he had a Messerschmitt he wanted to renovate. He does a show now and again, only small things, he don't seem too keen on the shows, like. One time he told me he was only interested in the big show – not quite sure what he meant by that."

"And where does Percy come into this?" asked Foxley.

"Well, old Percy wanted to get a good look at the plane when it was on the ground, like, but whenever he was here Erik wasn't, so he never did get a look at it. He said once he'd like to sit in it, but he'd not have got that far – Erik Lux keeps that plane well locked up. I never get near it for a really good look myself."

Detective Inspector Foxley nodded. "You mentioned the name Erik Lux, Mr Lake – is that the plane owner?"

George nodded in agreement. "Yeah, that's his name alright."

"German?" asked Foxley

"Reckon he is. Got a kind of German/Yankee accent. Seemed to be a nice enough bloke. Don't talk much, though, y'know."

"Not about now, this Mr Lux?" asked Monument, hopefully.

"Nope. Ain't seen him today, Sergeant. He rents a cottage in the village, though, out by the church. You might catch him in. Oh, by the way, I think he's doing one of the airshows tomorrow, a rare enough thing for him, out Bedfordshire way, so if you don't catch him in today he'll be up here tomorrow morning, that's for sure, getting that Messerschmitt of his ready for the off."

Detective Inspector Foxley thanked George Lake for his help and, along with Detective Sergeant Monument and WPC Hall, walked off towards the unmarked police car. He was about to get in when he stopped, and turned back to George Lake.

"Oh, Mr Lake – you don't happen to know if Mr Lux and Mr Brown knew one another, do you? To speak to, perhaps?"

George scratched his head. "Can't say they did. Never so much as a good morning, that I recall, Inspector.

"Thank you, Mr Lake. You've been most helpful."

As the police car drove away, George Lake stood, still scratching his head, wondering what the world was coming to.

Tim Watts flew over the manor estate, handling the Cherokee with the ease that comes from years of experience. He savoured the moment, the rich colours of woods and fields spread out beneath him. Up here in the air one could lose oneself in nostalgic memories, he thought, memories of a long time ago. A time when these very skies would have been filled with hostile enemies seeking to destroy him. Tomorrow, he would be back in the old Spit, taking part in the 50th anniversary commemoration of the most famous battle of that time. His mind wandered back to that day, in August 1940, that he had downed Hans Lux's Messerschmitt. Where was Erik Lux at this very moment, he wondered, and where would he be tomorrow? At these thoughts, Tim Watts felt a strange feeling in the pit of his stomach. There was sweat on his brow and top lip, but his body was ice cold. Angrily, he put the Cherokee into a sharp dive, skimming hedges and treetops, then came roaring skywards, then diving down once more, rolling the plane over and over. Abruptly, he levelled the Cherokee. *What the hell was all that about, old boy?* Tim asked himself. Aloud, he said; "To hell with you, Lux! Come and get me, if you want me!"

Roy Bigley sat back in his chair, watching as Erik Lux piled the fifty-pound notes onto the desk in front of him.

"It is all there, as we agreed, Mr Bigley." Bigley grinned.

"Good on yer, son. Everything will be delivered, and your instructions put into force, exactly as you requested. Mr Lux, I don't know what sort of caper you're planning, and I don't think I want to, but I'm guessing it's something big – that's why you've parted with a whole whack of cash. But Mouth Wilson'll see to it that everything is done on schedule, the way you want it."

"I trust nothing will get in the way to change things, Mr Bigley?" there was ice in Lux's gaze. Bigley gave him his own icy stare in response.

"Like I said, I don't know or care what your caper is. You came to me with a requirement, a deal has been done. Your requirements will be met at the right place, at the right time, in the right way." Bigley waved the fat cigar he was holding over the pile of cash, then pointed it back at himself. "I don't squeal on a deal, Mr Lux." Leaning forward, he scooped up the pile of fifties, stuffing them into the briefcase Lux had brought them in. Kissing his fat fingers, he touched them to the briefcase.

"So long, Mr Lux. I guess we have nothing more to talk about. Have a nice day tomorrow, and don't forget that Mr Wilson will want the rest of this when the job is done." He waved the briefcase, and watched Erik Lux walk away, still wondering what his client was planning.

Back in Elwood, the news of Percy Brown's murder had caused quite a stir, setting tongues wagging all over the village. His cottage was off-limits, tape across the door, a most unusual sight in this small, rural place.

Foxley stood in the centre of the front parlour, a square room just off to the right of a short hallway, while Forensics busied themselves about the rest of the place. It was well-kept, mused Foxley, the plain, 1950s furniture well-polished, the tiled floors swept, their rugs looking like they got regular beatings. Maybe Molly Stubbs, widow and neighbour, did a little light housework for him, Foxley thought, then shrugged his shoulders. What was to say the old boy hadn't learnt to keep house for himself?

There was a large, open fireplace, with deep-seated armchairs on other side, and a wedding photograph, showing a much younger Percy Brown and a blushing, demure bride, the old boy's late wife, Maude, hanging over the mantel. Other photographs hung in various positions against the faded floral wallpaper. A utility radio stood on the sideboard, and the clock hanging on the wall above it told him it was time to go back to George Lake's museum of an airfield .

Foxley could hear the Forensics team, who were now swarming all over the late Mr Brown's cottage, seeking clues, anything that would point them in a positive direction, something that would give them the break they needed to solve this unlikely murder.

It was Saturday, and Simon Foxley didn't want to be here. He had heard, on the late news the day before, that the Battle of Britain Memorial Flight, to commemorate the 50th anniversary of the Battle of Britain, was taking off from Duxford, instead of the usual Coningsby, a last-minute change of plans, for "reasons undisclosed." As Duxford was only about half an hour's drive from his home, Foxley had planned to take his family for a day out. On such a bright, sunny September day, it would have been a nice day for them all. He sighed, and, together with Monument and the Forensics team, left the cottage, locking it securely behind him. They would be heading back to that bloody airfield, the second time today Foxley had been there, though the first for the Forensic team.

It had been an early start for Wing Commander Timothy "Watto" Watts, an early start that had been preceeded by a late-afternoon telephone call from the Air Vice-Marshal.

"You're flying the Spitfire in tomorrow's display, aren't you?"

"Yes, Sir."

"Right. Well, your plane's been taken over to Duxford – the flight will leave from there, not Coningsby."

"May I ask why, Sir?"

The Air Vice-Marshal had been silent for a long moment. "Look, for God's sake, keep this to yourself, man…the IRA have threatened a terrorist attack on Coningsby, on the flight. God knows why – we weren't at war with *them* in 1940 – but can't take a risk that it's all a hoax. And it hardly ever is with those maniacs. Keeping it shtum, though – don't want a panic. The Press Office are putting out a statement to the national media, the BBC, "reasons undisclosed", that sort of thing. They're also telephoning everyone who brought tickets in advance. I'm contacting the pilots personally."

"I appreciate it, Sir."

"Well, Watts...see you tomorrow, at Duxford."

Tim Watts, with Patricia beside him, had left the manor early that morning, savouring the coming day, a celebration, old friends together again. Putting on a damn good show, slap-up dinner afterwards, no doubt a fair bit of drinking as well, singing and dancing and the like. He began to hum the tune to *This Is A Lovely Way To Spend An Evening*. He winked at Pat, as he had come to call her, their relationship having moved beyond the "just friends" stage.

"You are looking forward to this, aren't you, darling?" she smiled. "Will many of your old friends be taking part?"

"There are a few of us left!" he laughed. "Hopefully most of them will be there. Only one other chap will be flying, though. From the old days, I mean."

"Were you ever stationed at Duxford?"

"Yes, I was there with Douglas Bader, in 1941."

"Douglas who?"

" Douglas Bader - the man with the tin legs", Tim laughed, and, seeing the puzzled expression on Patricia's face, realising that she didn't have the faintest idea what he was on about, being several years his junior, he explained the Bader legend to her.

Soon, they arrived at Duxford. The huge hangars and buildings were impressive as Tim drove through the entrance gate. This would be the last show where he would actually take part, would actually fly. He intended to enjoy himself up there today. He would put the old Spit through her paces like never before.

The crowds were already starting to arrive, and there was a general bustle of activity everywhere. Tim pulled into one of the parking spaces reserved for pilots, and turned to Pat.

"Well, old girl. The big day, at last! Wish me luck."

"Good luck, darling. You will fly safe, won't you?" She kissed him, then walked with him to the administrative building, to report his arrival.

Foxley and Monument arrived at Elwood airfield, closely followed by the Forensics team in their van. Seeing them, George Lake walked over to them, meeting them in the middle of the yard.

"Caught up with your murderer yet, Inspector?" he asked.

"I'm afraid not, Mr Lake, but we will – don't worry about that." Foxley's eyes travelled over the area, taking in the yard and the buildings. "Our Mr Lux about today, is he?"

"I've not seen him yet, but he'll be here, no doubt about that – he's flying today."

Detective Sergeant Monument had moved away from them, and was peering down at the ground. As he did so, something caught his eye; a medium-sized, sharp-edge stone, its greyish-white surface spotted with dark stains. He called his boss over.

"Take a look at that, Sir." Foxley crouched down, taking a close look at the stone.

"Hmm, yes. Looks like dried blood, wouldn't you say?"

"I think so, Sir."

Foxley carefully took a pair of gloves from his right hand pocket, pulled them on, and removed a clear plastic bag from his left hand pocket. He picked up the stone, placed it in the bag, sealed the bag, and handed it to Monument, before removing the gloves and replacing them in his pocket, to be disposed of back at the station.

"I'm afraid I'm going to have to take a look round the premises, Mr Lake."

"You don't think anything happened *here*, Inspector?"

"Can't be certain yet, Mr Lake. We'll get that stone examined by our Forensics lads, and if you'd be so good as to show them where you found Mr Brown's cap and car, earlier?"

Falling. Dark, swirling clouds. He sees a young boy, perhaps ten, in blue pyjamas – somehow, the colour seems important. The boy is reaching for something, a child's smile of delight on his face, a smile that turns to a look of horror...

The boy had been reaching for a man, a Luftwaffe pilot, who was floating down from the stormclouds, a parachute covered in swastikas above his him. The boy had reached for the man, had opened his mouth to call something, say something...and the man's face had been revealed. It was no man, no living man. A grim, skeletal ghoul, with empty sockets where sparkling eyes should have been, a clean, white skull which should have been covered by a proud, noble face, a face full of strength and intelligence, with the leathery look of someone who spends much time out of doors.

A hand reaches for the boy, pulling him down, into a swirling mist, a harsh, awful laughter ringing in his ears. The boy can't turns, falling into the person who is pulling him down. An English pilot, flesh and blood, with an all too familiar face...

Erik Lux had woken suddenly, heart pounding, drenched in sweat, staring at the ceiling in the bedroom of the cottage Bigley had arranged for him a few weeks before. There was only one thought in his mind; kill the English pilot. If he killed the Englishman, he would be able to save his father.

Going downstairs, he ate a quick breakfast of cornflakes and coffee, then went about the few things he had to do before leaving the cottage. Once he had tidied up, he climbed the narrow staircase to the bedroom. Once in the room, he removed his jeans and shirt, folding them carefully into the suitcase on the bed. Then he went to the old fashioned wardrobe, with its long, oblong mirror. From the wardrobe he removed the suit bag that was hanging there, unzipped it, and removed a flying suit of the German Luftwaffe, the very suit his father had worn, which, as was traditional, had been presented to Hans Lux's widow. It was a miracle, the representative from the Luftwaffe had said, that there was so little damage to it. On his twenty-first birthday, Eva had presented the suit to her son. The suit was still in prime condition. Monthly sprayings with moth killer, and the services of a specially-purchased suit holder, had kept the suit in good order, and, as Erik Lux now held it against himself, watching his reflection in the mirror, he looked good. Erik had never worn the suit in public before, contenting himself with parading around the Montanan ranch in it, after Eva and Walter Chiltern had been killed in a car accident while on a trip to the Canadian Rockies. There being no other children, Erik Lux had inherited the ranch, cattle, and Walter's considerable fortune. Thus, at twenty-nine, he had obtained two things which he valued more than anything else – wealth and privacy. The suit was a perfect fit. The Iron Cross and Oak Leaves prominent at his throat. Erik had pulled on his father's boots, stamped his feet once, twice, then pulled on his gloves and helmet. He had looked at himself in the mirror for a long moment, then flung out his arm in the Nazi salute.

"Heil, Hitler! Mein Fuhrer! The Eagle will fly!"

Foxley and Monument had completed their inspection of Elwood airfield, and Forensics had finished examining Percy's cap and car. Nothing else seemed out of place. The area where the stone had been found was now cordoned off, so that it wasn't disturbed..

It was then that Erik Lux drove onto Elwood airfield, a frown creasing his brow as he took in the presence of the two strangers, who had "Police" written all over them.

Ignoring them, Lux drove straight to the shed where his Messerschmitt was stored, parked the Volvo, and stepped out, leaning back to pick up his helmet. He was standing there, helmet under his arm, as the officers approached. Still ignoring them, he unlocked the huge double doors, his back to the approaching men. He heard the shuffle of their footsteps behind him, and turned to face them.

"That's an interesting uniform you're wearing, Mr Lux – you *are* Mr Erik Lux, I assume?"

"You are well-informed. And you are..?"

Detective Inspector Foxley produced his badge, and introduced his Sergeant.

"Well, Detective Inspector. How may I help you?"

Foxley took in the tall figure, the strong face tanned and hardened by Montana weather, the grey eyes wary and sharp.

"We are investigating the death of a Mr Percy Brown. Did you know him, Mr Lux?"

Lux shook his head. "Never heard of him. But, then, I do not know many people here – just the men working here at the airfield, a couple of people in the village pub, and the lady at the Post Office. I do not really mix much with the locals, I'm afraid. So, no, Inspector, I do not know your Percy Brown."

Lux turned aside and pulled open the hangar doors. The two policemen stared in awe at the gleaming Messerschmitt.

"That's a fine looking machine, Sir" said Monument, admiration in his voice.

"Yes, she is, isn't she?" Lux replied, smiling.

"You're flying today, Mr Lux?" Foxley asked.

"Yes, Inspector. Just a small airshow out in Bedfordshire, at Long Hill. Nothing particularly noteworthy, but for me it will be a very special day indeed. My machine will set the skies alight!" He laughed aloud, turning away from the two police officers.

At Duxford, things were humming. Mechanics checked the vintage machines for any last minute problems, the old Lancaster bomber stood proud, waiting patiently for take-off, when it would escort the fighters of the Battle of Britain flight through the skies, and over London. Tim Watts' silver Spitfire gleamed in the sunlight, the name "Watto W" proudly emblazoned on the fuselage. Beneath it, 18 swastikas marked the number of kills credited to its pilot. Three had been over Malta, two over North Africa, and the remainder in the Battle of Britain.

The smell of high octane petrol and oil fumes mingled with the subtler scents of summer. Men in short sleeved shirts and women in summer dresses mingled with ground staff and pilots. Children ran and scrambled everywhere, their eyes wide with amazement at the scenes before them. The pilots were ready, making their way to their individual machines. Patricia stood with the crowd and watched as Tim clambered into the cockpit of his Spitfire. She waved vigorously, and he lifted his arm in response.

At that moment, an attendant came up to her.

"Excuse me, Mrs Lux, but there is a telephone call for you." The man recalled seeing her on a previous ocassion, when Tim Watts had introduced her.

"Oh, thank you. But, you see, I'm not Mrs Lux anymore. I'm divorced. Who is calling?"

"A Mr Erik Lux."

Wondering what on Earth Erik could want, Patricia followed the attendant to the reception office, and was directed to a telephone on a large desk, its receiver off the hook. She picked the receiver up, hesitantly.

"Is that you, Erik?"

Lux came on the line from the deserted office at Elwood airfield. "Hello, Patricia. Are you surprised at my call?"

"Yes, I am, Erik. What do you want?" Patricia was irritated; she did not want to miss Tim's take off.

"Is your Wing Commander ready for his celebration flight?" asked Erik. "Before he takes off, give him a message from me. Tell him we will meet soon, that the Eagle will be flying, and the Battle of Britain is not over. Goodbye, Patricia, my dear."

The phone went dead as Lux hung up abruptly.

Patricia felt a cold sense of fear come over her. There had been a ringing menace in her ex-husband's voice as he spelled out his message to Tim. That Tim was in some kind of danger Patricia had no doubt, but what it was she had no idea. She knew the motive of Erik's hatred, but could not guess exactly what terrible plan was in the man's evil, vengeful mind. She hurried out onto the airfield. Somehow, she must warn Tim. The engines of the vintage planes were warming up, and she could see Tim's Spitfire already taxiing into position. She ran forward, waving furiously, but, of course, he did not see her; his attention was on his instrument panel.

Back at Elwood, Erik Lux put down the receiver with a grim satisfaction. "I will be seeing you soon, Wing Commander" he whispered, then he spat, and, aloud, said; "Soon, Englander – very soon." He strode quickly to where the Messerschmitt was waiting on the runway, clambered into the cockpit, completed his instrument check, and taxied forward, along the weed-bordered stretch of concrete.

As the 109 rolled down the runway, a CID car drove through the entrance to the airfield. Detective Inspector Foxley sat in the front passenger seat, Detective Sergeant Ian Monument and WPC Kerry Hall behind him. PC Tony Cliveson was driving. Behind them was the Forensics team in their van.

Foxley wanted to talk to Lux; another call had come into the station, from a young woman who worked as a domestic at Elwood Hall. Her days started early in the morning, she explained, the family at Elwood Hall being farming folk, up with the sun, like most farmers, and, on the day Percy's body was been found, she had been cycling to work, as usual taking a route that ran past the old airfield, and had seen Percy Brown having what appeared to be an argument with a man she knew to be a foreigner living in the village. She couldn't give them any more details, other than to say she thought the man's accent was either American or German.

Foxley noted the fact that the doors to Lux's hangar were wide open, and soon saw that the hangar itself was empty.

Just as the others got out of the car, they heard a roar of engines. Monument pointed skywards as the 109 took to the air. Foxley stood, flanked by Cliveson and Hall, watching as the plane became airborne, like some giant bird escaping to freedom.

Foxley shook his head. "Missed him by a wing." Noticing Lux's Volvo, Foxley walked over to it, indicating to his team that they should follow him. The keys were still in the ignition.

"Strange thing to do," Monument commented. WPC Hall nodded. "Especially when he's going to be away all day." "Unless he's not planning on coming back", put in Cliveson. Foxley raised an eyebrow. "Now, Constable, what makes you say that?" "Nothing, really, Sir. Just a passing thought."

WPC Hall, who had been walking around the Volvo, leaned in and pulled the lever to open the boot. The boot flew open. It was almost empty, except for a car jack, a wheel brace and a shovel, which lay at an angle. As Kerry Hall peered closer, trying to get a good look at the shovel, she saw something that made her step back.

"Guv – I think you should take a look at this." Foxley beckoned one of the Forensic team over. "Get that shovel out, and be careful with it. It could be important." The man nodded, and picked up the shovel in gloved hands. Taking it out of the boot, he held it up for Foxley's inspection. Dark patches of dried blood, along with clumps of earth, were clearly evident on the scratched surface of the shovel's blade.

"Bag it" Foxley said to the Forensics officer, who merely nodded. "Where did Lake say that airshow was, Ian? Bedfordshire, wasn't it?"

"I think so, Guv, but if that shovel means what we think it means, will our man be going there, or leaving the country?"

The Inspector paused to think. "As far as we can tell, Lux doesn't know he's under suspicion. He could still be coming back."

Opening the back door of the Volvo, WPC Hall saw something on the floor. Pulling on her gloves, she took it out. It was a suitcase, old but still in good condition. Seeing it, Foxley motioned for her to open it.

It was packed with neatly folded clothes, on the top a red checked shirt, a pair of worn jeans, and a pair of brown brogues.

"Coming back, do we think?" Monument asked, pulling a face.

"Could be" Foxley replied, heavy emphasis on the word *could*. He shook his head. "Best get onto the control towers, get his journey monitored. Let's see if we can find out what airshow he's heading for in Bedford."

Cliveson laughed. "Well, at least it won't be the Battle of Britain flypast!"

None of them could have known just how wrong he was.

The Norfolk Constabulary at Thetford had not experienced anything like the matter now dominating their patch for some time. For a Force whose most exciting assignment might be helping a duck across the road, or having a quiet word with a pair of newlyweds whose nocturnal activities were disturbing the beauty sleep of an elderly neighbour, this was high drama. Detective Inspector Simon Foxley was in the control room with WPC Clare Farr, the wireless operator, listening to the chatter between Thetford control and Cambridge. WPC Farr turned her head. "He's just south of Cambridge at the moment, flying a pretty straight course. Looks like he might be heading for Long Hill after all." Foxley, deep in thought, bit his lip. "We'll see. Keep Cambridge in touch."

Just then, the voice of the Cambridge controller came back on the air. "Your man now turning left and dropping altitude, heading south."

Foxley turned to Ian Monument, whose attention was focused on a large map pinned to the wall just to the left of the control unit. The map clearly showed the counties of East Anglia – Norfolk, Suffolk, Cambridgeshire, Bedfordshire, Hertfordshire and Essex, and the sprawl of the London area. Symbols indicated major airports and lesser airfields.

Monuments fingers danced across the map, stopping at the symbol that marked Luton airport. Foxley turned back to Farr.

"Are we in touch with Luton?"

She nodded. "Luton control just coming through, they've spotted him, he's still on a southerly course, looks like he's heading London way."

Foxley grunted, and Monument's finger moved over the map to Heathrow. They'd have him next. Suddenly, Luton came back over the radio.

"Your man's done a disappearing act. We've lost him, no contact. Either he's flying well below radar, and blowing a few tiles off the rooftops, or he's done a quick landing somewhere. Over and out."

"Thank you, Luton." Farr turned to Foxley. "What do you think he's up to, Sir?"

Foxley shook his head. He had no idea what game the German was playing. All he knew was that the evidence told him the man had killed Percy Brown.

"I think he's landed somewhere", said Monument. "I mean, let's say he killed the old boy, he's making his getaway. Well, that Messerschmitt's not going to get him far, whether he stays under radar or not. He'll be forced down before he reaches the coast."

"I think you're right," Foxley said, slowly. "But, if he can't risk flying out, then his only option is to go by sea. He's got to get to the coast. I think he's landed somewhere near a major highway, got a car hidden out of the way there."

"I'd go along with that, Sir," said Monument. "Do we have any thoughts on his direction to the coast?"

Foxley rubbed his chin and stared at the map.

"I think he'll backtrack, come back into our territory. He's clever, and he's made himself very familiar with East Anglia. I think he'll make his way cross-country to either Ipswich or Yarmouth. I'd bet on Yarmouth – bit more isolated, fewer boats anchoring up, most of the ones that do put in are from the Baltic ports. A quiet word, a hefty roll of fifties and he'll be away in hours. I think we need an all-ports alert nationwide. This man is clever, and he could well be dangerous."

The Thetford station became a hive of activity, excitement racing at fever pitch.

Had Detective Inspector Foxley known of Erik Lux's real plans, he would have been wringing his hands, his usually calm face distorted in horror.

Thetford Constabulary were not the only ones interested in the plans of Mr Erik Lux.

Back at Duxford, Patricia had been almost beside herself, trying to think of a way to warn Tim about Erik's phone call, and his threat. She had finally found her answer when she had seen one of Tim's old friends, Air Commodore Peter Glanville-Jessup, crossing the airfield with a group of RAF dignitaries, all deep in conversation, and heading for the refreshment tent. Hurrying towards them, intercepting them alongside a Halifax bomber parked some two hundred feet from the refreshment tent, Patricia apologised for her intrusion, and asked if she might have a word with Glanville-Jessup.

Knowing that Tim and Patricia weren't married – indeed, that Tim considered Patricia merely a very good friend, and being able, despite his advancing years, to notice an attractive female when he saw one, Glanville-Jessup agreed, and lead Patricia off to the more private setting of the administration building, thinking that she was merely being silly, as women could be, that it was all a bit of a storm in a teacup that just needed some soothing and reassurance.

His face, however, grew concerned as he listened to her. There was no panic in her story, nothing that would suggest an hysteric female about to go off her rocker, and she really did seem as if she'd seen a ghost. Besides, he had known Patricia for several years now, and she had never seemed that type at all.

"Don't worry, my dear. Everything will be alright – I know planes better than anyone, and Mr Lux will be forced to meet radar height for a good while, if only to avoid crashing into the tops of various trees and buildings. I'll get on to the flightpath control towers, let them know what's going on, so they can keep an eye out for him. Come with me." With that, they both headed for the Control Tower building.

CHAPTER NINETEEN

At Lost Horse Farm, the mood was jovial, a welcome relief to the tensions of the past few weeks. Some of the men were even cracking jokes with old Horst, although Tony Knox and Eddie Small still had their problems with him. Mouth Wilson, though, had certainly warmed to him, and found he enjoyed listening to the old man's war stories. It was like having a grandfather, Mouth thought, an experience he'd never had. Mouth wanted to take Horst Block with them to the A1 rendezvous, but Bigley held firm against that, so the old German would stay at Lost Horse Farm tomorrow, while the rest of them went out on the final stage of whatever madness the other German was planning.

Young Vinnie Sampson had also quite taken to the old German, and seemed to have made a quick pupil; he seemed to know almost as much about aircraft mechanics as Horst himself, and Mouth had no concerns regarding Vinnie's performance tomorrow, on the big day.

Walking away from the barn, Mouth Wilson sat down on a moss-covered stump in what must once have been a thriving orchard. He wanted time to himself, to think. He had often come out here, when work had finally finished in the barn, just to wind down.

Smiling, he remembered their first attempt; they'd made a right balls-up of it, and the frame they were working on had collapsed as the inept crew had wrestled with the heavy machine guns, swearing like troopers as they tried to get the damn things in place, and hold them there. A couple of the lads had nearly walked away then and there. It'd been like an episode of the Muppets, he thought, with old Horst as Miss Piggy, always getting in a flap.

Mouth Wilson's thoughts turned more serious. He knew they would all have to lie low for a bit after this – whatever *this* turned out to be. A couple of months' holiday in Spain would see him right, he thought. He'd look up his old mate, Ozzie Stannet – Ozzie's missus could be a bit playful, he remembered. His thoughts went from Ozzie's wife to that maniac Kraut, Lux. No one, not even Bigley, knew what the man was planning, but they all knew what day it would be tomorrow, what anniversary. Or most of them did. Tony Knox didn't, but then, for people like Tony Knox, last week probably counted as ancient history.

Still, he thought, they'd done they job, they'd get their fair whack for it. What more could you ask for, really, in his game?

Suddenly, his mobile rang. His reverie shattered, Wilson noticed that the light was beginning to fade. He glanced at the number on the display, and swore under his breath. What the hell did Bigley want now? The man had been ringing him all day – it was a bloody wonder he'd managed to get any work done at all, with the constant interruptions.

"That you, Mouth?"

"No, Biggy. It's Hitler. You rang me mobile – who the hell do you *think* it's gonna be?"

Bigley's voice was steel. "Cut the comedy act, and get yourself up here. I want to see you."

"Tonight?" Wilson was really starting to get irritated, now. He was sick of being at someone else's beck and call – if he'd've wanted that, he would've got a legit job.

"Yes, tonight. Get your arse here, pronto." With a sigh, Mouth put the mobile back in his pocket, and headed into the barn to collect his jacket. Locking the door of the barn, he headed to the farmhouse, where the others were playing cards in the kitchen.

"I'm off to Walthamstow – the boss wants me. Behave while I'm gone." A few minutes later, he was on his way out.

The traffic was light, and it was an easy run to Walthamstow. Bigley was standing at his office window, blocking any light that might have been on, when Wilson pulled up. With a gesture, he indicated that the doors were unlocked, and that Mouth was to come straight up. As he entered the office, the door closed silently behind him, the lock clicking to like a bullet.

Bigley glanced at his watch. "You made good time for a dead man."

"What the hell kind of joke's that meant to be?" Wilson was tired, and his temper was frayed.

"Well, when I spoke to you on the phone, you told me you was Hitler, remember?" Bigley chortled, pleased with his own joke.

"Look, Bigley, can we get on to what this is about? I need my sleep."

"It's about the Kraut."

Wilson's blood froze. "Which one?" he asked, although he already knew the answer.

"The old man. He's got to go, Mouth. You know that, don't you?"

For the first time in his long life in the gangland, Mouth Wilson didn't want to kill the person he had been ordered to kill. For the first time, Mouth Wilson the man was gaining ground over Mouth Wilson the gun-for-hire.

"Surely he can't pose too much of a threat, Bigley? I mean, he hasn't got a clue what's going on, and there's his wife..." he trailed off as he saw the hard light in Bigley's eyes.

"You going soft on me, Mouth?" he growled, menace in the question.

"No, Bigley. You want me to kill the old man, I'll kill him."

Bigley shook his head. "Not you. Eddie Small can do it. Tonight. Midnight. Nice and clean. I want the Kraut out of the way before tomorrow, so no one's distracted before the big show, and I want *you* to be in charge of cleaning up – no trace anyone was ever at the farm, right? All the clothes, books, food – gone. You're also taking care of the vehicles, after the Meccano games on the A1. That should keep you busy for a spell. And if you could make it clear to Eddie that Jock Jackson won't want his chopper up too long, so he should be quick about it, yeah? I know Jock – he'll want to be on his way back from the estuary before the chimes call out one in the morning."

Mouth rose to leave. "I'll talk to Eddie."

"Ain't you forgetting something, Wilson?" Mouth turned, wary. Bigley had placed two briefcases, one black, one a dark red, on the desk. He indicated the black case. "Pay for the troops. Make sure they share nicely. The red one's got your cut, Mouth. God knows what kind of a mug I am, paying you in advance, but there you are. That's just your lovely Uncle Roy for you, treating you so nice. The Jerry'll bring the final payment in a rucksack to the meet tomorrow – you make sure it gets to me nice and safe, right? And if he tries anything funny, you have my permission to blast him out of the sky by any means necessary. Now – go and give Eddie his instructions."

Back at Lost Horse Farm, Mouth sat in the Rover, banging his fist on the steering wheel as he thought about what he was going to have to ask of Eddie Small. He gave a harsh, brutal yell. Once more, the bloody stopover would serve its terrible purpose.

As he walked away, Mouth Wilson wondered what Erik Lux was planning, and knew, with sudden and complete certainty, that he wanted nothing to do with it. He didn't have a choice with this job, but he *did* have a choice when it came to others. And his choice was made then and there; there would be no other jobs. He would keep the money, his own and the final payment to Bigley. The lads could have theirs. This wasn't about them, really, so it wouldn't be right to rob them of what they'd earned fair and square. Half of Lux's final payment to Bigley Mouth would give to Horst; he'd heard there was quite a large German community in Galway, on the West Coast of the Republic of Ireland. He'd get Horst and his wife a new passport each, new identities, help them disappear, then scarper himself. Bigley might choke on his cigar, but that was just tough. Mouth Wilson had heard Venezuela had some excellent plastic surgeons.

CHAPTER TWENTY.

The next day, it was a sombre group, the crew who would be directly involved in the A1 job, who sat around the table in the kitchen at Lost Horse Farm, eating a breakfast of buttered toast with Marmite, to give them an edge and energy for the job ahead, drinking mugs of hot, sweet tea. In the yard, the black Transit van was loaded, fitted with false number plates, ready to go. A low, light mist hovered over the countryside, but the weather forecast seemed to pose no problems. The job would go ahead, they would be paid, and then they'd disappear. Simple.

Tony Knox, at the wheel of the black Transit van, drove through the suburbs of Romford with the attitude of a man going nowhere in particular. He knew well enough not to rush this part of it, not to do anything that would draw the Old Bill's attention to him. Seeing a sign indicating the Newlands Industrial Estate to his left, he flicked his indicator on, and eased into the turn, driving past a row of cheap warehouses, home to small, struggling businesses. Outside the last – and largest – warehouse on the row, two nondescript figures were waiting. At the sight of the van, they slid open the double doors. Knox slowed down, drove through the entrance, and parked beside an older-model Toyota van, the same size and colour as his Transit. The only difference was the gold SAFELINE SECURITY lettering on the side of the Toyota. For a few brief minutes, the warehouse was a hive of activity as cargo was transferred from the Transit to the Toyota, and false number plates fitted to the latter. Less than half an hour after the Transit had pulled in to the warehouse, the Toyota was driving out, Tony Knox at the wheel, Mouth Wilson beside him. Both now wore the visored helmets and uniforms of security guards.

As they headed towards Romford, a uniformed police officer stood in the middle of the road, waving them down. Knox looked over at Wilson, who shook his head. This man wasn't one of theirs; had they been double-crossed?

"Where're you heading, mate?" A warrant card at the window told Tony Knox that this was the real Old Bill. He should know – he'd seen enough of them in his time.

"Got a meet-up and transfer just off the A12. Carrying on with the vehicle we're meeting to Heathrow." He hopped his directions were right. If they weren't, the police officer didn't seem to notice, just frowned at the two vans parked, either side of the road, a little way past the yellow diversion sign.

"You can't go this way, fellas. There's a burst watermain."

Wilson took over. "Look, officer, you know we've got a legal right, as a registered secure transport vehicle, to force our way through there, even if it means trashing the pipework completely, or writing off one of the vans. We're on a schedule, our route's registered – all Hell's going to break loose if we have to divert."

The police officer stared at them for a moment. "You seem pretty worried about your load, even for security guards. What're you running – gold bullion?" Wilson shrugged. "No idea. We just pick it up, get the docket signed at the other end. You want me to open up the van so you can check it out? Call my HQ, have them release the timelocks, all that hassle?" The police officer glanced at the works vans once more, then seemed to come to a decision.

"Come on, then. Follow my car, keep damn close. I'll give you an escort through here to the A12. The diversion sign should give any other idiots a bit of a clue not to drive along this stretch while I'm gone."

With a wail of sirens, they were away, both Knox and Wilson heaving a sigh of relief, and hoping they wouldn't be late at the rendezvous.

In a layby on the A12, what appeared, to all intents and purposes to be a police squad car sat waiting, its engine idling, the officer behind the wheel scanning the approaching traffic with a look of expectation, the clock on the dashboard telling him they couldn't be far away. As if reading his thoughts, Wilson's voice came over the officer's radio;

"Foxhunter Gold to Bloodhound One, receiving?" In the end, Roy Bigley had decided they needed a greater 'police' presence, but had agreed with Wilson that all the 'police' units should be known by the codename of Bloodhound, followed by a sequential number. "Receiving, Foxhunter, state your position, please." "Approaching position two, Bloodhound. Repeat, approaching position two, over." "Roger that, Foxhunter." Jack Wagg, dressed in the uniform of a Metropolitan Police officer, turned to the man sitting beside him, dressed in the same uniform, who went by the name of Willie Wante. "He's about two miles off", Jack Wagg said, interpretting Wilson's record of his position. Willie Wante shrugged, and flicked the ash of his cigarette out of the window.

Both men were hangers-on, bit-part extras that Roy Bigley called in for big jobs where a distraction or two was needed.

Wagg was the first to spot the Toyota, and, as it drew close, he flicked the switch that set the rooftop lights and sirens wailing. Knox slowed down, allowing the fake police vehicle to pull out in front of him, then sped after it.

The motorcyclists who waited in another layby furthur along the motorway were Mickey Meanes, Luke Miller and a third man, whose name no one had bothered to learn. He was Russian, really just there to make up the numbers, the son of a friend of Bigley's, brought into this job as a favour.

The three men sat astride their machines, watching and waiting, much as Willie and Jack had been doing in their squad car. Suddenly, simultaneously, their radios sparked into life.

"Foxhunter Gold calling Bloodhounds Two, Three and Four, approaching your position now." "Roger that, Foxhunter." Miller gave Meanes the thumbs-up as they heard the wail of sirens, then saw the squad car approaching at speed, the Toyota close on its tail. With a yelp of their own sirens, the riders forced their way across the flow of traffic and settled at cruising speed behind the Toyota, forming a miniature convoy. Motorists cursed as they were forced to slow down and give way to the security van and its escort, many speculating about the kind of cargo being carried – it must be of some considerable value, to merit such a show of force from the Met.

Wilson turned to Knox. "Easy, there. Just relax. We'll make it." Indeed, they were a couple of minutes or so early, no bad thing when you worked for Roy Bigley. Knox merely nodded; apart from the engine noise, the cab was silent. Words were not needed now. Soon, all going well, they would be on the A406. Irritably, Tony Knox began drumming his fingers on the steering wheel as he drove.

"Why'd that Kraut have to off the pensioner, eh? I ain't never done nuffink like this before – I mean, the bleedin' A1! Why can't we have a nice, smooth meadow, kind of place yer meant to do this sort of thing?"

Mouth Wilson laughed. "Ah, well, they do say there's a first time for everything – and this sure as hell is going to be the first time a Jerry plane's landed on the A1, I reckon! Cheer up, Tone – just think of all that lovely dosh at the end, eh?" Knox shook his head, irritation building.

"What's the Kraut's game, anyway? Eh? I dunno, you dunno – it's all Blankety Blank, innit? I don't reckon the fat man even knows what his client's playing at."

Mouth Wilson shrugged. "We just follow orders, mate."

"Yeah – and get landed in the proverbial when it all goes pear-shaped."

They were on the A109 now, passing through Barnet, then Tottenridge Village. Wilson consulted his Rolex. Tight-lipped, expectant, he scanned the skies.

Away over Epping forest, a large, greyish bird suddenly broke through the clouds above the treeline, its wings seeming to flap in a blur, in the split seconds before any onlooker realised that it was no bird, but rather a small helicopter. The more knowledgable among them would have known it was a Sikorsky, although no one would have been able to say why it was heading in the direction of the A1.

Jock Jackson, long-time pilot for Roy Bigley and his crew, manned the controls, a nameless Middle-Eastern man sitting beside him. He did not belong to Bigley, or any of the London gangs. His territory was Pakistan, and his speciality was the manufacture of high-velocity explosives – bombs.

The helicopter arrived over Apex Corner a few minutes early, and hovered, waiting. Down below, Jock saw the fake security van and escort approaching, dead on time, lights flashing and sirens wailing, giving anyone the impression they were carrying a shipment of diamonds or bullion. Jackson spoke quietly into his headset, the soft burr of his Scotts origins rumbling through like tiger's purr.

"Greybird, I'm over target area, and have you in my sights, Foxhunter Gold."

"We see you, Greybird. Drop your packages on my signal, over."

"Roger, Foxhunter." Jackson circled the chopper, watching as the convoy converged on Apex corner, then turn onto the A1, along Watford Way. Urging the helicopter forward, Jock pulled ahead of them. At a point midway between Apex Corner and the Mill Hill roundabout, three words came over Jock Jackson's radio; "Greybird, bombs away!" Jock nodded to the silent Pakistani, who began to work his contraption, specifically adapted, at Bigley's request, for this job, although Roy Bigley felt certain it could be useful for future ventures; in the belly of the Sikorsky, a small bomb bay had been fashioned, a steel hopper, mounted on three steel legs and bolted to the floor, was filled with top-class smoke bombs, manufactured in Pakistan, at great cost, but, Bigley had been promised, maximum effectiveness. The hopper had a hole at its base, which sloped down to a funnel, which then carried the smoke bombs through the open doors of the bomb bay. A steel shutter kept the smoke bombs in the hopper, operated by a lever that also controlled the bomb bay doors; left for the shutter, right for the bomb bay.

Jackson nodded to the man beside him, who worked the lever, allowing a shower of bombs to fall. Shutting both the bomb bay and the steel shutter, the man sat silently as Jock took the helicopter back a few hundred yards, where they repeated the exercise, as they would do several times along Watford Way, between Apex Corner and the Mill Hill roundabout, the bombs spilling out of the helicopter, landing and bursting on the traffic below.

Within seconds, the entire area was covered in a thick fog, vehicle after vehicle slamming on its brakes, cars slamming into one another, their drivers unable to see where they were going. The fake police motorbikes and squad car were now blocking off the exit of the Mill Hill roundabout, smoke coalescing around them. Wagg got out, and calmly opened the boot of the squad car, taking out a red and white fold-down road barrier and bollards. In seconds, the junction was completely blocked off.

In the confusion, the Toyota van had sped off towards London, then pulled onto the hard shoulder a few hundred yards after the roundabout. The rear doors were flung open and, while Tony Knox settled down to wait in the driving seat, Mouth Wilson leapt out, rushing to the back of the van, binoculars to his eyes as he scanned the skies for Lux's Messerschmitt.

Meanwhile, back at the roadblock, Jack Wagg and Willie Wante were leaning against the bonnet of their squad car, Kalashnikovs in hand. Bigley had told them, in no uncertain terms, that he didn't want anyone to get hurt – they were only to fire into the air, when given the signal from Wilson that Lux was about to take off, as a kind of final salute. If, however, Erik Lux failed to throw the rucksack containing the final payment down to Mouth Wilson, the two men were more then welcome to, as Bigley put it, "Blow the bloody Kraut out of the sky."

Lux had the Messerschmitt cruising at just under one thousand feet, the rural countryside spread out beneath him. By all accounts, and even by the last radar hit, Lux could indeed have been making for Bedfordshire, and Long Hill.

There was little cloud, and no other aircraft, in the sky as Lux held the Messerschmitt at a steady speed, keeping a level course a little to the south-west of Cambridge. Dropping to 500ft, he was over Royston in minutes, over Stevenage, and down to 300ft, skimming the rooftops, residential tower blocks seeming to rear up in warning. Welwyn Garden City, Hatfield...his chart told him he was close to the A1, over the A1... he followed the highway on its journey to London. Throttling back, both altitude and speed dropping. Being a Saturday, the A1 was busy. He was cruising low, at one hundred feet. Ahead of him, he could see a gathering cloud of smoke billowing over the carriageway. He spotted the helicopter. Flicking his throat mike, he made contact with Mouth Wilson.

"Foxhunter Gold, this is Red Eagle, altitude one hundred, coming in now – the smoke's not a problem. Over."

"Roger, and ready, Red Eagle." Wilson had come prepared; a white cross had been painted on the black tarmac of the A1, marking the spot where Lux would bring his Messerschmitt down.

As Lux slowed, dropping height, Wilson's marking came in sight. Lux landed perfectly, centred directly over the white cross. It was a landing even his old enemy Watts, the Englander, would have been proud of.

A low whine had announced the arrival of the Messerschmitt, and all heads had turned skyward. Through the coalescing fog of the smoke bombs, Lux's plane had seemed to descend in slow motion, hitting the smooth surface of the road, bouncing once, twice, three times, before braking to a stop just in front of the open rear doors of the van, which was parked just behind the aircraft's port wing.

Wilson and his crew were swarming over the plane in seconds, stripping off wing panels, dragging guns from the back of the van, spanners, hammers and other assorted tools becoming ready weapons as they worked themselves into a collective lather, racing against the clock to get everything done in time.

Curses flew, the sound of metal clanging off metal rang through the air, sweat dripped from hair into eyes, was wiped away by the backs of grease-stained hands or oily rags, tools were picked up, set down, picked up again. Through it all, Erik Lux sat, sentinel-silent, in the open cockpit of the Messerschmitt, while Mouth Wilson stood at the back of the van, stopwatch in hand, nervously supervising everyone.

Finally, a shout went up.

"Last gun on, we're armed and ready!" Wilson clicked the stopwatch off, and stepped forward, holding it up so that Lux could see. Eighteen minutes forty-six seconds; Roy Bigley's unlikely crew of misfits had done it, and Lux would be on time to intercept Wing Commander Timothy 'Watto' Watts at the central moment of the Battle of Britain 50th Anniversary Commemoration flight, when the formation of 168 planes, led by the Spitfires, was directly over Buckingham Palace, at about five minutes past midday.

Frustrated motorists cursed, craning their necks to try and see what was going on. Vehicle bumped vehicle. The Messerschmitt could be seen on the carriageway – the smoke from the bombs was not that thick – but, strangely, no one had got out of their cars to see what was happening, everyone simply sat, gaping, glued to their seats as if dumbfounded by the whole scenario.

A distant roar of old engines filled the sky, but no one could see anything for the smoke that shrouded the area. Lux had a feeling, though, that he was being passed by the vintage aircraft of the Battle of Britain Memorial Flight – which was indeed passing over the A1 at that very moment, bound for central London, where it would fly over

Buckingham Palace, Westminster Abbey and the Mall, in a fiftieth anniversary commemoration which would come to a spectacular finale - and he smiled at the irony of the situation. The finale, Lux thought, would not just be spectacular, but would have the added bonus of being completely unexpected.

Flipping back the cuff of his left-hand glove, Lux glanced at his watch. 11.39am. They had timed it right on the dot. Revving the 109, he watched as the gang leapt into the back of the fake security van, with the exception of Mouth Wilson, who had jogged up alongside him, and was looking at him expectantly, AK-47 in hand. Lux was not surprised to see the AK-47. Roy Bigley was a cliché of a gangster. Of course there'd be an AK-47 in there somewhere, of course he would not take anything for granted, would not trust anybody to deliver. With a grunt he tossed out the rucksack that had been resting on his lap. It landed in the road, at Wilson's feet. Waving a gloved hand in salute, Lux gunned the Messerschmitt's engines, and went roaring down the A1.

As Lux flew upwards, he glanced down, back at the A1. He was low enough still that he could see what was happening below him clearly.

He watched as Jack Wragg went to the back of the patrol car, and took out a bundle of rags and a petrol can. Piling the rags around the fake squad car, he doused them in petrol, and casually struck a match. As he tossed it onto the fuel-soaked material, turning to run to safety in the same moment, the three motorcyclists wheeled their machines over, leaving them at the edge of the gathering inferno. Equipment and tools were being hurled back into the van, followed by the gang, jumping into the back as Tony Knox roared away from the scene of chaos and destruction.

The weather forecast had said the skies would clear later, in time for the flypast, but, at that moment, there was still cloud, and it was through this cloud that the Messerschmitt roared away from the A1, the blur of burgundy on white whizzing past the pilot's eyes as he flew level with the side of an eighteen-tonne truck, carrying (as far as he could make out from the foreign lettering on the side) wine, exported from France, and no doubt bound for English supermarkets, where it would be sold at a price that would mean a loss for the growers back on the Continent.

As Lux entered London airspace, a clock chimed the noon hour, solemn, and full of purpose. Within minutes, a madman would be flying over the centre of the capital city of England, bent on revenge for one man. His madness had cost him a fortune; a fortune that, soon, he would not need.

Tony Knox, driving like he was on the home straight at Brand's Hatch, took the next exit left. The suburbs of London, the network of roads that wound its way, serpent-like, around the outer sprawl of the capital would soon swallow them up. To a stranger, these side streets and back alleys would be a maze in which they would soon find themselves hopelessly lost, but Knox knew the backstreets of London like the back of his hand, and in no time was in the industrial area of Haringey. He turned into a car park which held a large, desolate, and abandoned warehouse. The double doors were flung wide open as Knox drove up.

Parked inside the warehouse was a large removal van, its tailgate down. Tony Knox lost no time in driving up the ramp and into the van's interior, a loud shriek echoing as he slammed on the brakes. There was a dull thud as the tailgate slammed shut, and the sound of bolts slamming home. At the same moment, there was a shriek and clang as the rear doors of the warehouse opened.

Knox got out of the Toyota, and scrambled over the front seats of the removal van to get behind the wheel. He drove out of the open warehouse doors, and was soon in a narrow side street, barely wide enough for the large vehicle. In a short time, the whole caboodle – the furniture van, and the Toyota inside it – was in a breaker's yard in Newington.

The removal van would be driven to another area, abandoned, wiped clean of prints and with its plates stripped, from where it would be "stolen"...by someone who just happened to know Roy Bigley.

It was the perfect day for flying, Tim Watts thought. The perfect way to end one's career. It would, he knew, be wonderful to see all the crowds lining the route of the flypast, wonderful to see the landmarks of his country's capital city looming ever closer beneath him. He was at cruising altitude now, following the course of the Thames past the Houses of Parliament, and on to Buckingham Palace. No bullets or bombs, the organisers had laughingly reassured the Royal Family, as though anyone would even think of bringing murder into such a glorious event. This would be pure aerobatic skill.

The sounds of the powerful Rolls Royce Merlin engines carried the Spitfire over the London suburbs; Potter's Bar, Cockfosters, Haringey, ever nearer to the centre of the capital. Wing Commander Timothy "Watto" Watts was relaxed, in complete control of one of the world's most famous fighter planes, as the powerful engines carried both plane and pilot on to an impending conflict neither could be aware of.

The Battle of Britain flypast promised to be a sight to see, with more than 100 aircraft taking part. Toy-like figures, far below in the Mall, gazed skyward, eyes shielded, searching for the first glimpse of those birds of glories past.

At RAF Wattisham, in Suffolk, the whole station was on action stations alert, as a tower just south-west of London came online, warning of a possible major incident.

Tim Watts' R/T crackled into life;

"Duxford tower to Watts"

Tim flicked his headset. "Go ahead, Duxford tower."

"We believe hostile in your vicinity, pos -"

The R/T cut out, then began crackling once again.

"This is Heathrow tower, ghostrider on your tail, repeat, ghostrider on your tail."

Finchley fell away as Tim Watts pondered the situation. Duxford came on the air again;

"Command suggests you abort flyover, and return."

Tim flicked his mike; "You must be bloody joking! Bring this bugger on, let's see what he's made of!"

Tim scanned the sky around him, above and to his rear. Apart from the peaceful formation of the other vintage craft, all was calm. Tiny wisps of cotton wool clouds drifted high above, and the sun glinted off the Spitfire's fuselage.

Tim Watts looked at the sun, and understood. *That's where he'll come from,* he thought, summing up the situation. Although he knew Erik Lux had never flown in combat, the man was nothing if not his father's son. He would have studied and taken in all of the Luftwaffe tactics over the years.

Over the past few months, Tim Watts had become more aware that Erik Lux intended to kill him. What demons were convulsing in the man's mind, he could not imagine. Vengeance was not rational, there could be no end.

Tim Watts informed Duxford that he was leaving the flypast formation. He ignored the chitter-chatter coming over the R/T as Heathrow took over.

Hostile angels 1-5, Watts. Watts from Heathrow tower, hostile angels 1-5. Ghostrider. Repeat, hostile ghostrider.

"He's coming at me out of the sun, just like I thought" Tim whispered, his blood rushing at the fight ahead. A fight for his life. His life, or the German's. *What the hell did the mad Jerry plan to do?* Collide the two planes? Crash and burn in a midflight collision? *He can't shoot me down, that's for damn sure,* thought Tim. *Unless...*but, before he had even asked it, he had answered his own question. Somehow, Lux had obtained the ammunition for the Messchersmitt's .22mm canons. Each gun held 300 rounds. 2,400 rounds, assuming he was fully armed and loaded, in which to wreak deadly havoc upon Watts, his Spitfire, and anything else that took his fancy.

The London landscape fell away beneath the Spitfire's wings, Heathrow keeping Tim updated on Lux's position. Tim banked at 10,000ft, eyes scanning for the 109. He saw it to stern, then it flashed past on his port side. He saw Lux in the cockpit, as clearly as he could see his own instrument panel. Tim gunned the Merlin engines, giving chase, but the Messchersmitt had disappeared, and, save for the vintage flypast formation, the rest of the Spitfire squadron, a rearguard Lancaster formation, and two Hurricanes on the outside, making steady progress towards central London, the sky was empty.

Tim felt no fear. He knew there was no point hunting the German – Lux would come to him soon enough. Stalk him, then come in for the kill whichever way he was planning it. 1940 came back in a rush, filling Tim's thoughts as he found himself fighting the enemy in the skies once more.

Tracers fired, in front and above him. The German was firing, making it obvious he was armed and dangerous. Tim Watts felt he knew Erik Lux's thinking as well as he knew his own; the German would stalk him, play with him, make a mockery of him, before finally coming in for the kill.

Erik Lux was confident as he stalked his prey. Shaking his fist, he said, aloud yet to himself;

"This Battle of Britain you will not win; I have the bullets, you have only the wind. Goodbye, Wing Commander."

Erik Lux did indeed have the bullets, but he was overlooking some very important points. Aircraft enthusiasts, asked to pit a Spitfire against a Messchersmitt, a Battle of Britain ace against a relative novice, would tell Erik Lux; don't leave a forwarding address. You have no chance.

As if sensing this, Lux allowed his fingers to brush the bomb underneath his seat. This was the end, he knew, for himself as well as for Tim Watts. By killing Watts, and then himself, Erik could become a child again, and could be with his father forever.

The Eagle Will Fly

More tracers fly up, and over the Spitfire's hood. Not too close, though – Lux is merely playing with him, Tim realises. Glancing down, he sees the Red Arrows escorting the flypast formation across central London.

Suddenly, bullets rain off his hood. The German means business now. *This could be his final strike,* thought Tim, as he tried to tuck himself behind the 109. He gained a little on him, but the Messchersmitt came down and round in a tight bend. *Bloody hell, the bugger can fly*, Tim thought, trying to tighten up his own curve.

Tracer bullets smashed into his plane, somewhere underneath. Pieces flew off the Spitfire. Watts knew he had been hit. Erik Lux lined up the red circle with the small dot in the middle. This time, he would take the Englishman out. Thumb poised over the firing button, Erik Lux left it seconds too late, and was forced to watch the English pilot go screaming skyward.

It was now cat and mouse, two vintage fighters twisting and screaming through the sky. Bursts of rapid fire came from the ME109, Erik Lux, rank amateur, was being outflown by Tim Watts, master of the skies. Feeling the rush of battles past, yet knowing he was still at a madman's mercy if he should make the slightest mistake, Timothy "Watto" Watts played with the German, baiting him. Below them, Hyde Park, Buckingham Palace and the chaotic sprawl of colours, uniformed officers and civilians, were only a few hundred feet away. The roar of their engines mixed with drum rolls and trumpet blasts.

There were several mobile television units covering this special and historic event, among them Frank Berrison, the BBC's top reporter. Seeing what was happening above them, he fell silent, unable to believe it. Then he seemed to recover himself – he was a reporter, after all. As Seth Clark, Berrison's cameraman, relayed the scenes in the skies above London back to the public watching on television, while Frank Berrison started to speak once more.

"Ladies and gentlemen -" his voice was horrified, shaking with shocked disbelief - "this is...incredible...unbelievable. We have a major incident here. From what I can make out – from what you're seeing on your screens – it looks like an alien plane is attacking the Spitfire! Ladies and gentlemen, that was not fake gunfire you heard earlier, and these are live bullets. I repeat, there are live bullets being fired over Buckingham Palace!" Frank Berrison's voice rang with the excitement of a reporter sensing a scoop, the rattle of his commentary echoing the gunfire above him.

"I can see the other aircraft now – a German Messerschmitt – the yellow nose cone should be coming in to your screen just about now, you can see the swastikas on the fuselage, it's coming in for another attack on the Spitfire – ladies and gentlemen, this is *not* part of the display, and that is *not* fake gunfire I'm hearing up there! My word, this is incredible, bizarre. What on earth is going on up there?"

Seth Clark was capturing the drama, highlighting dramatic details with the skill of the true professional. Viewers that, moments ago, had been calmly relaxing with a can of beer or a cup of tea were now staring at their TV screens in horror, almost unable to believe what they were seeing. Could this really be happening? Surely it was some kind of stunt, some over-the-top trailer for one of those awful Hollywood movies that massacred history? The war had ended decades before; there couldn't really be a dogfight going on. Not now. Not in Britain, in this, the last decade of the 20th century. Not over Buckingham Palace, for God's sake?!

The rest of the flypast, and the escorting Red Arrows, seemed oblivious to anything else going on in the skies around them. The Spitfire came out of a steep dive, levelling low over the Thames, the four chimney stacks of Battersea Power Station flashing by on his right, Chelsea Bridge on his left.

The nose of the Spitfire dropped, and Lux's cannons screamed dangerously close. Tim Watts felt his aeroplane judder in the wake of a burst of fire from the Messerschmitt, but the big Merlin engines did not falter. The Spitfire was almost touching the grey waters of the Thames, Westminster Bridge coming up. Suddenly, the old Spitfire began to shudder as its pilot put it into a sudden stall, planning to hang just in front of Westminster Bridge, then shoot skywards at the last minute as the German came screaming after him.

Back on the ground, Frank Berrison continued his coverage of the action. "Well, ladies and gentlemen, it's been a day of drama here, and it's not over yet! It seemed like it, for a while there, seemed like the Spitfire would have to succumb to the Messerschmitt's cannon fire, but I'm not sure now – oh my word! I can't believe it! Look at this – there's the Spitfire, motionless a moment ago, gone in a flash...the Messerschmitt's going far to fast, he won't get out of this...he's heading straight for Westminster Bridge! Well, I can assure him, there's no sanctuary to be had there, he's going to crash straight into the bridge if he isn't...oh my word!"

Lux's arms were being pulled out their sockets as he tried desperately to steer clear of the underside of the bridge. He almost made it. There was a terrible sound of tearing as the perspex hood of the Messerschmitt was ripped off by the bridge it hadn't quite managed to clear. The cockpit was ripped away, nearly taking Lux's head with it. The port wing folded under the strut of the bridge, forcing its way through to the other side, as though sheer effort could deliver it from the insanity imposed upon it. Losing the battle, the Messerschmitt crashed into the murky waters of the Thames, the bomb Lux had carried exploding as, in one last, defiant act, Lux flicked the switch, sealing his own fate, and that of his father's plane. He knew this was the end.

As Seth Clark swung his camera round to cover the watery landing, Frank Berrison continued with his commentary. "That was a bomb – there was a bomb on board the Messerschmitt that you've just seen crash! I'm not sure what the pilot's intention was, but all he got for his efforts was a mighty big splash, and some wet passers-by – we'll be talking to them in just a moment..."

Erik Lux had, in fact, hoped to bring Westminster Bridge down with him, but, instead, as Frank Berrison remarked, his sole achievement was to cause the Thames the biggest splash it had seen at least since the Blitz, or possibly the river's beginning.

Wing Commander Timothy "Watto" Watts brought the Spitfire down, flying low over the wreckage, then, abruptly, its silver shape went soaring up into the blue sky. Rolling over and over in the most triumphant victory salute ever done, Tim Watts felt the tension and anxiety ease from his body. Speaking softly to himself, he said simply;

"War over."

"Ladies and gentlemen, those of us here, in the Mall, and all of you watching this on your televisions, have just witnessed a completely inexplicable scene here, a scene quite beyond belief, but we can go back to the flypast now..." Frank Berrison resumed his standard commentary as the flypast once again became the main attraction in then skies of the capital, with bands playing, and people of all nations cheering and waving flags down below in the Mall, the Red Arrows diving and swooping among the planes they escorted overhead.

A pair of silver wings slipped, quietly and unobtrusively, into the midst of the vintage planes, the aircraft they belonged to, although slightly battered, still retaining all of its dignity and magnificence.

CHAPTER TWENTY-ONE

When the news came through to the Thetford station that the German had landed his Messchersmitt on the A1 amidst a scene of chaos, Detective Inspector Simon Foxley had not spared a thought either for protocol or etiquette before heading straight down there, to see for himself what the hell was going on.

When the Thetford team finally arrived at the scene, things were indeed chaotic. The Metropolitan police were already on the scene, as were ambulances, fire engines, and air-accident investigation units. An air ambulance had already arrived, and left again when informed it was not needed. However, an RAF helicopter was still hovering, and a man Foxley recognised – Chief Superintendent Griffin – was talking to one of the officials, when Foxley and his team arrived. He looked up as Foxley strode over, PC Tony Cliveson and WPC Kerry Hall beside him, DS Ian Monument a couple of paces behind.

"Thetford, eh?" he commented, as Foxley and his team showed their warrant cards. "And what brings the County Mounties all the way out here, then, Foxley?" Griffin asked, unable to keep the sarcasm from his voice.

"Murder, Sir. We're chasing a murderer, and we believe he's responsible for this chaos at well. Sir, I know this is your patch, and so technically the man's yours, but the first offence – the murder – was committed on my patch. I believe that gives my team right of arrest. Sir."

Griffin smiled. "Indeed it does, Detective Inspector, but the Air Vice Marshall here" - he indicated the man he had been speaking to when Foxley arrived - "informs me that the man you're after has just crashed and burned in the Thames. I think even Thetford yokels realise that you can't arrest a dead man."

As Griffin proceeded to fill them on what had just occurred over London, Foxley's team listened in silence, a silence broken suddenly, when Tony Cliveson startled everyone by suddenly shrieking;

"The Battle of Britain!" Foxley turned to him.

"What about it?"

Taking a deep breath, Cliveson continued, in something approaching his normal speaking voice;

"Remember, Guv, old George Lake saying the German wasn't interested in showing his plane, only wanted to take it to 'the big show' – remember how we didn't know what he meant, how George Lake didn't know what he meant? Well, we should have been able to work it out – what 'show' could be bigger than the Battle of Britain Commemorative Flypast?"

Foxley clapped his hands together, and the team stood for a long moment in silence, WPC Hall with her hand on Tony Cliveson's shoulder. Finally, Foxley looked up.

"Oh well, lads. Back to the station – I'll get the teas in for you all."

An old Bedford van, yellow, with curtained windows, had been waiting at the breaker's yard in Newington, a scrawny individual behind the wheel. He was one of Bigley's "lost boys", people who worked for him because they owed him. His job was to pick up Bigley's main crews after a job, and drop them off in various, unconnected locations. The gang members sat in the van, Wilson with two suitcases and the rucksack Lux had thrown to him. He opened one of the suitcases, and handed each of the gang their cut, watching the expressions on their faces, which ranged from greed to relief, with some of the gang being more than glad it was all over. Mouth Wilson would be the last man to be dropped off, after Eddie Small, who was being dropped back at his flat in Golders Green. Mouth sighed. Among the many loose ends he had to tie up, he would have to pass on Bigley's orders to Eddie Small. Wilson waited until, apart from the driver, he and Eddie were the last members of the gang left in the van, and then told Eddie what Roy Bigley wanted him to do.

"No problem, Mouth." Eddie Small gave a sadistic smile, implying that he shared Bigley's reservations about Mouth's loyalties.

"Once it's done, you get as far away from the place as possible – out of England, preferably. You don't take anything from Lost Horse Farm – everything there's going to be burned, right?"

"Just like always" Eddie said, knowing how things went at the stopover.

"Yeah," Mouth muttered, "just like always. Look – make it quick and clean with the old boy. And let me talk to him first, tell him what's going to happen, let him make peace with whatever God he worships, right?"

"Never had you down as a priest, Mouth" Eddie sneered, but something in his eyes told Wilson that Eddie still wanted to be decent to the German, even though they'd had their differences and would never be what anyone'd call close. "Fine. Tell him. But you go soft, or try and get him out of there, and I'll make sure Bigley knows, right?"

"What else?" Mouth was tired, tired of being awake, and tired of the life he was living. He knew that this would be his last job. It was time to go straight, to start again. New life, far, far away from people like Roy Bigley. He remembered a resort he'd heard of, in Venezuala. Maybe he'd go there, open up a bar or something.

The van pulled up outside Eddie Small's flat. Mouth glanced at his watch.

"I won't be late, Mouth – I know the deal. I just wanna check the post, get some clothes, stuff like that, yeah?"

It was proving to be a long night for Horst Block; sleep was eluding him. His mind flicked back and forth over the events since the night of his kidnapping as he tried to work out what kind of bizarre game was being played here. It was only the threat to kill his wife if he did not cooperate that stopped him from thinking this was all some sort of prank. His mind could not really take in that other German, the crazy one, strutting about as though he were Hitler reborn, or the Messerschmitt, a dialpidated wreck that had been made strong enough to take the weight of fully-loaded machine guns and cannons. His mind rambled down a few dead ends, a few dark avenues, until it stumbled into that field in the middle of nowhere, where they had taken the guns and ammunition, and fitted them to a working 109, an amazingly beautiful machine to Horst's engineering gaze. There had been hard times with this gang of ruffians, times he had feared for his life, but, he felt, they had become more friendly towards him, especially the leader, Wilson.

Horst felt a cold sweat grip him as he wondered what would happen to him. Prisoners were never left alive, he knew...

Eddie Small stood in front of the mirror in his Golders Green flat, admiring his reflection as he pulled a comb through his hair. Dressed in black frog-mouth pocket jeans, a black polo shirt, reversible belt and top-notch Nike trainers, sunglasses pushed up on his head, he thought he looked good.

"Got to look the part, mate" he said to his reflection, smiling. Look the part of what? Of a hired killer? Oh, Eddie Small had put a bullet through a yobbo's brain before, in his younger days, but this was different.

"This is legit, him bein' a Kraut. It's like I'm fighting for my country." He laughed, a terrible, frightening sound, and, in that moment, he knew the life of the gang was the life he wanted, however much he may have doubted it before.

The Eagle Will Fly

Going to his bed, he knelt down and pulled out the shoebox that contained the automatic pistol he'd had since he could remember. Unwrapping a pair of thick football socks, he took out the silencer, and fitted it to the gun. Alright, so it wouldn't *completely* silence the shot, but it'd muffle it enough, he reckoned.

He pulled on his leather jacket, took one last look around the flat, and glanced at his watch. Still in good time.

As he stood in his house for what would be the last time, Mouth remembered the premonition he'd had at the start of all this madness, that this would be his last job. He thought he'd die doing the job, or because he *couldn't* do it, and he'd almost been right. It wouldn't have been beyond imagining for Bigley, believing Mouth's loyalties to be divided, to have killed him in his office, rather than simply telling him to instruct Eddie Small to take care of the German. But that hadn't happened. Mouth was alive, and, as long as he got the hell out of here pronto, that was the way he would stay. He'd miss this house, he thought, miss the football ground just down the road, miss the cosy local where he'd always felt at home. Miss old Blighty, come to that. As he fingered his passport – or, at least, a passport that bore his photograph – Mouth Wilson knew he wouldn't be coming back to England. He was leaving his country, the land of his birth, for the last time, was walking away from all that was safe and familiar into...he didn't know what. The future, certainly, but whether that future held good luck or bad, he couldn't say. Shouldering his hold-all, and tugging a wheeled suitcase behind him, he walked out, turning and locking the door behind him for the last time. He would drop the keys in to a Mr Paul Farmer, a retired estate agent who took care of the property procurement side of Roy Bigley's business. Paul would take care of the house, get responsible tenants in, take his twenty per cent cut of their rent, and forward the rest to an anonymous, numbered bank account somewhere with rather more relaxed tax laws than England. The Cayman Islands, perhaps.

Mouth Wilson sighed. This was a living, he reflected, but it wasn't life. Hadn't been life for a very long time. For at least as long as he'd known Roy Bigley.

But all that was over now. He was starting again, completely from scratch. Roy Bigley might well choke on his cigar at the mere thought of his best man deserting him, but Mouth was past caring now. He was going away. Was already gone. He just had to tie up a few things, take care of a few last bits and pieces of business.

Back at Lost Horse Farm, Mouth Wilson hesitated before opening the door to the annexe. Horst Block was on his feet at once.

"Horst…Eddie Small will be coming soon – you know Eddie, yeah?" Horst nodded. Mouth sighed, and continued delivery of his awful news. "He's been told to kill you, Horst. There's nothing I can do about it, okay? It's…orders. The way it has to be."

"To kill? But why? Everything you say, I do. I not talk, not to anyone! You tell me your boss say I cannot go with you today, do I argue? *Neine,* I am quiet, like a mouse. I cannot go. I accept this, make no trouble with you. Please, who will care for my wife, if I am killed?"

Mouth shook his head. "I'm sorry, Horst. I can't help you." The old German was sobbing, holding out his hands to Mouth as though Mouth Wilson, seasoned gangster, might, in fact, be a slightly hard-of-hearing God.

"Please, Mr Wilson! You not let this bad thing happen! Please! All you say, all you tell me, I do! No trouble, nothing! Not one thing I do to bring trouble on you! Please – my wife, my Rose – please! You stop him! You stop Eddie? Please – I beg you for this, for my wife…it is only for my wife, my Rose, that I care one little amount! You help me, please? Please, I just want to go home, to see my wife!"

Mouth shook his head again, sadness in his eyes. "I can't, Horst. I wish I could. I'm sorry."

As Horst Block sobbed and wailed in German, Mouth Wilson turned, and walked away.

Eddie Small arrived back at Lost Horse Farm at approximately 11.30pm, his pockets bulging with £50 notes. When he had finished with the old

Jerry, it would be back up to the West End. He'd been told to lie low, but what the hell – he was going to have a good time. He knew a couple of places where he could do that without attracting attention. He half expected to find the German gone when he got back, but everything was as it should be, with Mouth nowhere in sight. Horst looked up with a sigh as Eddie came in, the gun already in his hand.

"I was expecting you. Please, do what you have come for. I will not make trouble for you."

Eddie Small lowered the gun a little, so that the barrel was pointing straight at Horst's head.

"Too bloody right. Time to say aufwiedersehn, Kra-"

Eddie Small never got to finish his sentence. His head split open like a blood orange, and he fell to the floor. He seemed to half-turn as he fell, and there was a brief moment, before the light went out of Eddie's eyes, when he seemed to recognise his killer.

Mouth Wilson stepped out of the shadows.

"Stay" he said to Horst, as he picked up Eddie's lifeless body. "I'll be back, right?"

He ran out of the shed, and laid Eddie's body down on a clear patch of grass. Walking past the old Dutch barn, he went over to a run-down, dilapidated shed, its door securely fastened with a padlock. Mouth Wilson was one of only a very small handful of people who had keys to this particular padlock. Unlocking the shed, he ducked inside. The shed looked as though it could easily have belonged to a small builders' yard. One wall was lined with shovels, pick axes, lengths of rope, breeze blocks and bags of cement, while a wheelbarrow and cement mixer stood in the centre of the floor. Mouth Wilson grabbed a purpose-made bodybag, and ran back to Eddie's body, hearing the distant whirr of chopper blades getting closer. Laying down the bag, he ran back to the shed, and came out with two breeze blocks, which he slid into the bottom of the bag, one in each corner. He repeated the exercise, this time placing the blocks at the top of the bag, then, with slightly more effort, he slid

Eddie's body inside, and zipped the bag up, just as Jock brought the Sikorsky into view. Jock lowered the winch cable, and Mouth Wilson fastened the bodybag containing Eddie Small to it, making sure it was securely attached. He signalled to Jock, who turned the Sikorsky around, its deadly bundle swinging gently from the winch cable. Eddie Small – Horst Block, as far as everyone else knew – was on his way to a very watery grave. Since orders were to lie low for at least twelve months after a job like this, Mouth doubted Eddie would be missed for a long while. By that time, he would be in Maracaibo, Venezuala, running his beachfront bar, and Roy Bigely would have likely stopped looking for him, and promoted some other mug to Mouth's position as second-in-command. Life went on, Mouth mused, even in the gangland. Perhaps *especially* in the gangland.

EPILOGUE

"Thank you, Mr Wilson. I'll be sure to find responsible tenants for both of the properties you appear to have on your hands. I can see there being rather a lot of interest in both of them."

Paul Farmer, twenty-five years an estate agent, ten years Roy Bigley's man, smiled as he took the keys for Mouth Wilson's London terrace, and Horst Block's bungalow.

Wilson stood for a while, staring thoughtfully at the jovial man in front of him.

"How's that boy of yours, Paul? Samuel, wasn't it?"

Paul Farmer nodded, wariness clouding his eyes. "He's very well, Mr Wilson. Married a couple of years ago. Tamara, her name is. Tamara Ireland. Pretty young thing. She had a baby, a few months ago. A little boy, Garwent, they called him."

Mouth nodded, and pressed a thick wad of notes into Paul's plump hand. "I'm glad to hear that, Mr Farmer. Always good to have a family around you. You want to make sure that grandson of yours is well-provided for. Set up a trust fund for him, or something. Should keep him in touch when he's older, at least."

Paul Farmer swallowed, sweat glistening on his upper lip. "Ah...that's... very kind of you, Mr Wilson. Am I to...ah...assume this *gift* is being offered for a reason?"

Mouth Wilson spread his arms wide. "Paul, Paul, Paul. Why should there be a reason for me giving a good, loyal friend a sum of money to provide for his young grandson's future? Hm? But, of course, if you *want* there to be a reason...well, let me see..." Wilson grinned, wolfishly. "Let's not tell Mr Bigley about the property in Norfolk, eh? And, if you can, make it look like it's being sold, not rented out, got it?"

"Ah...yes. Yes, of course. Not a problem, Mr Wilson. Ah...do you... need a delay, perhaps, on the Norfolk property? I believe, ah, probate can take a fair while to, ah, come through, you see. If the owner is, ah, deceased?"

Mouth nodded, and clapped the man on the shoulder. "Good thinking, Mr Farmer. A probate period'll do nicely, I think."

"Right. Ah...so, your, ah, holiday...where was it you were going, again? I never do remember these things."

Mouth Wilson studied Paul Farmer for a long moment. That was the problem with people who could be bought, he reflected; they could very easily be bought by someone else.

"France, I think. Maybe hang out in Cannes with all those lovely young things. Or maybe Monte Carlo, live the high life a bit."

The estate agent gave a nervous laugh. "That sounds delightful, Mr Wilson. Possibly you could fit in both France *and* Monte Carlo?"

"I'm sure I could, Mr Farmer. I'm sure I could."

With that, Wilson walked out, smiling to himself. If Roy Bigley did get to Paul Farmer, he'd be sent on one hell of a wild goose chase.

A white-haired woman sat in a wheelchair, watching the surf crash against the rocks with unseeing eyes. An elderly man stood beside her, gazing out to sea. The other Germans he had met had told him the land he could see to the West was America, where the daughter of the woman he had married many years before now lived. It had been such a long time since he had heard from Amy, he thought, suddenly. He should write to her. Cards at birthdays and Christmases, a letter every so often from one of them or the other, really wasn't enough. As he stared at the raging surf, Horst Block remembered the events of the day that saw the Battle of Britain 50th Anniversary Commemoration as though that day were yesterday. He remembered Mouth Wilson, who had shot dead the man who would have killed him, Horst, and left his poor wife a widower, coming back the next day, when they job was evidently over, and giving him money, a lot of money, telling him about the German community in Galway, saying that he could arrange a false passport for Horst and his wife, that they could both start again, that Horst could forget what he had been a part of. Horst Block remembered how he had laughed, had quoted William Shakespeare at the Englishman;

"Oh, teach me how I should forget!" he had quoted, knowing that, like the prisoner of war camp, memories of the crazy scheme he had been a part of would stay with him forever.

Horst had not known what had taken place that day until almost two weeks later, when, enjoying a drink in the village pub in Rossaveel, a small port about five miles up the coast from Galway Bay, he had overheard people discussing the terrible events. He had gone over to them, explained that he had been unwell for some weeks, and had not seen the news, or read a paper. Could they tell him what had happened? It sounded like something he should not have missed. And they had told him, without knowing the part he had played in the drama, a part which made him feel sick. But, he told himself, he had had no choice. That is the curse of love, sometimes; in order to keep your love, you may have to sacrifice your conscience. Even as he formed the thought, Horst felt a flash of guilt; had he done what he had done for love, or merely self-preservation? He realised, shamefully, that he could not answer.

He gazed at the woman, whom he knew did not have long to live, and his heart slowed a little as he tried to imagine life without his beautiful English Rose. Perhaps, when she was no longer with him, he would make the journey to America, the land beyond the sea, that promised land, where he could disappear forever, an immigrant in a nation of immigrants. Perhaps he could stay with Amy for a while, see what her life had become. Or perhaps he would remain here, in the small chalet he had brought with the money Mouth had given him, a chalet set back a little from the cliff path, but from whose living room window he could still clearly see the sea. He could imagine himself tending Rose's grave in the local churchyard, having intimate conversations with her, although she was no longer there to hear him, much as he did now, if he were honest. The woman he loved was not dead, but she wasn't *there*, either. Horst Block's English Rose had gone a long time ago, just as the innocent, carefree man he had once been had gone, brutally killed by the ravages of life in a prisoner of war camp. The last shreds of that man were somewhere up at Lost Horse Farm, smouldering with the clothing, books and newspapers that Mouth Wilson had burned on their last night there, a task, he'd explained, that was carried out after every job.

The light was fading. Horst got up, stretched, and, taking the handles of the wheelchair, set off on the short walk along the cliff path that would take him to Bay View, Rose's new nursing home.

As he made the turn up the hill, and the modern, purpose-built house came in sight, its porch light burning and a friendly nurse welcoming back other residents who had also been out with their families that day, he felt something grip his hand, heard a quavering voice say;

"Pretty house. Pretty sea. Will we be staying here forever, Horst?"

As tears filled his eyes, and he whispered to the woman who was still his wife that, yes, they would stay here forever, Horst Block knew that Ireland was to be the country he died in. He would not run anymore.

Far away from Ireland, a raucous night was well underway at Wray's Wild Time, a beachfront bar in Maracaibo, specialising in cocktails and scantily clad females. Disco lights strobed, music blared, and gleaming, bronzed flesh paraded itself with abandon. The man tossing cocktail shakers through the air, and chatting up a particularly lovely young lady, was the proprietor, a Mr David Wray – who bore a passing resemblance, perhaps in the set of the eyes, or a certain way of moving, to a man known as Mouth Wilson, wanted for questioning in England. But the plastic surgeons he had used were very good at their job, his money meant a lot in this country, and the resemblance was never more than passing, and easily dismissed, especially since everyone knew Mouth Wilson had a badly broken nose, knew he was proud of it. He'd never change *that*. David Wray's perfectly straight, almost regal, nose had been well-crafted, as had his passport – done by an expert forger in Barcelona, known to one Mouth Wilson, but completely *un*known to one Roy Bigley - and no one looked twice at him as he spun tall cocktail shakers and taller tales in that beachfront bar, using laughter, banter, and booze to keep the memories of who he had been, and what he had done, at bay. All of that was in the past, and the past was long gone. There was only the future, now. The future; briefly, a memory came of an old, proud German, love shining in his eyes as he watched an elderly woman, frail, dying, confined to a wheelchair, being loaded into a specialist ambulance. With the memory came a fervent hope; Mouth Wilson hoped Horst Block had got away, hoped he and Rose were enjoying what little life remained to the two of them. He sighed. The only thing you could count on in this world, he reckoned, was regrets, and a man like Horst Block being caught up in something like what'd gone down that day, over the skies of London, and in the weeks before, would, he knew, be one of his biggest regrets. In a moment, though, the memories and the hopes – all that belonged to Mouth Wilson – were gone, and David Wray was back, laughing and joking as he answered a sexy black lady's request for some sex on the beach – the liquid kind that came in a glass with a parasol, of course, although, looking at the woman a second time, he felt he wouldn't object too much to the other...

Tim Watts, now in his ninetieth year, still lives at The Manor House with Patricia, who, on the 51st anniversary of the Battle of Britain, became his wife. The two of them spend a lot of time flying, Tim in his Cherokee Piper, and Patricia in a small bi-plane she saw advertised for sale quite by chance, when she had intended to look for a new car, her own having reached the stage of spitting oil and grumbling every time it was started. Tim and Patricia spend whatever time they're not in the air enjoying their garden, or walking along the cliffs at Cromer, enjoying the scenery they have both always loved. They still keep a full stable at The Manor House, although Tim had to admit, reluctantly, that horseriding was beyond him a few years ago. Still, there's something soothing about horses, he'd always thought.

Roy Bigley didn't choke on his cigar, although it was a close thing. The moment he realised he had been double-crossed, he hired assassins to track down and kill Mouth Wilson, but the photograph he gave them was six months out of date, and they searched for Mouth to no avail. A year after the battle over the skies of Buckingham Palace, Bigley sold all of his legitimate businesses, and Lost Horse Farm, and is now living the criminal high-life in Spain, staying true, in this as in everything else, to the stereotype of a gangster. The London underworld is quiet; while the big man is still alive, no one dares to try and take over the underworld that was his, and his alone.

Tony Knox brought out his boss, and now owns the garage he still works out of. The rumour mill has it that, if you want a hot car made legit, or a plain engine souped up, Knox's is the place to go.

Les Grant retired to the right side of the law, and manages to fit in a lot more time with his missus, between doing the *Telegraph* crosswords, and moving his money in and out of small Eastern European countries with high interest rates and no intention of sharing bank details with the likes of Great Britain.

The Sampson brothers gave up crime completely, and opened their own DIY and hardware store just off the Fulham Palace Road, round the corner from a Sainsbury's express, and a few hundred yards from a greasy spoon, the Half Moon, where they could usually be found at lunch time, toasting the memory of Eddie Small with bacon, eggs, sausages, chips, beans and a mug of hot, sweet tea.

Doc Little, as it turned out, couldn't handle riches, or his drug problem, and, one day shortly after the showdown between Watts and Lux, he took a long drive off the relatively short cliff that is Beachy Head.

The Eagle Will Fly

Poorly Manthorpe left Roy Bigley shortly after the Battle of Britain drama, and travelled the world collecting antiques. He died of natural causes in 2000.

DI Simon Foxley went on to become Chief of the Norfolk Constabulary, retiring on full pension at the age of sixty, glad of the chance to enjoy the countryside he'd spent his life policing.

DS Ian Monument, unable to see an end to men like Roy Bigley coming any time soon, left the police force in 1992. He emigrated to Canada, where he met and married a French Canadian beauty. Together, they now run their own cafe.

Foxley didn't forget his promise to PC Tony Cliveson, and, in 1991, on Foxley's recommendation, he was promoted to Sergeant. He still serves at the Thetford station, and never passes up the opportunity to get behind the wheel of a squad car.

WPC Kerry Hall transferred to Thetford CID in 1993, and passed her Sergeant's exams two years later. She now works with Dereham CID.

George Lake retired in 2000, curiously enough on the same day Poorly Manthorpe died, and his son now runs Elwood Airfield.

No one is entirely sure what happened to Big Sag ranch once news of its owner's death reached America. Some say the State took it over, eventually auctioning it off in sections, but who knows?

Lightning Source UK Ltd.
Milton Keynes UK
17 September 2010

160005UK00002B/2/P